STREET DREAMS

Visit us at www.boldstrokesbooks.com

STREET DREAMS

by
Tama Wise

A Division of Bold Strokes Books

2012

STREET DREAMS
© 2012 By Tama Wise. All Rights Reserved.

ISBN 13: 978-1-60282-650-2

This Trade Paperback Original Is Published By
Bold Strokes Books, Inc.
P.O. Box 249
Valley Falls, NY 12185

First Edition: March 2012

CREDITS
EDITOR: STEVE BERMAN
PRODUCTION DESIGN: STACIA SEAMAN
COVER DESIGN BY SHERI (GRAPHICARTIST2020@HOTMAIL.COM)

Acknowledgments

James Buchanan for pushing me to get Tyson out there. James Earl Hardy for inspiring me. I hope that Tyson will be there for people like Mitchell and Raheim were there for me.

Shout outs to Aotearoa hip hop, my rock and my fire.

CHAPTER ONE

Tyson had to remember to breathe. It was all he could do to stop himself from just staring as he stood there. He was all too conscious of everything right now, especially the fact that he was staring at another guy. Perhaps love at first sight, like he had heard all the kids talk about in high school before he had dropped out, was real.

Tyson felt the cold night air, but it was nothing next to the feeling in his stomach. His breath misted in front of him. His mind and heart fought, but all he wanted to do was forget the right and wrong and just exist in the moment.

The guy seemed so confident, so street. Dressed in all black, he was almost lost to the night. But to Tyson, the guy stood out and shined as if he were marked by a spotlight.

Tyson didn't even notice the music in his ears as his mind compared the guy back to his first love: hip hop. He was tall and solid like the rapper Flowz. His skin tone was pale like Con Psy's, a shade that made you wonder if he was just white. As he spoke and motioned to the few teenagers that stood around him, his presence and charisma reminded Tyson of Savage, extra large and impossible to ignore.

In Tyson's ears the track ran to its end. He wanted to stay and stare. The silence in his ears only made him want to fill it again with sound as he moved on. Tyson pulled his hood up over his head and bulky headphones. He spun his iPod on to the next album, still shaking as he glanced back one last time.

This is love. True love at first sight.

Tyson shoved his hands deep into the pockets of his black hoodie, worn from age. He tucked away his iPod and kept his hands in from the cold. At eighteen, he looked like any other Māori kid his age, perhaps a little out of place in downtown Auckland. He stuck out in sloppy street clothing, more so in all black. Even more with a head of short, ragged dreads. Suspicious and criminal.

Tyson had walked this way more times than he could remember. He just kept his head down and walked the same path. He quickened his step, his smooth, light brown face frowning in its usual expression. Staring at that guy had done more than mess with his head. It had cut off the time he needed to get himself down to the train. He could tell by the number of tracks he had already listened through. Missing the train would be a bad thing.

Life was just one day after another. Today, though, something different had happened and he had walked right past it. Tyson's frown deepened as he crossed the road quickly, stepping in between cars. In his ears, 4 Corners were tracing a melancholic path that matched his mood.

Tyson didn't notice the things that had become commonplace around him. Auckland at this time of the morning was all cold edges and unyielding glass. It was dispassionate concrete and grabbing lights. On any other morning he would have filtered it out for the music in his ears, but right now he wasn't even hearing that.

He stopped at the edge of street, staring across at Britomart. High above in the distance, a pale white clock face told him that he was cutting a fine edge with the time. Tyson lingered, holding off on that first step onto the street. Habit and routine willed him forward and worried him on the timetables he existed on, but his soul pulled in another direction.

He could still go back. He could find some way to say something to the guy. Confess his undying love. Tyson scowled and imagined the reaction he'd get to that, a fist in the face. Easier to just keep walking. By the time he got to the wide, empty expanses of Britomart, he had swept aside foolish notions of love, even though it hardened something inside him.

Tyson ran the last part of the platform and ducked through the nearest door just before it snapped shut. Given the time of the morning, the train was empty other than a few night workers. Tyson headed towards his favorite seat, next to the driver's door. He hated sitting with his back to things. He pulled his ragged satchel about and fell back into the seat almost as the train started pulling out. He was quick to get out his pass and shove away a wallet bloated by notes.

Tyson let himself relax, finally, getting comfortable. Getting to the train was the rough part. The long trip home gave him time to think, or create. Or if nothing else, it gave him time to just sit in the personal concert that ran the hour it took him to get from work to home. He reflected that he didn't need *that* sort of love when he had hip hop. Music was the air that he breathed and the blood in his veins. Sweet, local hip hop.

Tyson offered his pass to the weary-looking conductor without really looking at him. He was already thinking about the homeboy. His solid form. The way his sloppy street styles hung off him. If nothing else, he was a nice fantasy, something Tyson could share with himself before drifting off to sleep.

This felt different. Tyson didn't want to think about just sex with him. It disturbed him to think that he might think anything else. He wondered why he was having the feelings in the first place, why it was more than just hormones.

Tyson rested his head against the wall. The cold coming off the window soothed his forehead. He considered taking out his black book and losing himself in something else. Anything other than having to come back to the same thoughts again and again.

Tall. Solid. Looking all nice in those sagging black jeans and the oversized black Lakers jersey. He even had a hoodie like Tyson's, zip down and hood up. The white of his skin stood out as much as the gleaming shine of his wallet chain. If Tyson closed his eyes, he imagined he could see him perfectly. Maybe he could even imagine him staring back at him, with all that quiet self-confidence.

Silence rang in Tyson's ears again, and he jerked upright. Scribe's first album had always been short, and the lack of music stung him awake. His hours were getting too long, but he knew come tomorrow he would forget about the guy and just lose himself again in work. Five more minutes and Tyson pulled himself wearily to his feet.

One more day, work, sleep, repeat.

❖

When the train had pulled away, there wasn't much more sound than that of the dead morning streets of South Auckland. Tyson walked the same cracked footpaths that he always did, headphones down about his neck. The last stretch home was always the best. He left behind the run-down township, heading for the stillness of suburban streets. The air was sharp and crisp, and the stained blue of the night sky above was cut across by a spider's web of power lines.

Tyson felt comforted by the silence. It was broken only by the click of flicking streetlights or an electric hum from the lines above. Around him in low, quiet houses whole families slept. Some nights he wondered what it might like to be sleeping in the pale blue house on the corner, or the one down the street with the car always parked on its front lawn.

Tyson had grown up running along these footpaths and playing on the street. Almost being hit by cars. Eventually he had gone to school, walking in threadbare shoes, split along the side. Coming home now almost felt like walking back from school, even without the warm embrace of afternoon. His skate shoes held together a lot better than his school shoes. His destination still promised a warm bed.

Tyson cut across the street, into a short cul-de-sac that ran towards a creek overgrown and forgotten by Council. He still saw the same random tire and abandoned supermarket trolley. Beyond it was a thin line of trees that paled next to the skyward reach of the pylons. During weekends, if he was awake at the time, he could hear the sports they played just over the creek. He had stopped hanging out there about the same time he had stopped going to school. About the same time he had started working.

Then everything had changed.

Tyson's house was at the end of the street. His family had rented there almost as long as he had been alive. It was a typical Auckland villa, down and in need of repairs. Tyson always looked up at the house next door. The lights were off there. He felt comforted by it.

Tyson stepped over the short stone fence, feeling the soft squelch of the uncut lawn. The overgrowth and heavy trees further back were dark with shadows. Overgrowth had long since started to set up home in the old car tucked behind a tree that he had played in as a kid. The old wood house was almost the same color green, but rotten towards the ground in a way that made the wood a dirty brown. Tyson headed up the path towards the back door.

"Ty."

Tyson leapt, his heart hammering in fright. Back towards the side fence, there was a large shape sitting there near the blocked car. It took him a few moments to catch himself. By then he was worried for completely different reasons.

"Rawiri, bro, what you doing there?"

"What's it look like, cuz?" came the quiet reply. "Sitting out under the stars enjoying the night. What else?"

Tyson approached, more cautious because of all the reasons his friend might be there. He saw the hard face underneath the hood of his jacket. Rawiri was a bit older than him. Even though he shaved every day, his face still had a continuous dark shadow. It was like his permanent mood, all blunt, overcast features.

"You shouldn't sit out here." Tyson put his hand out to give his friend the usual shake in greeting. Rawiri didn't return it. "You'll get cold, bro."

"Just wanted to catch you before you hit the sack."

"You could have left a message with my mum." Tyson knew why his mate was sitting there. It gave him a bad feeling in his gut.

"Just wanted to talk to you, cuz. That too fuckin' much to ask?"

Tyson looked up through the line of trees that separated his house from his best friend's. The old wood fence hadn't seen repair in years, and there was enough room to get through back towards the creek, and the trees there.

"How long you been out here?"

Rawiri shrugged his stocky shoulders.0 "Long enough…"

Tyson knew Rawiri wasn't going to ask. "Come sleep up at my room, bro. I'll pull the mattress out."

"Sweet, cuz."

Tyson put a hand down to help Rawiri up, fighting his weight. Rawiri was a big guy, built for rugby. He looked the part in his favorite team jersey. Bars of blue and white. Matching blue jeans and a Blues jacket against the cold. Tyson got on Rawiri's right side, next to his bad leg. It took the two of them to get him up on both feet. Tyson tried not to look too deeply under the hood of his friend's jacket and dug his house key out from the string around his neck.

"Go up," Tyson said, after unlocking the door. "I'll be up in a minute."

"Sweet."

Tyson moved through the dark kitchen. Rawiri's stocky shadow headed straight for the stairs. Tyson took off his satchel. He saw the note popped up against the cookie jar on the kitchen table. Tyson read it by strained moonlight.

Hope we can catch up this weekend.
Got something for you.
Hold on to your money for this week,
we have enough.
Love Mum xxoo

Tyson took the thick wad of notes out of his wallet and put it in the earthen jar. They didn't keep cookies in it, despite that being its purpose. Tyson went into the hall to lurk near two of the doors there, waiting until he heard the sound of snoring within. Then up the stairs. Rawiri was already lying on the mattress on the floor. Right next to his own bed. Rawiri always beat him to the chase. Tyson was always willing to give up his bed for his mate. Rawiri was already snoring.

Tyson didn't do much more than kick off his shoes and slip out of his hoodie before lying down. He stared up at the ceiling, still worried about why Rawiri was staying this time. In the quiet, Tyson's mind drifted back to the big homeboy again. He just wanted to sleep.

CHAPTER TWO

The clock's *19:30* burned hot red in the dark bedroom when Tyson woke. No Rawiri. All he saw was the threadbare carpet, no mattress. The house had a ghostly stillness about it. Tyson knew he would be out of the house before his mother and two brothers got back from their grandparents'.

Tyson forced himself out of bed. Every day was like this, Sunday through Friday nights, with two days and a night off during the weekend. The routine was deadening.

Tyson stood up finally, looking out the window to see the deep shades of evening. Through the swaying forest of dark green, he saw a shine of light from Rawiri's house. It was dark enough that his bedroom was cast in the same shadows. There wasn't too much to see anyway. His room was small, but at least entirely his. From the walls, his local hip-hop heroes stared down on him. He liked to think they thought well of him and what he did day in, day out.

The single bed and a standing wardrobe took up most of his little space. A desk up against the wall near the window, stacked on top with compact discs and various local magazines—*Back2Basics* and *Disrupt*. Underneath was his computer, long since stripped of its outer shell. He only used it for putting stuff on his iPod. It was so old it barely ripped albums, and it gave off a dusty, hot smell whenever it was running.

Tyson turned on the desk light, which cast a strained light across the room and shined off the mirror on the back of the bedroom door. He stripped off his black T-shirt and dumped it in a washing basket heavy with clothes. He caught a glance of himself in the mirror. A worried, skinny young Māori stared back at him. Tyson had wanted to get rid of the mirror, but it was bolted down. He studied himself briefly, wishing as always that he was a little more Rawiri's size. He wished his skin was a little more dark.

Tyson grabbed himself his Usual Suspects T-shirt, uniform black. His routine was the same as always. Shower. Dress. Eat. His mother cooked dinner after she got home from working at the local supermarket and picking up his brothers from school. Then over to Tyson's grandparents' for a few hours. It was a precarious schedule that left the house empty when Tyson was home. He saw his family when he was home weekends.

Tyson was out the door thirty minutes after getting up, traveling the cracked footpaths into the town center. Fifteen minutes to get to the train, and then there was the train ride into central Auckland. He had forgotten how long ago it was that he had seen daylight when walking to the train. He pulled his hoodie closed and zipped it up against the cold, already feeling the sharp splat of oncoming rain. Nothing worse than getting caught before work.

He kept his head down, lips moving lightly as he mimed the words to Beatrootz's raps. Like every local hip-hop album he had, Tyson knew every word, every beat and sample. He was sure that if he hadn't had his music, things would have become unbearable a long time ago. It was his lifeblood. It kept him going.

Tyson stared at the huge hulks of the industrial buildings that dotted his neighborhood. It wasn't even too far from his quiet street that things got dense and depressing. The train station was just a little further on, and beyond that the town center. It was a landscape that had a soundtrack of local music, supplied by his taped and battered headphones.

Tyson picked up the pace as he headed towards the train station. A group of youths stood near a bus stop that marked the entrance to the station. For a moment, one of them looked as if he was rapping right along with the track in Tyson's ears. Tyson slowed, staring from under his hood.

Their dress sense was like his, borrowed from overseas videos but tipped sometimes by local flavor. The long hints of basketball singlets under oversized, heavy sweatshirts. Famous labels and images stolen and reworked to celebrate Polynesian culture. They saw the same rap music Tyson saw on television. Most of them dressed the glamorous life it portrayed. Young Polynesians. Hip hop spoke of hope and escapism.

Tyson worked his hand in his hoodie pocket a moment, hitting the pause on his iPod. The sound in his ears was replaced by the sharp, penetrating raps of a heavy-built youth. All power in his chest and shoulders, wearing a local tee over a long-sleeved shirt. Tyson couldn't help but be impressed. His style was sharp and just as hard hitting as those brawny shoulders. Sharp enough to be on Tyson's iPod along with all the others who had made it in the local rap game.

Tyson crossed the road and slowed as he headed towards the station gateway. The homeboy's crew cheered on what appeared to be rhymes straight off the top of his head. Tyson stared at them all, five or six of them. An athletic-built one with a black shirt tied back over his head stared back, smiling warm.

"Hey, uso…"

Their gaze lingered on each other for a few footsteps, before Tyson lowered his eyes and stepped through the gate.

Tyson hated himself for not having the nuts to hang with guys like that.

❖

Tyson went in through the main doors of Epicurious, subject to the bright glare and grabbing neon of the street. Normally he would have gone around back, like kitchen staff were meant to. Tonight the train had come in late and he had spent a little too much time dodging knife-sharp rain. Tyson preferred the back entrance. It was down an alley no one would know existed. Unlike the well-manicured and swept paving of High Street, it was part of the other side, which was all dirty backstreets and trade entrances.

Tyson went through the floor-to-ceiling glass doors, into the muted interior. He kept his head down, although his street attire and his reserved manner only drew further attention against stately white, and soft blues. Everything gleamed. It reminded Tyson of hip-hop videos from overseas, except this wasn't pretending. Tyson had seen people that rich come and go from Epicurious.

Tyson headed along the bar that ran along one long wall, towards the kitchen entrance. He didn't risk looking up to see which staff were on the floor, or if his boss was in. He hit the kitchens at a quick pace, straight to the lockers to put his things way. Although the front of the restaurant was still slow with early evening customers, the kitchen *looked* busy, if nothing else.

"Adams is going to have your ass," came a call over clattered pots and a cacophony of background boiling. Tyson almost managed a smile.

"Adams can have it if he wants it that bad." Tyson glanced about the kitchen, suddenly paranoid who might be within earshot. He saw Zadie smiling back at him, all warm looks and cheer. Tyson added, "He's not around, is he?"

"Not yet, but he will be. Something about having to come down on a supplier for messing up a shrimp order."

Tyson shook his head, heading through into the lunch room to dump his stuff. It didn't get much use, at least not that Tyson saw. Adams didn't believe in breaks. There was a lot that Adams didn't believe in. As Tyson shoved his satchel, headphones, and hoodie into his locker, he wondered what it would be like to be upset about something as simple as shrimp orders. He tied on his long white apron and headed back out. Zadie was checking on bread mixtures, while around her the kitchen was in a state of highly controlled chaos.

"How's your mum doing?"

"Busy as always." Tyson dodged kitchen staff as he made his way over towards the sinks.

The head chef, Faye, a heavy man who was notorious for his continuous stories about "how they did things in France," motioned towards a stack of pots. "There's a start for you there, son. Give me five minutes and I'll have you another five tables of dishes." Tyson had heard rumors that he wasn't even from France.

Zadie gave him another private smile as he started filling the sinks. He prepared for another night. A perfect repeat of last night. Life in Epicurious, where Adams liked to run his ship the old-fashioned way. He didn't believe in letting machines wash dishes that could be better done by hand. That's where Tyson came in, and occasionally some of the more junior chefs.

Tyson started washing and lost himself in the monotony of the task. With the evening crowd, the kitchen got inevitably louder, and hotter. Tyson had learnt it was best to keep your head down. When Adams came through or Faye got angry, it was best to just be doing what you were meant to be doing. Tyson had spent hours thinking how he contributed. An endless stream of clean, spotless white dishes. It was strange reading about Epicurious winning the awards it did. It never felt as if he was any part of that, even a small part.

The hours wound on. Tyson could tell how busy things were by the flow of dishes and how hot the kitchen got. His black T-shirt was clinging to his lanky body by the time the stream of plates began to slow. It had been a heavy night so far. The late crowd was always steady but usually scarce in comparison. Tyson woke from his mindlessness with a crack, feeling a wet towel sting against his ass.

"Best damn dishwasher this place has ever seen." Zadie smiled in reply to Tyson's look of discomfort. "You can do this stuff in your sleep."

"A monkey could do it in his sleep."

"Nah, you're cuter than a monkey," Zadie gibed. Tyson gelled better with Zadie's sense of humor than anyone else's in the kitchen. He was the only Māori, although there was a Fijian called Iosefa who covered his job during the day hours. "Come out and have a smoke with me."

"I gotta finish up these here."

"I said…come out and have a smoke with me." Zadie's tone was firm enough to be convincing, but she backed it up by hooking an arm under Tyson's and pulling. He put up a protest but it didn't slow her enthusiasm.

Compared to the heat and bustle of the kitchen, outside was a different world. Zadie always took her smoke breaks out here, just outside the back entrance. It was the downtown that Tyson was more comfortable with. There was no pretending here. This was what things looked like behind the glitz and polish. Back alleys like this that cut valuable minutes off Tyson's walk down to Britomart, the forgotten and dirty parts of Auckland.

Zadie's cigarette flared in a bright point of red as she lit it. Although it was raining lightly, little of it was getting down between the scummy buildings. It just ran down pipes and fell on air-conditioning ducts. Tyson leaned up against the wall near the door, feeling the flush of heat from the kitchen.

Zadie regarded him in silence for a moment, enjoying those first few puffs. Probably her first break of the evening, Tyson thought. Zadie was short and compact, long brown hair always worn up. She made Tyson feel tall. Her uniform somehow managed to stay impeccably white. Everything was formal and reserved, but Zadie made up for it with her personality. She was one of the young crowd of the Epicurious staff. He had never asked her age.

"So how's your mum?" Zadie asked. She let out a lingering puff of smoke.

"She's doing good, but busy. You know."

"And what about your brothers?"

Tyson smiled a bit. No one else at work even knew he had brothers, let alone asked about them. "Doing okay in school. You know, same old thing."

"You know, I asked you yesterday about when you were going to get out of here…"

Tyson frowned, and he knew Zadie saw it. "Probably not going to be much longer, I guess."

"Weren't you going to see about that chef course? I remember when you first started here you weren't always going to be a dish-hand," Zadie remarked, taking another slow drag. Tyson preferred looking at his battered skate shoes.

"Yeah, guess it just sort of fell off. I'm more worried about making sure money's coming in at the moment."

"Things are still okay at home, right?" Zadie asked. Tyson looked up at her. She didn't much bother with makeup, just as straightforward in her approach to things. She was starting to make Tyson worry.

"Yeah, of course. Why?"

Zadie gave a private smile. "I know you well enough to know you're always going to be the staunch one. Keep all that stuff bottled up inside. It's just been starting to show a little more the past few weeks."

Tyson was genuinely surprised. "Nah, I'm cool. Really."

"You're not your brothers' father, you know," Zadie said. She propped one arm under her front, cradling her elbow as she smoked. "You don't have to look after your whole family. You're too young for all that stuff."

"My mother's jobs ain't going to cover everything. My brothers gotta get through school. That's not cheap. I'm just helping out."

"Maybe, but you can't work this shithole for the rest of your life. Not unless you're doing more than just washing those dishes." Zadie reached over and touched Tyson's bare forearm. He looked up again, seeing her face. He could hear the concern in her quiet voice. "You're better than this place, Tyson. Don't stay here."

There wasn't really much he could say to something like that. Tyson was worried about the fact she had brought it up. Was it really that obvious? "I guess it's strange Adams still wants to stick with the hard way of washing dishes. He should get one of those machines."

"Don't go tempting fate. He's not even paying you what you're worth." Zadie took a long last drag off her cigarette and tossed it aside. It glowed a moment in the filth of the alley before fading out. "Hey, why don't you come out with me this weekend? You could use a break."

"My mum needs help with some stuff around the house," Tyson lied. He hoped that didn't show, but he couldn't see any hint that it did in Zadie's face.

"Well, I'm not going to push you, but the offer's there…"

Tyson glanced up again, noticing one of the junior chefs poking his head through the door. "Hey, Tyson. Faye wants you to clear the tables while the patrons are low."

"Why don't *you* do it?" Zadie shot back at the junior.

Tyson shook his head. "Nah, it's cool, I'll do it." He pushed up off the wall.

"Think about what I said, okay? I don't want to be having this conversation again in a month's time. I really mean it."

Tyson just nodded vacantly and headed back inside. The heat was a comfort after the temperature outside, which had started to turn the sweat on him to a cold chill. He wiped his hands down on his apron and made sure he looked as sharp as he could before heading out into the restaurant. Most of the night staff were starting to head out. From here on in it was just a skeleton crew and a few bakers, Zadie included. There was enough grunt work that he would be busy for the rest of the night, though.

The front of the restaurant was a tasteful oasis after the fuss of the kitchen. Tyson spotted the few tables that needed clearing and did them quickly, wiping them down as he went. Double-checking his work after returning the dishes, he grabbed a loose newspaper off one of the seats. Tyson stopped in the break room to toss the paper out, but paused at the bin. *Express*. A gay newspaper. Glancing over his shoulder, he seized the moment and shoved it in his locker instead. He froze in shock as Zadie walked in.

"There you are. I'll help you with drying up if you want."

Tyson slammed the locker door, murmuring a thanks. He walked away, still shaking with the fear of being caught.

CHAPTER THREE

Tyson woke with a start, feeling the heavy weight of a pillow slam down on him. He squinted against the bright light stabbing at his eyes. By all rights, if he could still see light, he should still be asleep. Tyson groaned his displeasure. He didn't need to see Rawiri to know it was him. Only his mate would wake him so rudely.

"Wake up."

"What time is it?" Tyson groaned. He tried to roll over. His blankets and sheets disappeared in a quick second, leaving him bare and trying to cover himself. He was wearing only his boxers.

"Time to get your skinny ass up, cuz. C'mon. We goin' for a walk."

Tyson didn't know whether to feel annoyed or not. He needed his sleep, but then he would gladly go without if Rawiri needed him. Rawiri rarely needed a reason other than wanting the company.

Tyson struggled to sit up on the edge of his bed. His clothes hit him next, no vague hint. It was an effort getting dressed, half-asleep. Rawiri was about the only person he would let see him this close to naked. Rawiri and him went back as far as he could remember.

Tyson stood up to pull on his jeans. Rawiri was still wearing the same clothes he always did, jeans and Auckland jersey. He had seen bruises on Rawiri enough that he never stared any more. It didn't mean that he didn't notice. Rawiri's right cheek seemed a bit dark, more so than his deep brown tones. He seemed his usual, dour self.

"What you starin' at, bro? Fuckin' hurry up," Rawiri said. "You already had enough sleep. I'll meet you downstairs."

Tyson just grunted a bit in reply. He was used to his mate's manner. Tyson figured that if there was anyone who deserved to be pissed at life, it was Rawiri.

He got himself ready as quickly as he could, sneakers, T-shirt, and then hoodie as always, scooping up his satchel and iPod on the way out. Tyson stopped mid step as he remembered. He dragged the newspaper out of his satchel and shoved it under his mattress before heading out.

"Tyson!" came a shout, down in the kitchen. "Rawiri has an excuse! How many times do I have to tell you not to thump down those stairs?"

Tyson muttered an apology when he got downstairs. He remembered the note as soon as he saw his mother, slowing his flight from the house. He felt guilty as he rounded the table to kiss his mother on the cheek. Tyson could hear the sounds of the TV from the lounge, one of his brothers' many videos.

Hine had the sort of skin tone Tyson wished he was closer to. She was tall, still young, but looking older from the stress of life. The life she had was strongest in her eyes, defiant. She was dressed as simple as she always was, worn T-shirts and jeans that had been made to last. Like Tyson, she preferred that his brothers were provided for first, but she still managed to force treats upon a begrudging Tyson, something she never did for herself.

Tyson looked at her expectantly. She smiled back at him. "Yes, you can go out with Rawiri. You don't have to ask me."

"I was just thinking about the note, that's all."

"Well yes, about that." His mother opened up the cookie jar on the table. "Think you left this in here…"

Tyson smiled a little and grabbed an apple out of the bowl of fruit on the counter before making for the door. "I'll catch up with you later about the note, then." Tyson didn't want to be caught on the subject of the money. His mother had too many ways of trying to give it back.

Rawiri was waiting outside, leaning up against the car under the tree. Tyson quickened his step, shouldering his satchel and falling alongside Rawiri. The brightness of the sun, even on the crisp overcast day, reminded Tyson of how much time he spent awake at night.

"What's so important that you got to wake me up, bro?" Tyson asked. His neighborhood looked totally different during the day. At least night hid a good deal of its shortcomings.

"Hanging with your bro, is what. I don't need a reason to wake you up. Ain't that what you said?"

"Yeah…"

Rawiri looked over at him, his walk stiff on account of his lame right leg. "Cuz, how many times I got to tell you this shit. Your ass needs to get a job that works days."

"You're not the only one telling me that," Tyson said. He tossed his hoodie up over his head. The weather was still sharp and cool.

"Oh yeah? Your mum tryin' to talk some sense into you?"

"Nah, just Zadie."

"That girl from work?" asked Rawiri. He was a big guy, but despite all his roughness his way of speaking had always been subdued. "Shit, you should listen to her. That and tap that ass of hers."

"Man, don't say that!"

"What? Maybe if you finally get your dick in something nice, you might not be actin' like work is all there is to life."

"You know why I work," Tyson replied, his tone hard. He cut Rawiri slack when it came to some things. Like how he got the bruise on his cheek this time. He expected the same back. "So don't talk about that, okay?"

"I just miss hangin' with you, cuz." Rawiri's voice was almost soft.

"I know, bro."

Tyson fell quiet, noticing how the subject had brought a downer on the both of them. They headed in the opposite direction from the town centre. Low-slung houses lined streets short on asphalt, some with mostly intact fences, all of which had been hit with tagging. Others had front lawns that spilled out onto the sidewalk, tangled chain link already overgrown with grass. The houses had the same drab similarities and tired color.

Tyson let Rawiri lead as they turned off the street and down a narrow walkway. He glanced down at his friend's stiff leg, which kept their pace slow. It reminded Tyson of the bruise on Rawiri's face and how he wanted to say something about it. It hit him. Two people in as many days were telling him to get a new job. Tyson wondered where else he was meant to work.

They headed along the walkway, either side corrugated-iron fences tagged up with signs and names. Then walkway gave way to a footbridge, crossing the creek, spreading out into the worn expanse of the local park. Most of the equipment there was in bad need of replacing. The half-pipe they had installed a year back crowded the park just off the bridge. It was busted in the middle, and the local council had refused to repair it on account of the fact it was a congregation spot for drunken teens. Some of whom had probably busted up the half-pipe.

A little way along the main path of the park was a basketball court, equally useless with two lone backboards minus the baskets. Beyond that, enough space for two full rugby pitches. There was a knoll that ran alongside them, with old rotted wooden bleachers that had been built into it. A line of struggling trees lined the knoll. Tyson knew they were headed there. They had always hung out there as kids and played in the trees. Now they used the bush for privacy.

Tyson couldn't help but notice the tangled mess of power lines and industrial blocks beyond the park, sharing the sky with a dirty brown haze. Somedays it felt like the lines tied him down into the hood.

Rawiri was still silent as they cut through gardens long since walked with tracks. Into the brush. He was wearing a blue cap, pulled down over straggled, greasy black hair that hid his ears and fell about his shoulders. Usually he wore it all tied back in a T-shirt.

Tyson followed, until a few minutes of careful travel later they were in one of the many brief clearings. Rawiri let himself down with effort and almost immediately plucked a blunt from behind his ear, confirming Tyson's suspicions. Tyson just sat down, watching as Rawiri sparked it up, taking a few tight, short drags to get it going. Tyson felt bad. Shit probably wasn't going good.

"Go on…"

Tyson shook his head, ignoring the offered blunt as he stared at Rawiri's face. The bruise on Rawiri's broad cheekbone wasn't as obvious as Tyson had thought. It was a moment longer before Rawiri took back the offer and stretched out on the stunted grass. The earth beneath was hard packed and unforgiving.

"You oughta smoke, cuz. At least you'd have something else to look forward to other than work."

The pungent odor of it failed to carry far, and despite the stout, cold breeze that had been upon them coming into the park, it was fairly sheltered here. Tyson looked down at Rawiri, the way his rugby jersey pulled across his solid frame. His good leg was bent, the other straight and awkward. He watched in silence as Rawiri puffed away. It was an old ritual. Rawiri always offered him a smoke. Tyson always turned it down.

He felt less like holding out lately.

"You ever think about things other than the dole?" Tyson asked, after a while.

"Nah, why?"

"I mean you talking about *me* getting a different job."

"I just want you to get a normal job so I see you more," Rawiri said. Tyson watched as his friend took another long drag. "You work too much, cuz, for real."

Tyson thought about it for a moment. He couldn't remember

a time when things were different. Someone had to help make sure his mum and brothers were all right. It only bothered him that he was starting to feel a hole inside. Working was just a good way to cover it up.

"You never dreamed about doing something else?"

"Like what, cuz? With my leg I'm pretty much fucked. And sure as fuck I'm not gettin' some job like buildin' roads or something," said Rawiri. He was getting down to the end of his blunt, all too quick. Tyson could see the look in his eyes as he stared up at the sky. "Why bother? I'm not gettin' out of this shithole any time soon."

"If you could, would you do it?" Tyson ventured.

"It's not gonna happen, so why even think about it?"

Tyson shrugged, staring off idly at the trees around them. He glimpsed the telltale signs of bright colors moving beyond the swaying foliage, people in the park. "Don't want to be doing this all my life…"

"Pity you got born poor, then, cuz. Maybe we oughta do over a 4-Square and get us some cash to get out of here."

"Whatever…" Tyson stared down at Rawiri, surprised to see the expression on his broad features. "You're joking, right?"

"Yeah, I'm jokin'."

Tyson kept staring. Part of him felt like Rawiri wasn't. He was sitting slightly behind the stocky Māori, so that he could see his mate but Rawiri would have to stretch to see him. Tyson felt worse the longer he stared. The more he looked at Rawiri, the more he saw how tired he looked. There was a dead stare in his eyes that seemed to be caring less and less.

Tyson's attention drifted awhile before he noticed the occasional bird and the distant sound of people and traffic. At least here he could hide from seeing his neighborhood. Compared to where he worked, coming back to this day after day only made it worse. When he saw things by daylight, they always came down with an oppressive weight. At least he got to get out of here, even if it was just to work.

Tyson considered trying to ask about the bruises, but saw Rawiri closing his eyes. It wasn't too much longer before he heard a soft snoring. He found himself thinking of the white homeboy he had seen on the street those few nights back.

Tyson felt bad for himself. More for Rawiri. It didn't take him long to get pissed off enough to pull off his satchel and dig about in it. He put his headphones up over his head and cued up some tracks. The silence was starting to get to him.

Nesian Mystik filled his ears as he dug about in his satchel. The track "Brothaz" always made him think of Rawiri. The warm tones and gentle sentiment made him think of everything good that they had. Even these quiet times together, when both of them were so unsettled. He pulled out one of his many black books. Usually Tyson reserved drawing and thinking for the train, but Rawiri wasn't going to wake up any time soon.

Tyson paged through the endless scratchings as the music continued to warm his soul. He had filled countless books like this, about the size of a schoolbook. Some pages had poetry, words and thoughts scratched out in pencil, but for the most part it was artwork.

At first he had started out just reproducing from his mind what he saw on his rides to and from work. The colorful scrawls that enriched a drab concrete corridor from downtown Auckland to his neighborhood. He had maps of the route. Notes of which graffiti was where. Then he started making up his own. Tyson flipped through to the last page, seeing something that he had done in the last few days.

It was a large comic image, a staunch figure with oversized feet in typical street pose. Big and stocky, in all black with a hoodie. Seeing that homeboy, even as brief as it had been, had burnt his appearance into his mind. It had been an easy enough job to get it down on paper.

Tyson looked back at Rawiri, asleep on the grass. The music continued to play at his ears. He felt the large, tired hole within him, the longer he sat. He lay back on the grass next to Rawiri with his black book on his chest and imagined what it would be like to be close to that white homeboy. Tyson wondered if it would make life seem easier, having the love of someone like that.

Tyson lay there, watching the sky, then watching Rawiri. He felt himself stir slightly, excited as fantasies began to play out in his mind, and he slowly closed his eyes.

Chapter Four

Y ou want to talk about it?"

Tyson almost dropped a plate, swearing under his breath as he saved it with slippery hands. His iPod beat his ears with angry raps, someone from the Breakin' Wreckwordz crew, but not so loud that he couldn't hear Zadie. Tyson glanced up to see her concerned face. He muttered an apology.

"Don't worry about it. Think you should take a break."

The kitchen of Epicurious was its usual busy, perhaps a little more than usual with the Sunday night diners. Up to the elbows in soapy water, Tyson tried to calm himself, shut himself off from the world. All he wanted was to have the waiters keep the dishes coming. Hot water started to turn anger into brooding pity.

"I don't have a break for another half hour."

Zadie grabbed him by the elbow. "Yeah, well, you taking one now. This rate you're going to end up breaking dishes. You don't want that. Jansen, take over washing. Tyson and I are taking our break."

Tyson stepped outside, almost feeling like a kid called in on detention. He ran his hands up through his short, ragged dreadlocks. Zadie was already starting to light up a cigarette.

"So, what's up?"

"Nothing," Tyson lied. "I'm sweet."

"I know you better than that, Tyson. You can play it straight with me."

Tyson ignored the irony of the remark. He wasn't about to tell her that he had the hots for another guy. Tyson leaned his head up against the wall and stared up at the impassive brick face of the building. Somewhere above he thought he could see stars.

"Are things at home really okay right now?"

"Sure."

Truth be told, Tyson hadn't been able to stop dwelling on what Rawiri had said. Between that and his yearning for the big white homeboy of his dreams he had managed to drum up an incredibly foul mood. He shook his head quietly and summoned the courage to reply.

"Everything's okay, really. Life is just a bit heavy at the moment."

Zadie took a puff on her cigarette. "You should see Adams about getting some leave. You've been here long enough."

Tyson replied with a noncommittal shrug. Zadie's sigh broke the inevitable silence that fell between them.

"You might find this hard to believe, Tyson, but I really do worry about you. I can tell when things are bugging you."

"Thanks."

"I know you're not going to take time off."

Tyson shrugged again, glancing up. "I might think about it."

"I know you better than that." Zadie shoved playfully at his shoulder, smiling. "You're just all talk. Look, if you're not going to take leave, then what about doing coffee with me?"

Tyson tried to hide his worry. "You mean like a date?"

"Not a date. That would mean we were going out, right?"

The silence that lingered between them wasn't lost on Tyson. Zadie tossed aside her cigarette. "I don't have to tell you that I like you a lot, Tyson. But I'm not going to push anything. I think you could use a night on the town, though. If you're not going to tell me what's up, and you're going to keep it bottled up, the least you can do is try and get a little release..."

Tyson nodded. He felt cheated that a girl would show him so

much attention and concern. He wondered why he couldn't just feel like everyone else and be flattered by it. Why couldn't he just feel like any other guy? Tyson tried to draw up the courage to truly play it straight with Zadie.

"You trying to work out how to say yes?" she asked.

Tyson watched her with a guarded expression. He wanted to speak his mind. Instead the words stayed hard inside.

"Where you want to go?"

"Oh hell, Tyson, it's just a drink. Just somewhere nice. I want to see you relax a bit."

"Sweet. Sure," Tyson replied. What the fuck, what did he have to lose? Maybe sleep. Zadie put a hand on his forearm, easing it upwards a little to rub lightly. He lowered his head, confused.

"Take life by the balls, Tyson. You already play hard, but just make sure you don't do it alone, okay? You know I'm always here if you want to talk."

"Thanks. I will. No, serious. I will."

Zadie regarded him for a long moment before seeing the truth of it in his face. Tyson felt strange enough with her touching his arm like she was. He felt just as strange when she took it back and smiled, stepping back in through the door. He wondered if he could ever find what it took to return her feelings.

❖

Tyson felt more exhausted than usual when he finally left work. He hadn't talked much more to Zadie after their break, instead wandering out into the dark streets to clear his mind when his next break rolled around. The rain and the long walk served to quench the frustration and anger inside him.

He felt heavy as he walked his usual route back to Britomart. Maybe Zadie was right. Maybe he did need a holiday. He couldn't remember the last time he had taken a real break. Tyson thought about Rawiri. He was almost the opposite. Where Rawiri did nothing day after day, all he ever thought about was work. Someone had to look after his brothers.

The air was crisp as usual. Tyson put on his headphones, pulled his hood up. Settling into his usual routine. He spun his iPod about to Dam Native, listening to old-school raps about Māori poverty, trying to wrestle with his situation.

His thoughts kept coming back to Rawiri, and Zadie. Either thought felt dirty.

Tyson crossed the road, ignoring the usual early morning walkers. Downtown was never all that quiet. There was always someone on the street, even if it was just the homeless.

The beats continued to play in his ears, lending more subdued colors than the myriad of shopfronts and neon lights that fought for his attention. Tyson cut through a tight, open lane before slipping into one of the many backstreets that he used to get down to Britomart. He had done this run enough times that he knew he was still running to time.

The gloom of the back alleys matched his bad mood. Tyson almost stepped into a puddle, dodging it at the last moment. His mind was preoccupied. Like how thinking things through logically could explain why he couldn't feel anything when Zadie looked at him, yet his stomach erupted in butterflies when he thought of that damn homeboy.

That damn white homeboy!

Tyson sucked in a tight breath, stumbling a short few steps to a stop as his eyes caught the movement. He froze, just like he had before, taking this time as sudden as the last. Although as much as he had thought about it, nothing seemed to make it any less challenging. He stood and stared, but at least this time his wits were about him enough to stop him fleeing after a few brief moments.

Tyson hadn't expected to see him there, much less see him again. He was dressed exactly the same, in his sagging blacks and whites. Clothes clean off the rack and immaculately groomed. He looked as if he had stepped right off the set of some U.S. rap video. Tyson stayed his movement, even though his gut raged and bubbled. He felt hot and flushed.

Damn, he's so damn good-looking.

The fantasies he had entertained since that last moment ran through his mind. Tyson's hand worked in the pocket of his hoodie, stopping the track that was thumping in his ears. He watched as the homeboy handed out what looked liked heavy rolls to two guys about his age. Tyson couldn't catch what he was saying to them, so quietly pulled his headphones off.

He was still frozen, still staring. It was like seeing a dream again the second time, still recognizing the bold features but picking up on the infinite details.

The guy was solid, but in a different way from Rawiri. There was something different about the way he carried himself. Tyson recognized the numerous white guys who dressed and acted like all the videos they saw, hanging off every latest style and fashion of guys like 50 Cent. There was something posturing about it, artificial beyond the fact they were white and doing it.

There was nothing posturing about the way *he* looked. He carried himself with an air of confidence. He looked the way he did because it was how he dressed, not because he was trying to look a certain way. Tyson stared at him, wondering about his pale complexion. Maybe there was some Māori in him. He had a shade so pale it made him wonder.

He continued to hand out what Tyson figured might be posters. Tyson became conscious of the fact he was just standing there, watching. Tyson was too used to blending. Even dressed in blacks, the homeboy stood out by miles, but he looked like he was meant to be there.

"When you finished along Quay, make sure you come back. I still got another two hundred I need to get up downtown."

Tyson felt giddy, and then entirely stupid when he realized it.

He soaked in the sound of the guy's husky voice like he basked in the sounds of his hip hop. Like everything else, there was something entirely comfortable about it.

The two young bros began to head back up the alley. Tyson felt trapped when the homeboy looked his way. He was shouldering a hefty rucksack from which a number more rolls poked out. Tyson panicked, shaking and sweating as the guy made eye contact, heading up the alley towards him.

"What's up, my man?"

Tyson gave a staunch nod, a stout salute of the eyebrows. He tried to force himself to speak as the homeboy strode towards him. Inside everything in his mind was fighting and ultimately tangling and tripping. Tyson let out a quiet word, wondering if the guy even heard it.

"Hey…"

The homeboy smiled in recognition, nodding a bit as he passed by. Strong and confident strides. Tyson started walking, making it look as if he was checking on his iPod. His stomach was in knots by the time they continued in opposite directions. It had felt like two worlds passing each other by.

Tyson had known it the first time he had seen him. There was no question he liked guys like *that*. The second time around, he only longed more painfully, needing rather than wanting. As he kept walking, he struggled to think of any real reason to turn and call after him, glancing back a few times as the homeboy headed back out onto the street.

Tyson still couldn't ignore the warm smile and what it had done to him.

CHAPTER FIVE

Tyson's trip home was preoccupied with thoughts and recollections. He sat in the back of the train, in his usual spot, with a clear view up the relatively unoccupied carriage. He wore his hood up, over his headphones, the sounds of PNC beating at his ears. The solid rapper's equally solid delivery matched the exhilaration that sat deep in Tyson's being as he drew quick and sharp strokes in his black book. PNC was a good thing to be listening to, given how he looked stocky like Tyson's subject.

Tyson looked down at the many images he had drawn in the time that the train had rattled and swayed through five stations. He was catching the homeboy's appearance in more and more appropriate poses. Hood up, or hood down off that short shaved head. Everything about how he dressed and looked seemed so exact. So perfect. Tyson felt obsessed.

By the time he got close to home, Tyson had started drawing the white homeboy with his shirt off. His hand shook. There was a dangerous thrill at it, not as if he hadn't already imagined the sight, but to commit it to paper was different, more real. He stroked out the slow, easy strokes, guiding outlines to sketch the extension of what he saw, broad chest and strong shoulders.

Tyson glanced up, paranoid as he came to what his character might wear waist down. He looked at the various other images he had made up, half-completed concepts, posed this way or that.

T-shirt in one, the T-shirt sleeveless in the next. He put his feet up against the seat opposite, hiding his work and chubby groin from an empty carriage as he kept drawing. The artwork felt crude, but no less so than what he was doing.

Thought given form. Tyson looked at the page. He felt bad. It was one thing to undress the guy in his mind while staring up at the sky on a Saturday afternoon. It was another to strip him off on the page. A perverse part of him wondered about dimensions. He considered ripping the page out, but was too paranoid to just throw it in a rubbish bin where someone might see it.

Tyson closed the black book and shoved it away, slouching back on the chair. He was still shaking, playing over and over the brief seconds in his mind. It wasn't like he didn't want to see what he had just drawn. Fuck...how bad was he to draw *that*? Tyson frowned, finding little comfort in PNC's easy, effortless flow. He turned off his iPod.

Tyson knew he wanted to do more than just see it. It cheapened the whole thing. Lewd thoughts mixed with the romantic in a desperate miasma of fantasy. He kept coming back to the same thoughts. What would it be like if he was with someone like that? Life would be so much easier.

How wrong was it that the first time in his life he felt this, it was for another guy?

Tyson pulled himself up off his seat as the train rolled into his stop. Everything had drained from him when he had run into the homeboy. Right now he just felt very tired. Tyson was too aware of what was still lingering in his jeans as he tried to straighten himself up. He stepped out into the early morning.

There were guys hanging about the station when he got off. He was too distracted to notice them too much beyond the basics. Māoris, Pacific Islanders. Tyson took in the bandannas and common colors. There was some shouting that he didn't pay any attention to as he headed out onto the street. Even the cold air did little, it only focused his problems more.

Tyson wanted to tell someone. He wanted to tell them how much of a thrill he felt inside just to hear a few words from the guy. To tell them how seeing the guy made him feel. If somehow Tyson had the courage to talk to the guy, he could tell him how strongly he felt. That would make it okay.

Tyson figured he should have been feeling this way for Zadie. It troubled him that he didn't. As he headed up the street to his house, he decided he didn't care. All that mattered was this one guy. Being held by him. To feel that big stocky frame against his.

To feel his lips press against his own, soft and strong.

Tyson was aroused again by the time he got home, slipping off his shoes as he closed and locked the door. He was up the stairs in moments, closing and locking his bedroom door behind him. Fatigue pulled at his lanky limbs, exhaustion that was bared only by emotions. Tyson dumped his satchel and stripped off in the darkness, slipping under his sheets.

Tyson's mind kept him awake. He studied the ceiling above him. The house was as quiet as it always was. He wanted to look out the window, just out of habit. Just to check the house next door.

Tyson found a new, giddy thrill at being finally in his bed. He thought on what he had drawn in his black book, so lewd and impulsive. He frowned as his hand eased down about his dick. His breath quickened as he pleasured himself. It wasn't the first time he had done it while thinking about the homeboy, but it was different doing it so soon after having seen him. Tyson pulled firmly yet gently at himself, his soft moans touching the air. His mind filled with thoughts far more vivid than the one he had illustrated in his black book.

The homeboy looked so good in those clothes, so new and fresh. It didn't escape Tyson that he had been dressed the same way. He realized that he recognized his basketball singlet, a throwback LA Lakers one that he had seen in shops, well beyond what he could afford. The homeboy cared about how he looked, and he looked sharp. Tyson liked that.

Tyson squirmed beneath the blankets, his breath light. He played out walking up to the guy. Everything from there was sexual, bold and flagrant. Every time the big white guy took him, guided him. Every time Tyson felt safe and warm, imagining his own pleasure was because of what the homeboy was doing to him.

For some reason he found himself thinking about Rawiri, in the scattered, unorganized dreams. Tyson wondered curiously about his friend's size, comparing it to the homeboy's. He stared at his friend's stocky form, holding Rawiri close as they touched and embraced. Tyson was far too close when he realized he was thinking of him only. As he came, Tyson found himself telling Rawiri everything would be okay. Tyson felt guilty almost instantly, left with a mess on his stomach beneath carefully held back sheets.

Tyson tossed back the sheets and blankets, feeling the sudden shock of cold. He groped under the bed, pulling out a towel. As he cleaned himself up, his mood felt as bad as it had going in to work, but for all different reasons. He had thought about Rawiri before when he wanked, but it had been innocent curiosity, nothing as deliberately sexual. He thought with shock that he was thinking about his best friend like *that*. No guy should think about his best friend like that, straight or gay.

Tyson shoved the towel away, brooding. He got up and checked out the window at the house next door just to be safe. The night beyond his bedroom was dark, and silent. For a long time, he just stared out of the window, thinking.

He felt so utterly alone.

Chapter Six

I'm taking Tamati and Taine down to the park for a run around. You coming?"

Tyson pulled himself up a bit in his bed, still shaking sleep from his head. The blankets fell back on his bare chest as he looked over at his mother, standing near the door. He nodded vacantly.

"I'll catch you downstairs, then." Hine took the basket of washing near the door. Tyson caught a hint of a smile, something that made him wonder. "Five minutes."

Tyson waited until he heard his mother's footsteps on the stairs before getting up. He didn't need to worry about wondering what to wear, pulling on his usual sagging black jeans. The only real decision was working out which of his local hip-hop T-shirts to wear. They hung inside the ancient freestanding wardrobe that smelt its age. He picked out his Disruptiv tee, black with a large white "d" within a circle, slipping it on.

Then his hoodie, then his satchel, like a ritual. Tyson figured that he would catch a shower later in the evening. He never bothered to correct his sleeping during the weekend if he could help it. He didn't mind the night so much, but like now, he often felt the pang of missing his brothers. Tyson was looking forward to it, even if he was woken up a little early.

Tyson checked the charge on his iPod as he headed down

the stairs. He dodged Tamati, who ran screaming towards the door, followed closely by his brother. They were at that age where running around was a constant occupation. They were both eight, and twins.

"Don't run in the house!"

Tyson put his iPod carefully away into his satchel, mussing his dreadlocks as he headed towards the kitchen table and sat down. His mother was packing away plastic containers and loose fruit into a backpack. Tyson eyed a large brown bag on the table. He frowned.

"That's for you," Hine said. "Go on. Open it up."

Tyson pulled it towards him and glanced inside the bag. He couldn't hide his surprise when he saw the box inside, pulling it out carefully. He put it on the table, looking it over rather than opening it. The box was emblazoned with images of the DJ-quality headphones inside.

"Mum…damn…you didn't need to get me these," Tyson said. He looked the box over more closely. "These are really expensive… how did you afford them?"

"I've been putting a little away each week. I know how you like your music." Hine finished packing the food. "Your other ones are starting to look past it."

"Mum, I can't take these, they're too expensive."

"Too late, I've lost the receipt. Plus I can't remember where I bought them…"

Tyson glanced over at his mother, still hesitant about opening the box. When she turned her back and went to the fridge to get out some drinks, Tyson let himself get a little more used to the idea. It had been a long time since he had bought headphones. There was no point on skimping on those. Sound quality was important. Tyson noticed his brothers running outside past the window. He stared out at the backyard for a while before finally opening the box.

"Thanks, Mum."

"That's okay, dear." Hine put the drinks into the pack and rounded the counter to stand near Tyson. She stroked his dreadlocks a moment. "You do a lot, helping provide for your brothers and us. You have to treat yourself every now and then."

"Yeah, but I'm not. You are. What about you?"

Hine smiled a little, but it was fleeting. Tyson recognized that in himself, seeing it in her. "You don't need to worry about me. Making sure you three grow up safe is my reward."

Tyson was about to complain, frowning again already, but there was a knocking at the back door. He glanced past his mother, seeing Rawiri standing there. He was back to wearing a T-shirt tied back over his shaggy hair, keeping it all hidden. The pair of black shades he was wearing made him look like a Black Power member.

"Hey, Ty." Rawiri hesitated when he spotted Tyson's mother. "Hi, Mrs Rua."

"Afternoon, Rawiri."

Tyson saw how Rawiri lingered near the door. "We're going down to the park. Give my brothers some time to stretch." He pulled the headphones out of their box with pride. "Check this out. My mum got them for me."

Hine leaned over to kiss lightly at Tyson's forehead before leaving him to finish her preparations. Tyson managed a smile for her as Rawiri walked slowly inside. Tyson wasn't entirely sure what to say, feeling the nagging concern he always felt when he saw his friend. His mother solved half of the problem.

"Are you going to come down to the park with us, Rawiri?"

"Yeah. Sure. Thanks, Mrs Rua."

Tyson gave a questioning look at that same, stoic expression of Rawiri's, but didn't see any reply. He held up the headphones for Rawiri to see, checking them out for the first time himself.

"Pretty sweet," Rawiri said. He was more reserved than usual.

"Come on, then," said Hine, shouldering the backpack. "Help me round up your brothers, Tyson."

"Sure, Mum." Tyson got up, pulling his old headphones off their usual place hooked into the strap of his satchel. He put the new ones in their place, getting up and ready.

Tyson headed outside, keeping the same slow pace he always did when Rawiri was around. It was bright outside, the afternoon sun still strong in an overcast winter day. As always, a sharp breeze stung Tyson's cheeks, but it was a bracing rather than truly cold breeze. He followed the shouting from around the back of the house, walking an overgrown concrete path. Their backyard was a wild, overrun tangle of grass, trees, and somewhere further back, fence. Tyson could remember climbing through it as a kid, but now it was something his brothers did.

Taine and Tamati were already dressed for the weather, in jeans and jackets. His mother avoiding dressing the twins too similar. Tyson knew that she could tell them apart anyway. They were both overenthusiastic bundles of energy. Tyson was sure that he hadn't been like that. He had thrown around a rugby ball with his father at their age. Now he was doing the same with them. Tyson was becoming more aware every time he took them down to the park that he had been the same age as his brothers when his father died.

"*You're* it!" Tamati shouted with glee, almost shoving Tyson. His twin laughed as Tyson grabbed Tamati. Tamati might have been all energy, but he was still as ropey as Tyson.

"Nah, you're it," replied Tyson, grabbing onto his wriggling brother, holding him tight even though Tamati's thick, kinky hair brushed at his face. It took a moment longer before Tamati got free. "We're going down to the park now, so make sure you stick with us. No running off."

"You sound like Mum," Taine complained. He gave Rawiri a fairly wide berth, but Tyson noticed the look in both brothers' eyes when they realized he was coming along. It was a look of quiet respect. They seemed to curb their shouting and screaming a moment.

Tamati reached and slapped Taine on the back. "You're it."

"Nah!"

"Yeah, you're it."

"You're it!"

The two ran about the front of the house. Tyson smiled as he watched them. He noticed Rawiri, all too obviously quiet, ignoring the twins' aimless, playful banter. Tyson put a hand on his friend's shoulder as he followed after his brothers.

"You cool, bro?"

"Yeah, cuz."

Tyson frowned and tried to keep his worry down. He noticed that his mother and brothers were already halfway down the street. Rawiri came to his side, walking stiff on his leg. Tyson knew they'd never keep up. He lost sight of them as they headed into the alley that led to the park.

"K-1's on tonight," Rawiri said. "You up for the usual, cuz?"

"Yeah, sure." Tyson warmed to the idea almost instantly. He started to ignore those dark shades Rawiri was wearing, rather than feeling the usual paranoia about his well-being. "What time you want to come over?"

"Yeah, well, that's just it, cuz. I got some business I need to take care of, then I'll roll on over to your place. All good?"

"You can come over whenever you want. You know that. You need any help?"

"What you mean?"

"I mean with your business."

"Nah, it's nothin' like that, cuz," replied Rawiri. He paused for a moment. Tyson thought he was reconsidering. Rawiri's face was unreadable.

"Can I borrow twenty bucks?"

Tyson raised an eyebrow. "What you need it for?"

"I'll tell you later."

Tyson was already reaching for his wallet, tucked away in his satchel along with all his other worldly goods. He handed the twenty over without a second thought. Rawiri slipped the single note away almost as quickly as Tyson had brought it out.

"Thanks, cuz." Rawiri looked guilty. Tyson figured it was for weed. It usually was. "I'll catch you tonight, then."

"You're not coming to the park?" They'd finally reached the alley.

"Nah, I better bounce, cuz. I'll catch you tonight."

"C'mon, man," Tyson said gently. "Is it really going take that long to take care of it? Come and sit with me, else I'm going to get run down by my brothers. You said I got to have something to look forward to other than work. Well, you're it."

Rawiri gave him a sideward glance. Tyson smiled. "Plus, you said you wanted me to get a day job so you saw more of me. I want to see more of you too, bro."

"Sure, cuz," Rawiri said.

"We both need to relax, right? You got any weed?"

"Not on me." Rawiri looked surprised. "But not like you gonna blaze up with me."

"Nah, but it's worth a shot," Tyson said, smiling as they headed down the alley. The sun shined sharp on freshly broken glass.

Tyson crossed the bridge to the park, to see his brothers already running wild on the basketball courts. Tyson noticed a number of youths slow strolling across the park, towards the clubrooms on the far side. Otherwise there were only a few lone people, a few joggers, a couple of people kicking a ball. The only reason Tyson ever came here was because it was the only park in the area.

Hine was setting up near the tree-covered ridge where Tyson used to watch games as a kid. Tyson eventually sat a fashionable distance from where his mother had taken up, only because his friend was with him. Rawiri didn't seem to be in the talking mood. He sat down, and the two of them sat in silence. Tyson tried not to let the quiet get to him. He longed to fill it with music.

Everything always looked different by day. Tyson looked past the fields and his brothers, who were now running and throwing about a ball. He tried to look past the large industrial blocks and the endless spider's web of power lines. It was like they somehow kept the city tied down, giant pylons standing eternally vigilant. Tyson put his forearms down on his knees, staring. Somewhere beyond that dirty brown haze were coils and ropes of motorway.

And beyond that, a totally different world.

Tyson stared at his brothers, watching his mother sitting with the same solitary mood. He felt something horrible inside that Tamati and Taine would have to stay here forever. Unlike Rawiri and his mother, Tyson knew that he saw a hint of that different world every day he went to work.

Tyson thought how he didn't want to be here for the rest of his life. And he certainly didn't want to wash dishes for the rest of his life either.

CHAPTER SEVEN

Tyson hauled the family's television upstairs to his bedroom. He guessed that it would be a while before Rawiri was back. The two of them hadn't spoken the whole time at the park. Tyson had taken some time to throw around a rugby ball with his brothers. Part of him had wished Rawiri would join in, but he hadn't touched a ball since the accident. Instead, his friend had wandered off, saying he would be over later.

Tyson sat on his bed, his desk lamp setting a pale light over his dark room. The television added a bit more glow. He didn't want to listen to his iPod—even though he wanted to check out his new headphones—as he might miss Rawiri's arrival. Tyson looked through his old black books, which he kept in a box in the bottom of his wardrobe. It was strange. Like visiting a younger version of himself. He couldn't remember the last time he had really looked through his older books. When the current one was filled, he tossed it in with the others and changed to a new one that he had bought in advance. The box was a mess of successive black books, piling up in the back of his wardrobe. Then there were times like this when he dragged it out from behind all the clothes.

Tyson could easily see the themes, where perhaps others might need to look harder. Tattered fragments of rhymes and words reminded him as readily as some of the graffiti of moods and times. They were dark and lonely phrases, lyrics pulled from songs. All just idle jottings that connected into a depressive image. Tyson frowned at himself, sitting slouched on his bed.

He glanced towards his satchel, lying atop his desk. Tyson saw the book there, suddenly reminded of the images that he had worked on in the last few days, born of hormones and desperate yearning. Each book seemed to paint a lonely path that led to those few pages and that lewd image he had scrawled.

Tyson heard a familiar tap on the window. Then a second, as the pebble hit its mark. He saw Rawiri's unmistakable dark shape down on the lawn. His friend tossed aside the rest of the stuff he had gathered to throw. Tyson went down quickly to let him in, nodding staunchly in greeting when he opened the door on the stocky Māori.

"You get your business done?" Tyson asked. Rawiri looked like he had expected Tyson to forget it.

"Yeah. It's sweet."

Tyson closed the door once he was in and locked it. He kept his voice quiet, a hint to Rawiri to do the same as they headed through the kitchen.

"You buy some weed with the money I gave you?" pressed Tyson. Something still struck him as strange about it.

"Yeah. I left it at home though, cuz. Why? You want some?"

"Yeah."

Rawiri gave him a look, "You shittin' me."

"Yeah, man, I am. A few more weeks of this bullshit and I might be serious, though."

Rawiri looked at him suspiciously. Tyson locked the bedroom door behind Rawiri, mostly out of habit.

"You staying over, right?" asked Tyson. He got up to pull the spare mattress out from under his bed.

"Yeah, if that's all good. You got any drinks?"

Tyson was distracted as Rawiri started undoing his jeans and shoved them down. Rawiri used the bed to balance himself and pushed his jeans awkwardly down over the tight black leg brace that strapped the big thigh, knee, and calf of his right leg. Tyson never got used to seeing it, especially not when Rawiri got to work on taking his brace off.

Tyson stared as Rawiri pulled at the Velcro straps, loosening the whole brace. His thighs were big. Although they lacked the power Tyson knew they once had, they were still something to look at. Rawiri had all the look of someone who would be a natural rugby player. Tyson looked down over those smooth, hairless legs, his eye drawn to the mess of scars and ugly flesh that made up his right knee.

Rawiri cast aside the brace like it was something to be loathed, off the end of the bed. Tyson kept taking in the sight of his big legs, his eyes wandering up. He caught himself staring at Rawiri's cotton boxers, scowling at himself the moment he did.

"I'll get us some Coke, okay?"

"Sweet."

Tyson unlocked the door and went back down to the kitchen, quietly cursing himself. He remembered what he had done a few nights before, and what he had been thinking about. Tyson's stomach felt like it wouldn't settle. He remembered everything, that horny soup that boiled inside him, stirred up whenever he thought about that white homeboy. And for some reason Rawiri had got caught in that mix.

Tyson grabbed a bottle of Coke from the kitchen, heading back upstairs. He wondered briefly if he had the nuts to admit to someone he had known most his life that he liked guys.

When Tyson got back up to the bedroom, things didn't get any easier. Rawiri had stripped off his jacket and Auckland rugby jersey. His permanent clothing. Stripped down to just his boxers and white singlet. Tyson was taken by Rawiri's arms, wondering if they had been that big last time he had seen him like this. The singlet was loose enough that Tyson could see the hints of the scars he knew lined Rawiri's broad back. One ran along the thick ball of his shoulder.

"Figured what I want to do," Rawiri said out of the blue. Tyson noticed that his friend had slipped off the bed and was sitting on the mattress now. Tricked again into offering his mate the bed.

"What you mean?"

"Cuz, you was the one who was askin' me all that shit. You remember? About jobs and shit?"

"I remember." Tyson put the bottle down on the desk, trying to ignore his hormones for the moment. It felt obscene looking at Rawiri so undressed after what he had thought. It had never been a problem before.

"Yeah well, I ain't talkin' about gettin' a job, but I still know what I wanna do," replied Rawiri. Tyson didn't ask, so Rawiri answered after a pregnant silence. "I been workin' out a bit."

That made sense. Tyson tried to play it casual, sitting on the floor next to his friend. He was conscious of how close Rawiri was. It made his breath tight. "Yeah, thought you had."

"Huh? How you know that?"

"I just mean…I didn't think your arms were that big last time I saw them. How long you been working out?"

Rawiri gave a rare smile, obviously taking it as a compliment. His shaggy black hair was out, and that, along with his stubble, gave him a rugged handsomeness that didn't always seem so apparent. "Few months."

"Why?"

"What you mean why? 'Cause I wanna."

Tyson thought of his mate's knee. Rawiri hadn't seemed interested in anything physical after what had happened to his leg. Before that, his life had been nothing but physical. He had spent more time on a rugby pitch than Tyson thought anyone would want to. He took this latest piece of news in stride. He was glad that his friend had found some new dream in life. He blamed his hormones when he thought what Rawiri would look like after a another few months of working out.

"It looks good," Tyson said quietly.

"Yeah, I think so too, cuz. Guess pretty soon I'm gonna be all cut up. Hey, pass me that Coke."

Tyson pushed himself up and grabbed the Coke, passing the bottle down to Rawiri. He smiled, trying to shove aside all his guilty feelings as he expressed his honest happiness for his friend. "Well, if you working out, you going to have to cut out stuff like Coke, right? You eating all that health stuff, and all that protein stuff?"

Rawiri shrugged. "Yeah, something like that. Anyway, you was askin' me all that shit about what I wanted to do, so that's it. So what's your answer?"

"What's my dream?" Tyson asked. He frowned. He didn't have time to think about stuff like that with work and now all this shit about him liking guys. He shrugged dismissively, "I dunno. Don't have time for that."

"Workin' too fuckin' much. Get a real job."

Tyson ignored the edge in Rawiri's voice. He watched as his friend skulled back on the Coke. It was nearly a quarter of a bottle before he stopped, letting out a huff. Tyson stared, his mind sitting on the edge. The words hung on his tongue, waiting to be uttered. Rawiri was too busy watching the silent television to notice.

Bro, I think I'm gay.

"Hey, K-1's almost on, you gonna turn that shit up for me?"

"Yeah, sure, man."

Tyson pushed the thoughts aside. What would Rawiri think about always being so undressed around him if he knew the truth?

Tyson pulled himself up again, putting up the volume on the TV and turning off the desk lamp. Rawiri seemed more relaxed. Tyson tried to keep from looking at Rawiri, or at least his big shoulders. Why hadn't he told Rawiri earlier? He felt stupid for feeling guilty, but with everything that was going on at the moment, he couldn't help it.

K-1 was an unspoken ritual between the two of them. Tyson always guessed it was an excuse for Rawiri to come over, but he didn't mind. Privately, he sort of liked eying the brawny guys who fought, swinging devastating kickboxing blows in those shorts. But it was cool to have Rawiri over, no matter what the reason. The coolest thing was seeing Rawiri like he was getting now, excited about something, distracted from life.

Rawiri had his kickboxing. Tyson had his music. There had to be something to take the taste off life.

Tyson was only half watching the fights, distracted by his thoughts. His mind was a flood of situations and images. It occurred to him to wonder what the white homeboy had been doing in that alley. His manner was confident, and the other guys with him seemed to hang off his every word. The thoughts eclipsed the sexual feelings he was assaulted with every time he thought about the guy.

Tyson brooded in the dim light of his bedroom. He kept looking sideward at Rawiri. Tyson thought about everything they had been through together. He kept thinking about Zadie's advice, about taking life by the balls. Rawiri was the one person he should be talking to about it.

Tyson couldn't think of how to say it. He couldn't get the words straight, and they just lingered pointless and half-formed. In the end, it was too difficult. Tyson felt crushed inside, hateful. Scared of all the things that might happen. The words were powerful and dangerous, even if he was to say it at its most simple.

I'm gay, bro.

Tyson watched the guys beating away at each other on the television, promising himself not to think about it any more. He knew how to fix that painful absence in him, but he couldn't. So failing talking about it, Tyson decided to just not think about it. The chances of seeing that homeboy again anyway were slim.

The time between fights seemed like agonizing hours of weighty silence. When the opportunity allowed itself, Tyson broke into dulled conversation.

"Hey, Rawiri. If you're working out now, you think you might get back into rugby?"

Tyson didn't like the expression that took Rawiri's face,

especially after how light-spirited he had seemed during the fights. The stocky Māori swigged at the Coke. "Nah, cuz. Not gonna happen."

"Would you ever consider teaching my brothers a few things about the game?" Tyson asked cautiously. "Tamati is pretty good for his age, I think."

Rawiri shrugged, his only answer to the question. He stared at the television in that ambivalent and stone-faced way. Tyson just muttered a quiet apology, getting about as much answer. "It's good that you're working out, though. It's good to have something to look forward to. Probably about the closest thing to a dream we got, right?"

"Yeah, guess so, cuz."

Tyson let the whole subject drop. It wasn't too much longer before he got back up onto his bed and pulled a sheet up over him. He half watched the late-night movie, half studied Rawiri's features and strong, stubble-covered jaw. Those solid, scarred shoulders. Tyson thought about having dreams. He dreamed that if he was going to get out of this shithole, then he was going to somehow take Rawiri with him.

CHAPTER EIGHT

Ignoring things worked surprisingly well. The start of Tyson's working week went fast as he drowned himself in music and dishes. The new headphones kept everything out. His nights were soapy hot water and his days were restful sleep. He felt life's heavy pall over him. In some ways, ignoring everything helped life to douse him in a mist that made him see nothing but the day-to-day.

All that changed Wednesday morning, just home from work.

Tyson turned on his desk lamp, already noticing his sharply made bed with stark dismay. He locked the door, not bothering to push off his hood or take off his satchel as he headed straight over to it. His heart was pounding. Since when did his mother *ever* make his bed for him?

Tyson dug under the mattress, feeling the folded paper underneath. He dragged it out, messing a bit of the bed as he did so. He could smell the crisp, fresh smell of the well-made bed, but it paled next to the terror. Tyson couldn't do anything but stare at the all-too-obviously gay boy on the front page of the paper. He trembled as he sank down next to the bed.

Had his mother seen it? He tried to remember if that was exactly where he had put the paper. Was there any chance she might have discovered it when she was making the bed? Since when did his mother ever make his bed? The thought of it made him angry.

Tyson stared down at the well-groomed white boy on the cover of the paper. *Fuck you if you have gone and ruined things for me*, he thought. Tyson couldn't stop trembling as he wondered what his mother must have thought. *Damn, please don't let her have seen it.*

Tyson dumped the paper down on the bed and made an effort to get with his normal routine, pulling off his satchel and then his hoodie. He dumped them down on the desk before staring out the window. The house next door was silent, behind trees that swayed with the heavy winds that were starting to pick up.

The gay boy was still smiling up from the bed. He couldn't believe he had been so stupid as to grab the fucking thing. Tyson pondered what he was meant to do with it next. Tyson wandered over towards his bed, still shaking in part from his anger and worry. His dreadlocks fell into his face as he stared down at the paper. The gay boy stared back.

He seemed so typically gay in Tyson's eyes. Hard-looking body, well dressed. Mussed hair that had probably taken a long time to get just right despite looking so casual. His T-shirt was pulled tight over firm, broad pecs. He looked no older than his early twenties. He looked like the sort of person Tyson would have expected to be gay. He didn't need to be on the front cover of a gay paper for Tyson to work that out.

Tyson sat down on his bed, resigned and angry, yet it boiled away to leave him tired. He pulled the paper open with shaky hands, finding himself unable to ignore the fact that he was curious now he had the thing alone. He paged through it with a certain detachment.

Everything was cut in stark greys. A full-page spread on what must have been the event of the year regaled with larger-than-life drag queens and overly eager grins, some obviously sauced by ample alcohol. Tyson felt his groin charge a little at the bare flesh, hard bodies, some down to just a mere g-string. He searched the pages, turning one after the other.

Photo spreads turned to articles, intermingled with advertisements. He felt his light cheeks burn as his eyes fixed on an erect cock, an advertisement for condoms. He stared at the huge, seemingly ugly thing, all uncut flange and balls and pubic hair. Other advertisements showed off sex toys, things just as big, things that Tyson hadn't even considered or entertained in even his fantasies. He shook as he read through escorts promising their wares in brief language he didn't fully understand.

Tyson stared, both excited and for some reason empty as he looked at the magazine. All he could think was the same thing as he stared at the huge queens, bare-chested boys and rough-looking dykes.

This is what you are.

Tyson searched through the personals. So much was packed into so few words, cut down into abbreviations and shorthand that he tried to guess at. He scowled at himself, and at the thing that seemed to represent everything he wanted to be, just by dreaming of that homeboy. He sat, his mind empty. He wondered if it was worth it.

Confused?
Wondering?
Just want someone to talk to?

We can help. Private and confidential.

Tyson studied the advert, nestled between ones for explicit DVDs that emphasized the fact. It was almost lost but stood out to him in its plain simplicity. He looked at the number a moment, then reread the advert. He was beginning to hate how he was feeling inside. It had been growing long enough, but the first time he had seen the big homeboy, the feeling had only festered deeper.

Tyson stared at the paper and only felt more alone because of it.

Grabbing it, Tyson unceremoniously dragged it off the bed and got up to shove it away in his satchel. The pages creased and screwed as he pushed it deep inside. He thought fatalist thoughts as he pulled off his T-shirt and tossed it at the washing basket near the door. It missed. He caught the mirrored image of himself, boxers showing as his jeans sagged off his hips. His dreadlocks shadowed his face and veiled his stare. He looked at himself, wishing he could be a bit bigger, like Rawiri. His groin leapt as he thought about what Rawiri might look like in a few more months.

Tyson undid his jeans and went to bed. As much as he wanted to try and ignore it all, it kept coming back. The empty wounds wouldn't heal. Life was just going through the motions, day after day. Tyson slipped under the sheets, praying that he would dream of the homeboy. That he would take him into his arms and tell him everything was going to be okay.

❖

Tyson was sore by the time he woke. He pushed back his blankets, feeling the ache in his limbs. He rubbed his neck as he looked over towards his bedside clock. It reported 18:49 in red numbers. With the sound of heavy rain beating against his window, Tyson swung his feet about and sat on the edge of his bed. Too many things had been on his mind. He had gone to bed with them and slept. Instead of the homeboy he had hoped to see, all he had got was restless tossing and turning. It was an hour or so before he was meant to get ready for work.

Tyson stared down at his satchel. It was bulged at one side where he had shoved away the newspaper. He entertained the idea of calling the number in the advert. If he got ready an hour early he could call before work and still get there on time. He felt the apprehension and guilt chewing at his stomach. This was worse than just thoughts and fantasy, wanking alone in his bed. Calling someone and talking about it set it in stone.

Tyson seized the idea almost as impulsively as he had grabbed the newspaper that night.

He set about getting ready in the silence of the house. He

showered, ate the food his mother had prepared before going over to his grandparents'. Dressed. He kept staring over at the satchel, wondering at other ways to deal with the problem. Talking with Rawiri wasn't going to happen any time soon.

Heading down the stairs, he grabbed the phone. Leading it back up to his room, he made sure the long extension didn't catch on anything on the way up. He made sure twice that the door to his bedroom was locked before sitting down just under his window. His heart was racing, but he knew that if he didn't do it now he might not get the nuts to do it again any time soon. Things couldn't get worse.

Tyson dragged the paper out and smoothed it open at the page where the advert was. His fingers trembled as he punched the number in. He kept thinking he heard his mother, or movement outside. Nerves knotted him in on himself. Tyson sat back against the wall, cheeks burning as the sound of dialing filled his ear.

Tyson half expected no one to answer, but they did.

"Hi, you've reached the support line for gays, bis, and lesbians. How can I help?"

Tyson froze. As much as he had thought everything he had, and wondered it, it sounded so strange hearing someone say the word "gay," especially when he was involved. He mustered himself as best he could.

"Uh...yeah, hi."

"How are you doing?" The voice sounded cultured, an older man's. He sounded like he should have been some sort of radio announcer.

"Doing okay, I guess."

"Is this your first time calling?"

Tyson was still a tight ball of nerves, muttering into the line. "Yeah."

"It's a bit of a step, I know. My name's William," the man said. "You don't have to tell me your name if you don't want to. I'm just here to listen if you want."

"Cool," Tyson replied. He added, not sure why he did, "My name's Wiremu."

"Nice to talk to you, Wiremu. I'm guessing you're Māori?"

"Yeah."

"Is there anything in particular you want to talk about?"

The line fell silent as Tyson sat there. His nerves were still getting the better of him. Eventually he remarked quietly, "Not used to this sort of thing. Never called one of these lines before."

"That's okay," William replied. "Can I ask you where you got the number from?"

"Yeah. From a newspaper." Tyson looked down at it, still crumpled somewhat, laid open beside his bed. He felt a lump in his throat as he stared up at the ceiling, and committed himself. "I think I might be gay…"

"You find yourself having feelings for guys. There's nothing wrong with that."

"Yeah…well…not all guys. Just some guys."

"You think about girls like you think about those guys?"

"Nah…don't think I ever really liked girls," Tyson admitted. He felt so small, feeling the cool air coming down off the window above him. He could almost feel the rain as it beat against the glass. "I feel pretty fucked up."

Tyson could feel the sympathy in the man's tone. "I can imagine. You sound like a young guy. Dealing with feelings like this is never easy, Wiremu. But it's good you've made the move to talk to someone about it."

"I can't talk to anyone else. I don't want them to know…"

"They don't have to know. If you're more comfortable talking to me on the phone, then that's how it will be."

Tyson wondered how it could be that easy, but hearing William put it like that made it seem obvious. He sat on the end of the line for a while, still lost in that silence that took his voice from time to time. He was just concentrating on breathing for the moment.

"I think I got the hots for someone."

"You want to talk about that?"

Tyson stared at his shoes as he picked over the thoughts. It was hard to put into words now he had someone to talk to about it all. He felt stupid that he felt so deeply, given that he had only seen him a few times. Maybe it wasn't how it seemed somehow.

"I just really like him…I think I want to do stuff with him."

"Is this a friend of yours?"

"No. I don't really know him all that much."

"It might not be so safe telling him your feelings if you're not sure how he might react," William remarked.

"I know."

"Doesn't mean you have to give up, though," replied William. Tyson wasn't expecting that, already somewhat resigning himself to the fact that what he wanted was impossible. "How long have you been having these feelings for guys?"

"I don't know…it's been a while, I guess. It's just I saw this guy and I really felt it," Tyson said. He was feeling that lump again in his throat.

"Well, if seeing this guy eventually prompted you to call and talk about your feelings and maybe do something about them, then that can't be a bad thing." Tyson sat in silence as William spoke. He felt weird hearing the sympathy from a stranger. "What you're feeling is normal. And you don't have to deal with all this all at once, or overnight. There's no rush."

"I don't know."

"One step at a time, Wiremu. You're doing fine."

"What am I meant to do?" Tyson felt panicked.

"You don't have to do anything if you don't want to. Probably the best thing for you would be to talk to other people who are in the same position as you."

"Why's this shit happening to me, man?" Tyson asked. He scowled. "Why's this shit got to be so heavy for?"

William took a moment before he replied, his voice solemn. "I can't answer that, Wiremu. But you're not alone. I know it doesn't count for much, but I feel the same way you do about guys. What's it feel like knowing that you're talking to someone else who likes guys?"

"Weird."

"It will get easier."

"It just feels like everything's so messed up," said Tyson. He didn't think how hard he was releasing, wishing that William would somehow have the answers to fix everything. That quick, magic solution. "Feeling like this for that guy. And I don't even know him! And work's so hard…"

"Well, maybe we can try and work things out for you."

"How?"

"Well, a group of us meet up on Ponsonby Road every Saturday night. There's a café up there called Quartet. Maybe if you wanted you could come along and meet some guys…"

"I'm not really into that sort of thing."

"Meeting people?"

"Yeah," Tyson said, panicking. "Not really into that."

"It might be a bit too soon for you. If you want, though, you can call here and ask for me. I'm usually up here until about eight thirty."

"Cool."

"It does get easier, Wiremu. I promise."

Tyson frowned. It felt good to talk to someone, but he still felt trapped. Eventually, he replied, "My name's Tyson."

"In that case, I do promise it gets easier, Tyson. I really do. Just don't feel like you're alone, okay?"

"I'll try not to," he replied, thinking how William didn't seem fazed about him lying about his name. "I got to go. I have to get to work."

"Sure. And thanks for calling, Tyson. And thanks for telling me your real name. Trust is a good thing. You take care of yourself, okay?"

"Cool. Bye."

"Bye."

Tyson hung up the phone, still feeling the nerves eating at him. He sat in silence, listening to the rain pounding against the window above him. He couldn't believe he had just done that. But somehow, it felt okay. Outside it was getting steadily darker.

CHAPTER NINE

Zadie had been acting strange ever since Tyson had got into work Friday night. She wore a private smile that bugged him. Tyson didn't question it, knuckling down with work like he always did. The call with William seemed like a world away, doused in a train trip's worth of local music and poor weather. He had even felt like scribbling in his black book again. For once, he felt like maybe things might be going back to normal.

Friday night was busy like usual. Tyson lost himself as he washed and listened. He drowned himself in Adeaze's smooth harmonies, quickly consumed in the rhythm and flow of work. Nothing worried him when he was like this.

Tyson hadn't seen Zadie during his break and didn't even think about it until he was about to leave for the night. He stepped out the back door, into the alley behind before being startled. Zadie was slipping an arm under his, walking quickly in step with him.

"Don't tell me you've forgotten?"

Tyson knew she would recognize his usual frown as he looked down at her, surprised at the touch. He turned his iPod off. "Huh?"

"You promised that we could go out after work and get that coffee?"

Tyson wracked his brains trying to remember. "I don't think I said that."

"Sure you did. You said after work Friday would be the best time for you, because you wouldn't have to get back to sleep."

Tyson fell silent. Maybe he had. Given everything that had happened lately, it didn't surprise him that it might slip his mind. If he had said it, it would probably have been to placate her. The rain had let up a little, yet it still managed to penetrate the tall divide of the buildings.

"So we're going?"

"I guess so."

Zadie gave him a strange look. "You're really not that keen, are you?"

"Well, if I said today, then I guess I owe you."

"Sure do," Zadie said. She wasn't going to take no for an answer. It felt strange having someone so close to him, arm within his. He did his best to fall in pace with her quick walking.

"Where are we going?"

"You have any preferences?"

"Not really," said Tyson. He was already been whisked down the street. "I don't do this sort of thing all that much."

"I know this place downtown. We won't go all the way up to Ponsonby or K Road, seems you probably want to get home."

"It's not that."

"It's okay, Tyson."

Tyson remained quiet as Zadie guided him through more populated streets, even for this time of the morning. The streets shined with neon off wet sidewalks, and he could hear the raucous roars of modified cars on Queen Street.

Caught up in Zadie's quick pace and lost in his thoughts, Tyson almost tripped up as she pulled him off the street and up a narrow staircase. The wood protested with every step, and the stairway was lit in a strange fluorescent glow. When they arrived at the top and pushed through a bead curtain, Tyson was assailed by the smell of incense, thick on his senses. The small dark room was awash with fluorescent, DayGlo colors. Tyson wondered if this was what Rawiri saw when he smoked.

"What you want to drink?"

Tyson shrugged, taking the place in. It was a little too hot, and the low booths, in which were equally low tables rounded by stiff-looking cushions, were lit by lava lamps of numerous colors. The music was a little too dance for his tastes, a low thump that never seemed to stop, giving the place its own heartbeat. The whole place startled him somewhat, especially the fake volcano behind the counter that glowed red, and the gaudy Hawaiian shirts the staff wore.

"Two mochas, Grant, thanks," Zadie called to the guy behind the bar. The place was empty except for a table near the back where two people sat, sometimes giving in to loud guffaws. Zadie gathered him and headed towards booths near the windows that lined one end of the long café. "Guess you don't have places like this out south?"

"I don't think we even have cafés out south."

Zadie slipped into one of the booths and Tyson did his best to struggle into the other side, given how low they were. It was strangely comfortable among the cushions. He noticed that Zadie was still wearing her uniform under her large jacket. The black-light lamps along the ceiling were making it glow neon white.

"Might have to make this a weekly thing, if you want."

"Why did you drag me out here?" Tyson asked. He couldn't shake his suspicions. "I'm pretty sure I said that we could go out *sometime*, but I don't remember saying when."

"Tyson, you need a social life."

"How do you know I don't have one out south?" he asked, staring at her across the table. Tyson could see she was calling his bluff in a second.

"Because you don't. I know you, Tyson. I know you very well." Zadie added after a moment, "Damn, I should have had a cigarette before I came in here. Anyway, I know you work too much, and I know you go home from here and sleep. That's it, right?"

Tyson shrugged rather than further incriminate himself. Zadie was pushy, but she wasn't usually *this* pushy. Her look softened a bit, her features lit by the strange glow hanging off the walls and the lava lamp between them. She smiled.

"I'm just helping you unwind, Tyson. I don't want to see you get chewed up by work. If you're not going to think about getting another job any time soon, then this is the only way I can help you out. I don't want you ending up on the front page of the *Herald* with the headline 'Māori youth kills family of four.'"

Tyson scowled. "Doubt it."

"You know what I mean. You given any more thought to what you want to do? I mean, you still want to go for your apprenticeship as a chef?"

"You really think I look like a chef to you?" Tyson asked. He couldn't even remember having mentioned it, but he couldn't rule it out. He had been washing dishes far too long. "Faye isn't going for that."

"He will if you want to do it. You know we're always looking out for 'nother chef. By the time you sort your shit out, I'll be head chef." Zadie glanced up, thanking the tall guy who put their coffees down. She slipped him five dollars and change.

"I don't know."

"I do…you don't look happy with life. I know something's up. I know it's probably working all these long hours. You can't be doing much more than sleeping or working. Or worrying about your family. Look, I know your mother probably worries about you. And your friend…what's his name?"

"Rawiri."

"I'm sure he worries about you too."

"He just wants my ass working normal hours so he can see me more," Tyson snorted.

"Nothing wrong with that. He sounds like he's got the brains out of you two." Zadie sipped at her mocha. Tyson just played with his cup, pushing the handle about the cup in circles. "I'm not going to pester you about this forever…but I still think you should have dreams beyond just washing dishes."

Tyson didn't know how to explain how things were. Life was regular enough that one day blended into another, blended into weekends. Sometimes it stung enough to make him think, but for the most part it seemed like a malaise. He frowned. Zadie was bordering on lecturing.

"Why do you do this?" he asked, looking her in the eyes.

"Pester you?" Zadie answered frankly. "Because I'm your friend? Because I care about you?"

"Yeah, but why?"

Tyson saw the hint of frustration pass over her features. Zadie pondered over her mocha. She looked up at Tyson with an expression that was disarming. "I really like you, Tyson. A lot. Actually, I don't know why we aren't going out. Why aren't we? Do you want to?"

Tyson almost spluttered, glad that he wasn't drinking his mocha and feeling his light-skinned cheeks flush suddenly. She saved him, mercifully, a hint of a playful smile as she remarked, "We go well together, I think. I always figured that you didn't have the guts to ask or something. But you being all shy all the time is sort of cute."

"I guess," replied Tyson. He barely managed to get even that out. He was light skinned enough that blushing showed bad.

"What about it, then? Do you want to go out?"

"I dunno…"

"You know that's not always the sort of answer a girl wants to hear." Zadie ignored her cup a moment. "It's either yes or no."

Tyson felt the heat burning in his cheeks, his mind working overtime as he tried to think of excuses. He wished there was some way that he could open his mouth and have the words come out: *Sorry. I only think about guys.*

It would solve so many problems.

"You're cool," Tyson said. Better to avoid it. "Why me? What's so cool that you want to go out with me?"

Zadie raised an eyebrow, "You want me to list the reasons

for you, then? Because I think you're sorta hot. Well, sorta is an understatement. I think you rock those dreads. Because you're caring, you show that with all this work you put in to look after your brothers." Tyson had never felt so uncomfortable, feeling Zadie's gaze linger on his. He glanced down as she continued. "Because I like you, Tyson. I really do."

"I'm not really looking for a relationship right now," he said. The excuses came easy, tumbling from his lips. "With work and all, you know…"

"You like guys."

"Huh?"

"The cutest ones are always gay. Is that why you don't want to go out? Because you're into guys, not girls?"

Tyson tried to stifle the look of shock and dismay on his face. For a split instant he thought to say "Yeah," but instead he just blurted, "Hell no! Why did you think that for? You think I look gay?"

"No," Zadie grunted. She looked put off by Tyson's sudden defense. "You don't need to be a queen to like guys, Tyson."

Tyson sat in shocked silence, his heart thumping along with the quick beat of the music. He busied himself with his coffee, slurping in quick gulps. He realized a few moments later that he was almost holding an empty cup.

"I'm sorry, Tyson. I didn't mean to make you uncomfortable with all this. You know I like you." Zadie took a casual sip of her mocha. "I guess I just hoped the feeling was mutual. This seriously wasn't the reason I pulled you out here. It just sort of came up."

"It's cool," he murmured.

"That's your answer to everything. You say that too much."

Tyson looked up, but she was smiling across the table at him. He was scared what she thought, about why he had turned her down. He hated himself again for not having whatever wiring it took to get a hard-on staring at her. Zadie smiled warmly. "One day you're going to make some girl very happy."

"I hope so," he replied, all that he could think to say. Maybe she didn't think he was into guys. Not for real. Why the hell hadn't he said yes?

"You want to come back here next week? Not as a date. Just so we can work out what you're going to do with your job."

"Sure," said Tyson. "I guess it wouldn't hurt."

"'Course it wouldn't. And stop frowning, fuck ya." Tyson looked surprised, staring over at Zadie, but she was smiling still. "You look better when you smile. So do me a favor."

The sentiment was enough to tug a hint of a smile out of him. Tyson took another gulp from his mocha. He tried to relax, but his mind was busy. He felt bad that he hadn't brought up his sexuality when he had the perfect opportunity. Tyson shuffled about on the cushions a little, thankful at least that the air between them was lighter and that she didn't seem to think he was gay.

Chapter Ten

The rain was assaulting the inner city in great waves as Tyson and Zadie left the café. The lights were losing their shine to the haze of the approaching morning. Tyson felt tired, already thinking about his bed. He pulled out his iPod to check the time, watching as Zadie made a dash to cover, heading back to her car. Tyson looked after her for a time. He had lied to her. Even after all the compliments she had paid him.

Heading out onto Queen Street, Tyson opted for cover, rather than ducking and twisting through the backstreets. Glad that it was the end of the week so it didn't matter so much if he got soaked on the way home. A chill still hung in the air as he kept away from the rain's cold touch. He pulled his deep hood up over his head of dreadlocks, already shoving his hands low into the pockets of his hoodie. He wondered when the next train would be pulling out. His life worked on routine. He didn't often have to deal with deviation.

His conversation with Zadie kept bugging him. He hadn't *really* lied, had he? Tyson tried to remember if she had asked him the question directly, whether he had said no, anything to justify it. In the end, he decided he had lied. Tyson scowled at missing his chance to finally admit it. The opportunity had been handed to him and he'd fucked it up.

Tyson's gaze lifted from the pavement long enough to catch on someone coming up the street towards him. The guy looked about his age, although he was browner, more rugged. He was wearing an orange construction hat. It reminded Tyson of what Rawiri had said about not wanting to build roads or buildings for a living. It was true that it seemed to be the sort of thing you did if your skin was brown.

Tyson couldn't help admitting to himself that the profession certainly made the bros look phine. The guy was heading closer towards him, up the street, with a wide-legged swagger. His clothes were grimy, and he was wearing a few singlets over an old white T-shirt that had been forcibly divorced of its sleeves. Tyson stared at those arms. Tyson felt the suddenly excited weight between his thighs. At the last moment he stared up at the guy's face, finally. The guy raised his eyebrows and gave a sharp nod of greeting. Tyson nodded in reply.

Cursing himself, Tyson slipped his hands into his jeans pockets and tried to rearrange himself discreetly. It didn't make it any easier that he was wearing boxers. He found himself staring after the guy for a moment, half hoping, mostly dreaming that the guy would glance back at him. It didn't happen. The whole thing left Tyson with a half hard-on and a head full of hard feelings.

Tyson wondered if anyone like that turned up to William's café on Saturday nights. That made the whole idea appealing.

The pale haze of morning was breaking over the downtown as Tyson headed into Britomart. It was early enough that trains were probably running frequently, but he couldn't vouch for a Saturday morning. He headed down to the platforms, briefly glancing up at the electronic board as he passed. Half an hour later and Tyson was sitting on a mostly unoccupied carriage, pulling out of the station.

Tyson set himself up quickly with his black book and headphones. Although he was tired, he still had a nervous energy. As the train rattled along, swaying and rocking, Tyson busied himself in his book, scratching furiously with his stump of a pencil. He had started a new page, working on various versions of the word "hope."

The latest was barely distinguishable as a word, angular in graffiti style.

Tyson paused to glance up at one stop, Con Psy rapping in his ears. By chance he stared down the mostly empty carriage, his heart skipping a beat.

Him!

Tyson felt his cheeks flushing instantly. Even if he hadn't been dressed in the same black and whites he had seen him wearing the last two times, Tyson would still have recognized that pale face and flawlessly shaved buzz cut. The homeboy was sitting near the door, hoodie and feet up, head back as he leaned back in his seat. He looked like he was sleeping.

Tyson let himself stare at the homeboy's broad chest. He could see how his unblemished white T-shirt hung off it and his stocky shoulders. His hands were shoved deep into the pockets of his oversized, sloppy hoodie. Tyson felt himself getting up again, second time in less than half an hour. He shuffled uncomfortably in his seat, his hands somewhat shaky as he pushed himself down.

What was the homeboy doing on the same train as Tyson? Did he live out south as well? Why hadn't he seen him before? Tyson was overwhelmed by the questions. He couldn't believe that he could have been traveling a few trains before this guy for so long. All it took was being broken out of his schedule.

Tyson felt a painful longing as he stared at the guy. Surprise quickly turned to more melancholic thoughts. In his mind he sang praises and made a litany of promises, of how the guy would never have to worry about anything ever again. Just if he had that one chance with him.

Tyson couldn't take his eyes off the guy. Maybe he had fallen asleep. What stop was he going to get off at? Tyson panicked when he thought it could be the next one, for all he knew. He willed the guy to look up, to notice him. He begged, but he knew his luck, knowing the homeboy wouldn't.

For some reason he entertained the impossible for a moment.

Tyson had fucked up one perfect opportunity already, not telling Zadie he liked guys. He sat staring at the white homeboy, seeing the situation for what it was. Another opportunity that he could fuck up.

Or he could grab life by the nuts, like Zadie told him.

Tyson almost fell back down into his seat as he got up. He did what he could to steel himself and ignore the feelings in his stomach. Shoving his headphones off his head, hoodie going back with it, he put his black book under one arm and made his way up the carriage.

What was he meant to say?

Tyson stared at the homeboy, looking at the way he filled out his sloppy attire while it still hung on his frame. Closer and closer. His cheeks felt like they were on fire as he dropped himself down in the seat across from the guy's, eyes still not leaving that face. Words formed on his lips but they lay trapped in the top of his throat.

The guy stirred and glanced casually over at him. Tyson froze, like a cat caught. The guy nodded to him in staunch greeting. Tyson slouched back in his seat, the homeboy resting his head back again, closing his eyes. Tyson forced himself to form words.

"I saw you in that alley."

The homeboy glanced back up again, looking him over a moment, as if trying to place him. A look of vague recollection passed over his features before he remarked in his bold, husky voice, "Oh yeah, I remember. What's up, my man."

The homeboy pulled a hand out of his pocket and reached over to Tyson. Tyson fumbled with himself, managing the close approximation of a street shake. He mostly fucked it up, in his nervousness.

"You write?"

"Huh?" Tyson asked. He was still shaking somewhat, still not fully comprehending the fact he was talking to the guy of his dreams.

He looked so confident and casual. It came so easy. The homeboy nodded towards Tyson's black book.

"You a graff artist? You write? What name you tag?"

"Oh…uh…nah…not really. Just some stuff I mess around with," Tyson forced out. He was shaking again.

"Can I check it out?"

It might have been a question, but Tyson heard it as an order. He handed over his black book without a second thought. The homeboy sat up a bit straighter, and started paging through it from the front.

"And you telling me you don't write, man? Fuck, what a waste."

"Nah, I'm not that good…it's just sort of stuff…nothing serious."

"You oughta get serious, my man," the homeboy replied. "You checked out any of the shit in *Disrupt*? Some of this shit would look sweet up on a wall." Tyson watched as he paged through. He kept pausing to give various parts of it closer attention. Tyson murmured something of a reply, but wasn't paying much attention to his voice.

"Name's Marc."

Of course it was. It fitted. Tyson was staring again. "Uh… Tyson…"

"Yeah? Like the boxer? Pretty hardcore name."

"Yeah…My dad was into boxing."

"No shit."

Marc kept paging through the black book, reading over some of the words scribbled here or there. Tyson noticed the passage of time on those pages. He could tell the weeks and days in a steady stream forward. He stared as Marc stared at a small work he had done. Tyson thought it was sort of ironic that he had first seen Marc around the same time he had done that one.

Fuck.

Tyson reached over and grabbed the book out of Marc's hand,

a gut reaction as he panicked. Marc looked surprised. Tyson shoved the book into his satchel. Another few pages and Marc would see a whole lot more of Tyson's mind.

"I'm not that good…it's just some shit."

"If you say, man. I think the only shit around here is the fact you're bullshitting yourself about your skill."

Tyson glanced back up, annoyed at the sudden bluntness in Marc's husky voice. He forgot his infatuation for a moment. Marc was staring back at him with light brown eyes. "What?"

"You think Mouli or P-Money or any of those cats sat around thinking they weren't shit? They're DJs, but still, get off your ass. Do something with it."

The words stunned Tyson for the moment. He had hardly expected for things to go this way. Marc's tone was forceful and disarming. Tyson just managed a sort of a quiet "I guess so."

"Fuck that. Work it out, my man. I could hook you up with someone to help you with that."

Tyson just sat in silence for a moment, Marc's words still sinking in. He found himself curious, unintentionally changing the subject. "What were you doing in that alley anyway?"

"Oh. Downtown? I'm a street promoter. Well, that and a few other things." Marc dug about in the back pocket of his pants and handed something over towards Tyson. "Guerrilla Advertising. I get people up and out there. I promote gigs and artists. I could promote your shit once you get out there."

Tyson looked down at the card. It looked like a business card, other than the graffiti title of his business on it. Marc Westing. And a cell phone number. His name didn't seem too thuggish, seeing it written there. Then again, Tyson always had problems with his own name. His brothers got the good names. Strong Māori names.

"Cool."

"You heard of the Dodgee Dozen?" Marc asked. Tyson looked up from the card, still too occupied to be totally infatuated.

"No."

"You will. They're a group from out south," Marc said, shoving his hands back into his pockets. He leaned in heavily on them, pulling his sweatshirt down tight over his solid shoulders. "All four realms represented. Should hook you up with those guys. They got a few graff artists up in there."

"Wouldn't really be twelve of them if I joined," Tyson tried to joke.

"It's just a name. I think they got about fifteen confirmed members," Marc said. Tyson felt a raw blush coming at him again as Marc regarded him for a second. "Guess you ain't going to the freestyle battle down at the Barge tonight, then?"

Tyson knew the place. It was in his hood. He tried to remember what Rawiri had said about the place. All bars were the same to Tyson, small, dark, dingy, and stinking of beer. "No."

"You know the place?"

"Yeah, it's just up the road from where I live."

"Sweet. I'll roll by your place about eight, then, and we can go over there. Introduce you to them. They pretty cool bros."

Tyson stared at Marc like he was crazy or something. After a moment Marc gave him a rather frank and questioning look, then asked, "Why? You got some shit on you need to do?"

"No...but...I don't really go in for that sort of thing."

"Well, if you wanna sit on your ass for the rest of your life, mate, it's on you. Or you can give me a call when you finally get your shit together..."

Tyson frowned. He wanted to open up his black book and try and work out what it was that Marc was seeing in his stuff. Tyson only had to think about things a few moments longer. Another opportunity. He pushed himself.

"Nah, okay. Eight, then."

Chapter Eleven

Tyson walked home, although it felt like he flew. He should have been tired, but the energy was keeping him on a high. Not only had he talked to Marc, but now he was going to a bar with him. Marc seemed to pay him more attention than Tyson ever thought he would, even in his fantasies. Suddenly all those thoughts and dreams seemed pale in comparison to the reality.

Tyson headed up to his room and dumped his stuff. He looked over at his bed, pondering what he would usually do. He didn't feel like sleeping, instead he wanted to tell everyone, anyone who would listen. The guy's name was Marc. And somehow Tyson had worked up the nuts to talk to him! Tyson looked out the window at the grey, wet skies, trying to work out if Rawiri might be home.

He headed back downstairs, passing his mother, who was busy loading up the washing. She smiled at him, seeming to sense his strange, madly happy mood. "You're up early...or have you even gone to bed yet?"

"No. I stayed in town for a bit after work." Tyson tried to curb his smiles before asking, "It cool if I go out tonight?"

"Don't need to ask me. You're old enough to make your own decisions." Tyson saw the private enthusiasm on his mother's face. She leaned in close to him as he passed and kissed him on the forehead. "Just make sure you take care of yourself."

"Yeah, I will."

Tyson headed back outside. He missed the tired expression that slipped back over his mother's face as he stepped out into spitting rain. He headed towards the break in the fence in the backyard. Tyson started to slow as he lifted and ducked in under the sodden wood. Standing up on Rawiri's side of the fence put a damper on his high spirits.

Compared to his place, Rawiri's was a tip. It looked about as run down from the front as Tyson's place, but out the back most of the yard was packed dirt; what little grass grew clung to life and was twisted into hard tussocks. Towards the creek was a garage that had been turned into a sleep-out. Stacks of corrugated iron and wood lined the back of the property, overgrown and destroyed by neglect. Nearby sodden rubbish bags lent a rich stink to the air, and escaped rubbish blew and snagged here or there.

Sobered somewhat, Tyson headed over towards the garage. There was a side entrance. Some of the windows had been broken and boarded, or filled over by plastic bags. All of them were curtained by mismatched or dirty materials. Tyson knocked a few times, noticing the stillness about the yard. He glanced back at the mean house, its off-cyan paint long since cracked and peeling.

Hearing no answer, Tyson pushed open the door, peering into the yawning darkness that presented itself. The place was cramped, the floors strewn mostly with mattresses or discarded bottles or cigarette packets. Compared to the prevalent stink of the backyard, the musty, damp smell was a relief. Tyson went in, half-hoping to see Rawiri lying asleep on one of the mattresses.

He didn't, disappointed. Tyson saw a rather rusted-looking exercise machine and scattered weights down the back that he hadn't seen last time he was here. That was a long time ago. Tyson hated the oppressive weight of the place. He dreaded what he was about to do and considered whether he really needed to talk to Rawiri as badly as he thought.

Heading towards the house, Tyson lingered at the bottom of the concrete steps that led to the back door. It was a while longer, the rain spitting at his face, before he headed up and knocked on the door. No answer. He knocked again, knowing that Rawiri would be home. The only other place he ever seemed to be was Tyson's house. Tyson opened the door, knowing it would be unlocked. He stared into the kitchen. His heart sank.

The place looked so totaled that it was hard to believe anyone could live there. Dishes were stacked everywhere; that and pots filled with old food made the place smell ripe. It seemed stupid to think anyone would bother emptying the bin, given the rest of the kitchen. It was piled high. The kitchen table was stacked with empty beer bottles and Tyson could smell the yeasty scent permeating the air.

"Rawiri..."

Tyson lingered at the door, unable to bring himself to step inside. He hoped calling would rouse Rawiri, scared of what else it might awaken. He called again, before someone he didn't recognize came wandering into the kitchen. He was large, middle age compounded by a self-abusive urban life that had mangled his appearance. Thick, unkempt hair, dark stains on his bare brown arms that were probably at one point legible tattoos. His gut hung tight against the inside of his threadbare rugby jersey. Tyson didn't recognize the team colors.

"Who the fuck are you?"

"Rawiri's mate," Tyson shot back, annoyed that he was seeing someone unfamiliar in his friend's house. "Who are you?"

"His uncle."

"Where is he?"

The guy nodded back towards the darkness beyond the kitchen door. Tyson stood his ground, his nerve slipping. "Tell him I came over..." The guy nodded again, looking put out. Despite the day's triumphs, Tyson didn't want to push his luck.

Tyson grew bored on the back steps, waiting, not hearing

anything inside. He was starting to feel the effects of the cold morning, thinking of leaving, before he heard the back door open. Seeing Rawiri coming out pulled a smile to Tyson's face. His gaze lingered on his friend's arms. He was wearing only a white singlet and blue sports pants that lost their domes further down the legs, falling open on his lower calves, and thick wool socks.

"Shouldn't you be in bed, cuz? Why you up for?"

Tyson got up as Rawiri headed awkwardly down the steps. Tyson sobered somewhat as he caught himself staring at Rawiri's wide ass and the way his singlet hugged down over it. They started towards the garage-cum-sleep-out.

"I haven't gone to bed yet…"

Rawiri gave him a strange look, his thick, greasy mane dancing about his shoulders as he scratched at his head. "Why the fuck you smilin' so much? You still ain't said why you up."

"I had coffee in town after work with one of the people I work with."

This time it was Rawiri's turn to smile, and he pushed open the side door to the garage and went inside. "Oh yeah, well, that explains it, then. You finally got your cock in some cunt, cuz? Only reason your ass would be grinnin' like you on drugs. You fuck that girl you work with?"

Tyson felt the wave of heat wash over him, embarrassed. "Hell no!" It was all he could think to say.

"What then?"

"I just came over to say I'm going out to the Barge Bar tonight."

Rawiri's expression bordered on confusion. He dodged mattresses, pulling on a light cord, before sitting down on the exercise machine. The ceiling light added a morose hue to the garage. "Why?"

Because the guy who I got a massive crush on invited me, after I had the guts to talk to him. At least that's what was going through Tyson's mind. He pegged back the ambition of it.

"This guy I met on the train told me he knows some guys," Tyson tried to explain. "I mean, he looked at my book and said he thinks I got skill and I should get into graffiti."

Tyson smiled widely. Rawiri was staring back at him like he didn't know who was standing in front of him. He shrugged his thick shoulders. "I told you that a long time ago, cuz. You just told me your stuff was shit."

"Well, yeah," Tyson replied, frowning. He sat on the arm of a couch frame that sat along one cluttered wall. It had long since lost its cushions. "Was a while ago…guess I got a little better…" Tyson couldn't shake how suspicious Rawiri looked of him. It was starting to worry him.

"Sweet. Go hard."

"You want to come?"

"No."

"What you doing tonight?" Tyson hadn't expected Rawiri was going to say yes. He was enough like him, they both hated crowds.

"Was gonna check out the K-1."

Tyson frowned. He had forgotten. "You can come chill over at my place. I can set the TV up in my bedroom. I'll just get in a bit later." Rawiri was shaking his head.

"Nah, cuz. I don't wanna be over your place if you're not there. That's fuckin' weird. I'll just catch it over here or see it someplace else."

Tyson knew there wasn't anyplace else. He toyed with the idea of not going, but the idea was fleeting. "You'll be okay, though, right, bro?"

"Sure. I ain't your mother, Ty. Maybe I'll come check you out in the mornin' if you ain't sleepin'."

Tyson grinned, his mood still bright. "Like that's ever stopped you, man."

Rawiri managed a hint of a grin, but it wasn't an honest one. He ran his hands through his thick hair. "Nah, guess not."

"Come over my place for now, bro," suggested Tyson. "You can have a shower and chill out until I have to go."

"You sayin' I stink?"

"Nah. Better than me hanging out by myself. Think I might just stay awake until tonight."

Rawiri struggled up with considerable effort. He shook his head again, remarking in his quiet tones, "Almost like you goin' on a fuckin' date, cuz. Guess I can't complain if it's got you in a good mood."

Tyson let Rawiri pull him up, feeling the tightness of his grasp. He let the remark lie. In some ways it almost did feel like a date. Tyson wondered if this was what dates felt like. How many people were lucky enough to go out with someone they had fallen head over heels in love with? He just smiled quietly to himself as they went back over to his house.

CHAPTER TWELVE

The main gig don't start until nine," Marc said, pulling his usual hoodie against the cold. "But I usually roll in to gigs I've advertised early. Check out who turns up and who doesn't. Get me some more work."

The Barge Bar was up ahead of them, a great block of a building with a sizable car park in front. The front was plastered in beer sponsors. It was down the far end of the town that Tyson usually never had reason to visit. He kept his hands buried in the pockets of a jacket he had borrowed from Rawiri, a heavy, long one with a big hood, lined with faux fur. Other than that, it was his usual uniform of black, a Disruptiv tee. Tyson avoided the puddles as they walked, hearing the thump of a familiar beat from inside.

"You advertised this gig?"

"Yeah, wallpapered a whole lot of places downtown. Then hit up a few places around here. You ain't seen the posters? Southstyle Freestyle Battle?"

Tyson shook his head, but he couldn't help but show he was impressed. "You do all that stuff?"

"Yeah, my man. Told you I was in advertising."

It had never occurred to Tyson before. He always figured that it was people a lot older than him that got into running businesses. Marc looked around his age, early twenties at most. He wondered at what it took inside to have that sort of drive in life. They stopped at the doors of the bar, letting a group of noisy homeboys in first. Marc slapped him on the shoulder, shocking him back to reality.

"C'mon. If there's any of the Dodgee Dozen up in here, I'll introduce you. They'll probably turn up a bit later. Probably end up taking out this whole thing anyway, ain't really too much competition."

"They really that good?" Tyson asked. He fell in step beside Marc.

"Yeah, I'm backing them as the next best thing in local hip hop. Sorta like New Zealand's answer to Wu Tang."

Tyson had never been into the bar, but it was everything he had expected it to be. The place was a warehouse with a long bar down one side. It had a smell of beer about it that worried Tyson, reminded him of Rawiri's place. A stage had been set up at the far end, where a DJ was already digging through crates, picking out tracks. There were already a decent number of people in the bar, most of them gathered around an area in front of the stage.

Marc was stopped at almost every turn, greeting with people. Tyson kept his head down, doing his best to sink into the background. He couldn't help staring at Marc's obvious popularity, jealous at how everyone knew him. As they weaved closer to the stage, a whoop went up. Tyson saw the movement of breakdancers through the press of the crowd. He knew track the guy was dancing to word for word, 4 Corners' "On the Downlow."

Tyson stared, mesmerized by the energy of the guy. He tried to recall where he had seen him before as the guy hit his top rock perfect beat for beat. He was dressed in Adidas sports pants, black tee, and another tee tied back across his head. The gathered crowds cheered as he transitioned to the floor, spinning into the famous windmill move that Tyson had seen in videos before. The b-boy kept at it, the crowd hollering louder with every passing moment, each turn making Tyson think he was going to drop. Finally, he pulled into a freeze that dropped his T-shirt on his abs.

"Hey, my man," Marc said, slapping at Tyson's arm. Tyson had to stop himself staring at the b-boy's stomach. "They over here."

Tyson followed behind Marc, who was heading over towards a table near the side of the stage. The group there were a scattered lot, but all had the sloppy dressed air of hip hop about them. Tyson recognized the overly bling rocks in some of their ears, chunks of stuff that had to be glass, all too large. Tyson wouldn't have dreamed of approaching a group like these lot; they intimidated him. Marc started to shake with them, a few of them giving him staunch, one-armed hugs, so brief they barely betrayed any emotion behind them.

"'Sup, Marc?"

"Not much, man. Fuck, you better be ready for tonight. I already been telling people you lot gonna take it out."

Tyson looked at the guy, tall, long and lean, towering over everyone else. His complexion was dark, so much so Tyson wondered if he was entirely Polynesian. He looked like he would make a better basketball player than rapper, and other than the athletic bands on his corded, thin forearms his attire was strictly plain in blacks. His jeans did a poor job of staying on his narrow hips. He wore a towel draped over his head, dark eyes regarding Tyson suspiciously a moment. Tyson tried not to stare at the guy's thick lips.

"Who's this?"

Marc slapped Tyson on the back again, remarking in his husky tones, "This my boy, he's an up-and-coming graff artist. Figured he might be able to get some tips from you or some your boys."

The guy stuck a hand out, and Tyson did his best not to screw up the handshake. "Name's Loot. Or S-A-Loot," he explained, spelling it out. "South Auckland money and all that shit. Plus S. A. is my initials." Loot looked at him expectantly, and Tyson froze up instantly. Marc came to his rescue, quickly.

"Yeah," Marc replied. "Soon to be undisputed champion of local graff, Tyson. He writes Dred1. You seen any that shit?"

"Nah…"

"He does most his shit downtown, so maybe you haven't seen it. I seen his black book, it's fucking sweet. Just needs him some help to take the next step and start hitting up the walls."

"That's cool," Loot remarked. He seemed to regard Tyson with a little less hardness now. Tyson couldn't get past what Marc was doing. How could he lie like this? Tyson knew he was going to get in deep shit once Loot found out he wasn't all that. Tyson glanced back towards the door when he noticed Loot stare past him, Marc doing the same.

"Oh yeah, there's the fucking big man of the hour." Marc couldn't contain his grin. Tyson noticed a large islander had just come in with a group of other guys. Marc waved to try and get his attention before hollering, "Fat ass!"

The guy walked over towards Marc, smiling a hint when he saw who it was. Tyson checked him out as he swaggered over slow. He was a big guy, but most of his size and weight was poised up in his chest and shoulders. An oversized T-shirt hung from solid muscle that had Tyson trying not to gawk. He smiled a bit as he read what was written on the T-shirt: "Lock up your mothers too…" The guy had a bit of a chubby face, long hair separated into five thick braids that stuck out at weird angles.

"'Sup, my man?" Marc said, giving the guy a staunch half hug. He made Marc look small. "Want you to meet someone. My boy Dred1 here. You oughta see his artwork. He wants to become a graff artist. And he's local too, so I'm guessing your crew's gonna have competition pretty soon unless you snatch him up."

Tyson just tried to keep himself in one piece to Marc's hard sell, nodding a bit, hands shoved deep in the pockets of Rawiri's jacket. He was learning to keep face, despite the fact he was wanting to kick Marc in the ass. The group's leader looked down on him. Tyson shrank. The guy's gaze didn't relent, almost like a blunt physical challenge. Tyson found somewhere else to look and wished he was actually someplace else too.

"This is Siege, he's one the main rappers in the Dodgee

Dozen," said Marc. Tyson stuck out a hand rather than make a fool out of himself by not moving. Siege didn't take it. Tyson wondered if this was how boxers felt just before the first round bell rang. "Best fucking battle rapper in NZ. Wouldn't mind seeing Mareko go head to head with him."

Sweating, Tyson nodded vacantly, shoving his hands away. He wondered again why he had come here. This whole scene wasn't him. Siege walked past him to greet the rest of the table. Tyson sent a look toward Marc, who was already starting to pull him away.

"Shit, bro…"

Marc laughed. "Fuck, forget that, my man. Siege is like that with everyone. That's just half of who he is, he's always trying to psych people out. It's part of his game. Doesn't mean he doesn't like you."

Tyson frowned, suddenly realizing that he had seen Siege and the b-boy before. Out on the street one night, in front of the train station. He remembered Siege's hard raps, the rest of the boys there cheering him on. The b-boy had spoken to him.

Tyson also recalled thinking how he would never have the nuts to talk to guys like them. And here he was meeting them all in a bar. Funny how life messed with you.

"You want a beer or something?" Marc asked.

Tyson looked past him, seeing the guy's grin. "Fuck, you sorta out of it tonight, my man. Better stay sharp."

"You sure it's cool telling them all that stuff about me?"

"What? You mean about your artwork?" Marc shrugged his solid shoulders. "I said I would. And I'm not lying to these guys. Your shit's worth hyping, man. Whether you want to follow through and do something with it is up to you now. I'm just opening the doors."

Tyson wanted to ask Marc if he really felt his stuff was that good. He was at the bar, trying to keep out of the way of the swell of people that were starting to get drinks. The music was starting to get louder, and more people came into the place. Tyson wanted to keep his head down. He could already start to feel how his T-shirt was clinging to him, and the smell of beer was starting to permeate the air.

Marc stepped back from the bar with two bottles of beer. He passed Tyson one before he had a chance to say he didn't drink. It was sobering seeing Marc in this light, but Tyson couldn't bring himself to be angry. Why was Marc taking as much interest in him as he was? But then wasn't that what he wanted in the first place? Tyson frowned, feeling the chill of the bottle in his hand.

"I'm just gonna check out the rest of the crowd, catch up with a few of my other mates," Marc said. Tyson felt out of sorts. "You want to come along, or…"

"Nah, I'm gonna chill over here for a bit," Tyson replied. He glanced over to where he had pointed, seeing that it wasn't as empty as he had hoped.

"Not gonna dump you and leave you to fend for yourself." Marc put a hand on Tyson's shoulder. "That'd make me an asshole. I'll be around." Tyson tried not to melt under those words. He savored the way that Marc looked him straight in the eyes, the feeling of his hand on his shoulder. Tyson knew he couldn't be mad at that.

"Sweet."

That didn't help the loneliness that Tyson felt when he saw Marc walk away. He tried to find himself a place to chill as the bar started to get ready for the main event. He tried to spot Marc through the crowds who were pushing towards the stage. Tyson couldn't stop the jealousy that he felt seeing him laughing and talking with others. Soon enough he was swallowed up by the crowd entirely.

He got a job to do, that's all.

Tyson started questioning why he had even agreed to come, feeling his mood sink.

"Hey."

Tyson felt a tap on his shoulder, glanced over to see the b-boy that he had seen breaking before. The guy was smiling at him, high cheekbones and strange grey eyes. He had a shadow of stubble that made Tyson think of Rawiri. He remembered the guy's abs, saw the cords in his forearm as the b-boy pressed a handshake into his hand. His grip was strong. It matched the obvious athleticism that he could see in his body.

"You're Dred1, right? My name's Ihaia," the guy offered, putting out his hand. Tyson ignored it. "Most people call me Crunch, though."

The nickname got the better of Tyson, and he asked despite himself, "Why?"

"Depends who you talk to. It's either because of the fact everyone thinks I only care about my abs…or because of something that happened once when I was breakdancing."

"My name's not really Dred1. It's Tyson."

"Sweet name, uso," Ihaia said. Tyson tried to spot Marc again in the crowd. "I'm one of the Dodgee Dozen. Loot told me about you."

Tyson nodded, frowning when he saw Marc further over, talking to Siege. Already the bar was starting to gear up for the first round of the battle. The heat was starting to get to Tyson, he could feel his T-shirt starting to cling to him under his jacket. That, and the smell of beer on the air. Tyson tried to keep an eye on Marc as a stringy-looking homeboy took to the stage and started announcing. The weight of the noise started to press in around Tyson.

"You doing okay there, uso?" Ihaia asked, standing in close to Tyson. Tyson just nodded again. Marc and Siege were holding court near the tables where he had first met him.

Tyson felt a deep longing as he watched Marc. Even as small as he looked next to Siege, Tyson kept staring at Marc's solid shoulders, the confident way he looked. Tyson felt the cold glass of the beer bottle he was still holding, the way that the moisture was starting to make his hand wet. When it was evident that Marc wasn't coming back, he felt the mood weigh heavy on his shoulders.

The first few rounds of the battle were fairly straightforward. Thirty seconds a side, one on one. The gathered crowds had moved closer when the first battle started and Tyson lost sight of Marc. Probably for the best. Tyson found it hard enough to focus on the raps that were happening on the stage. The beat thumped in his head, the cheers of the crowds steady on him. His feet were starting to ache from standing so long.

"You live around here, right?" asked Ihaia. The latest round came to an end. "I seen you around, I think."

"Yeah, I'm local."

Tyson thought he saw Marc again, briefly. He caught Ihaia's easy smile, felt his hand on his arm. "Hey, well, hope you do end up running with Dodgee, uso. Be good to have some new blood in the group."

"I dunno, man."

"Looks like it's our turn up."

Tyson turned his attention back to the stage. He could see Siege going up, amidst cheers. Tyson could tell the guy was lapping it up, despite his intimidating stare. He watched as Siege began his round. His raps hit like punches, thinly veiled threats and insults on almost every level, knotted together in rhyme. Tyson felt bad for the guy opposite. He could see his confidence dropping a peg with every line. The raps were vicious, cruel. Demoralizing.

"On your knees, you sick mah'fucker, faggot, suck my cock," Siege ended, to a roar of applause. Tyson felt sick as Siege stood toe to toe and shoved the microphone at the other rapper. He looked shaken. Around them the crowds were ecstatic.

Tyson watched the rapper who walked off the stage rather than reply, the cheers turning to hard jeers. The last phrase had left Tyson as shaken as it seemed to leave Siege's opponent. Tyson felt guilty, scared.

"Damn, Siege," Ihaia remarked, shaking his head. Tyson just nodded lightly.

Tyson felt edgy for much of the next few rounds. He said good-bye to Ihaia to go in search of Marc. He couldn't find him for a long while, before coming upon him back near the bar where he had started. He tried to talk to Marc over the noise of the rapping. He made a few motions towards the door, and Marc followed. As they approached the door and headed back out into the cold night, Tyson finally managed to get his words out so Marc could hear them.

"I'm gonna go back home."

"You cool?" Marc asked, surprised. Tyson could see Ihaia lingering near the door, watching.

"Yeah, man. You know me and crowds." Tyson paused, then remarked. "Thanks for inviting me, though…"

"Sweet, my man," Marc replied. Tyson was startled as Marc pulled him in for one of those staunch half hugs. He felt himself throb, sucking in a tight breath as he spent an all-too-short second up hard against him. Tyson's mind panicked as he pulled back, recognized the finality of the situation.

"Uh…you going to be downtown…I mean, you going to be doing any work down there?"

"Yeah, I'm always down there doing this or that, I'll run into you."

It didn't feel like enough of an assurance, and Tyson felt scared he might not see him again, something screwed up only by his inability to cement it. Marc added after a moment, "You got my card, ain't you?"

"Yeah."

"Well, just gimme a call, we'll hook up."

Tyson smiled, seeing the easy smile on Marc's face. That confidence that Tyson loved so much was there. He nodded to him and then made his final farewells, heading back out onto the street. Once the thump of the music had died down into the mindless drone of the streets at night, Tyson started to realize how tired he was. His mind was a storm of thoughts, not focused enough to make sense of anything. Despite everything, there was something deep inside that drove him, like something had finally been stirred. He had something outside work and the day-to-day.

Marc had given him hope.

Tyson kept as quick a pace as he could returning home, eager to be in bed. He entertained ideas of staying in bed late tomorrow. It made him wonder about Rawiri. He had stopped worrying about him at some point of the night. But as Tyson rounded into his short street, his heart sank. He saw the flickering of blue and red light a while before he saw the police cars parked outside his friend's house.

CHAPTER THIRTEEN

Tyson panicked as he jogged towards his place, keeping to the far side of the road. He cursed himself quietly for leaving his best friend to this shit. He thought back, trying to remember if he had noticed any sign from Rawiri.

Heading back towards the deep shadows of his front yard, Tyson vaulted the short brick fence and walked quickly around to the back door. His mind raced as he worked out what he should do. Dump his stuff and then see if he could scope the place out. Try and find out where Rawiri was. His mind swam with dark images. He consoled himself with the fact that at least it was only police cars. It could have been ambulances too.

"Ty."

Tyson glanced back, hearing the quiet call as he started to unlock the back door. He saw movement in the shadows near the abandoned car and knew instantly who it was. Tyson walked quickly towards him, fearing the worst, hesitating. But when his friend pulled himself up out of the front seat and nodded a greeting, Tyson felt an almost overwhelming wave of relief.

"Fuck, bro…there's police outside your place." Tyson wondered why he was keeping his voice down.

"Yeah, I know."

"What happened?"

Rawiri shrugged his big shoulders. "Party got a bit outta hand. Someone called the police. Was probably the noise."

Tyson could not see past the shadows of his friend's hood, so he shoved it back off Rawiri's shaggy locks. Rawiri slapped back his hand with a force that hurt. A defiant anger was kept in his friend's eyes. Tyson just stared at Rawiri's rugged features. There were no bruises.

"Don't fuckin' touch me," Rawiri snarled. "You think I can't take care of myself or something? Fuck you."

"Bro…" Tyson shrank, instantly sorry he had done it.

"You think I got smacked around or something?"

Tyson's heart was thumping and he felt the urge to just back down and let the whole issue lie. He felt guilty thinking it was harder for him to deal with than Rawiri. Rawiri's stare cut through him, but Tyson felt a sudden defiance build in himself.

"Yeah, I did. Sorry if I give a fucking shit about you, bro."

The words hit Tyson about as hard as they seemed to hit Rawiri. Tyson saw his friend's expression drop, all guards down now. He felt sick inside, talking to his best friend like that. "Look…bro…I didn't mean that…"

"It's all good, cuz," Rawiri said. Tyson knew that self-denying tone.

"No, it isn't. None of this shit is, man…" Tyson looked back at Rawiri and almost instantly wanted to look away. He didn't like what he saw in his friend's eyes. There was no mask hiding those emotions. "Bro…"

"It's cool, cuz."

"C'mon, bro…you staying up at my place tonight."

Tyson didn't expect any resistance, and none was offered. He groped for his key again and headed back towards the house. The flashing lights of the police car still dappled the dense trees between the two worlds of their homes. Tyson felt a lump in his throat, choking him as he unlocked the door. He just wanted to get back to his bedroom. Fuck everything.

Tyson locked the door behind Rawiri as he let his friend go into the bedroom first. Rawiri seemed to just stand there, staring out the window, as Tyson quickly turned on the light on his desk. Rawiri stared back over at him, murmuring, "Turn that shit off, cuz..."

Tyson obliged, working by memory and the scant light of the dark, grey night outside. He pulled his jacket off and got the mattress out from under his bed. Tyson stood there, out of sorts for a long time. He eventually pulled his friend down towards the mattress. Tyson sat down with him, listening to the sound of the wind and then the sound of cars moving out in the street. He didn't bother to look—all he cared about was sitting here next to him.

"I can't do this shit any more, Ty..."

"I know."

"I fuckin' can't do it."

Tyson didn't know what to say, again. His throat hurt as he sat. He couldn't think what words would make it better. It seemed a stark comedown from what he had just been through. Marc and Siege and the deafening thump of the Freestyle Battle seemed like a world away. Everything here was quiet and hard and uncomfortable.

"We need to do something," was all Tyson could come out with. He risked looking over at his friend. Rawiri was rubbing slowly at his big thigh. The brace was making his jeans bunch up a little as he rubbed.

"Forget it, Ty. It's how shit is."

"It doesn't have to be, man. You remember what I told you about dreaming? About trying to think of something better?"

"Some people don't deserve better, cuz. Sometimes you can't change shit."

"Bro, that ain't true. I—" Tyson cut himself off. He couldn't talk about that part of his life. It stunned him into silence.

"Look, I don't fuckin' wanna talk about all this shit, cuz. Just drop it."

"Cool."

Rawiri was breathing tight and heavy next to him, and Tyson was feeling it himself. The dim light from the window fell on Rawiri's hard expression. Tyson could see everything that was getting locked up inside, and it hurt him seeing it. Rawiri bent over beside him, covering up his face. Tyson felt stunned as Rawiri started sobbing. This wasn't Rawiri. Rawiri never cried. Neither did he, for that matter.

Tyson sat there, feeling as if his body was locked in place. He couldn't move or speak. Instead he fought the battle inside him to try and change it. Right when he needed to do something, speak his feelings, or take that risk. Rawiri's big shoulders shuddered as he cried and Tyson hated himself, sitting there silent, everything bottled inside him.

Rawiri wiped at his eyes, choking back the few last sobs that wracked through him. Tyson watched as he dragged his rugby jersey up and wiped his face with it. The expression that revealed itself after was sullen and ashy. Tyson's throat was still raw and painful as he held back his own tears. He managed to work up the strength to mutter quietly to his friend.

"It's cool, bro…"

❖

Compared to the emotional rush of Saturday night, the week's work was a welcome escape. Seeing Rawiri cry had sobered Tyson. He wanted to tell someone about how his night out had gone. Usually Rawiri would have been the first to know. Awkwardly, he avoided bringing it up. Rawiri had slept about as long as he had Sunday.

Work was like coming down off a high, the usual grind that he had wanted so badly to escape from. Meeting up with Marc and going out to the Freestyle Battle seemed almost like a dream, distant and ethereal. Tyson buried himself in dishes and hot suds. Drowning himself in the endless seas of the local music on his iPod. Welcomed escape.

The night streets seemed more base, the temperature starting to pitch night after night. Tyson half expected to walk into Marc, like some street general, giving out orders to his ranks of young employees. The backstreets on the way to and from work were empty, occupied only by biting winds and blank stares from the streetscapes.

His weekend was eventless. Rawiri showed himself, but ultimately stayed away. Tyson kept to himself, scrawling in his black book and starting a new one. He thought to call Marc, but the surreal feeling of running into him kept him from doing it. It was halfway through his next week of work before things began to catch up on him again. Things began to feel like they had before, the emptiness inside, feeling trapped. He hated what had happened to Rawiri.

Wednesday night, he left for work early. Pulling out an old phone card he had tucked in his wallet, Tyson shut himself in a phone box near the bottom of Queen Street. He was wearing Rawiri's jacket against the cold. He had left it there since that night, and Tyson had become accustomed to it. It was comforting, slightly too large, and had a slight mustiness to it that reminded him all too much of Rawiri.

Tyson leaned up against the glass of the box as the call went through.

"Evening, this is the support line for gays, bis, and lesbians. How can I help you?"

"William." Tyson felt relieved he was hearing the older man's radio announcer–like voice.

"Ah, Tyson, is it? Good to hear from you again. It's been a while. How have you been?"

"Good. And not so good."

"Things are still a bit rough for you?"

"Yeah," Tyson replied. He played with the metal cord of the phone, keeping the receiver inside the big hood of Rawiri's jacket. "I dunno why I called again, though."

"Maybe you just wanted someone to listen. That's not a crime."

"I guess…"

William's voice reminded Tyson of the smell of smooth coffee, strong and full. "What have you been up to since we last talked?"

"I met that guy...the one I was talking about." Tyson looked out over the street, paranoid that someone might hear or see him talking about Marc. "We went out to this bar. Went to this event. He introduced me to some guys."

"That's good. I'm assuming a straight bar, and straight friends?"

"Yeah, it was a Freestyle Battle. I mean, like a rap gig."

"I'm sure you enjoyed yourself. The company would have been good, at least."

Tyson frowned. "I don't like crowds much. Makes me feel uncomfortable." Tyson fell quiet for a moment, and William seemed to stay the same. "One of my best mates is having problems..."

"Do you want to talk about it?"

"I don't know if I should. I wanna help him but he doesn't want me to do anything."

"That can be pretty hard. I don't want to make you talk about it, but without knowing anything, I would have to say that you should just follow your instincts," William said. That sympathetic tone that was so common to his voice was returning. "Sometimes your gut is the best thing to follow if you don't know how to proceed."

"I guess," said Tyson, picking his words all too carefully. "I don't wanna see him get hurt..."

"It sounds like you have some strong feelings for your friend. There's nothing wrong with that."

Tyson stayed leaning up against the wall of the phone box. The rain was dancing patterns down the glass in front of him. Outside, the streets were grey as people dashed between buildings. Tyson let out a slow sigh, catching himself, not meaning it to come out quite as loud as it did.

"What about your feelings for this person you have just met?" asked William. "Have they changed now that you have actually met him?"

"I dunno…he seems real cool. I really like him…" Tyson frowned as he murmured into the receiver. It sounded stupid, to say it like that. It was tough to express, and it made him sound like some schoolgirl.

"Big, handsome guy?"

Tyson let out a small smile despite himself. "Yeah, he is. He's real cute. Makes me happy thinking about him. Like everything's going to be cool. When I went out with him I didn't think about anything else. Was like nothing else mattered and I didn't have any problems…I sorta forgot about everything else."

"That's good. It's good to have someone who makes you feel like that." William paused on the other end of the line, then spoke again, carefully and measured. "How do you feel that you might not be able to have the relationship with him that you want?"

"I dunno." Despite all the looks and fantasies, he had to admit the thought had crossed his mind that maybe Marc might not even be like that. It seemed strange that it hadn't occurred to him earlier. "How can you have feelings like that for someone and nothing happen?"

"I know, and sometimes people don't return the feelings you have for them."

Tyson felt a bit of a lump in his throat, and things began to feel heavy. He stared at the rain that wriggled and ran down the glass, his head against it. "No one else has just been my friend like he has… no one. I still don't know why he is doing all this stuff for me…He saw some of my drawings and then went all hard out to try and get these guys to help me with it. I dunno why."

"It might be that he sees you have a talent. I wouldn't mind having a look at your artwork." Tyson just grunted, stubbornly noncommittal. William continued talking. "I'm not saying this guy doesn't feel the same about you. I can't say what his feelings might be. But I would still be very careful."

"I know…"

"You sound like a very wonderful person, Tyson. You've

already proved to me you're caring, with your concern for your friend. And talented with your artwork if this guy can see that in it. Have you considered talking to your parents about all this?"

"No." The answer was blunt.

"Have you considered it? Talking to your mother or father?"

"I don't think I want to." Tyson knew the hardness he was feeling inside from what he saw of Rawiri. "My father's dead."

"I'm sorry to hear that," William said. He asked after a polite pause, "Can I ask when he died?"

"When I was about seven...so...I dunno...maybe ten years ago." Even after all these years, Tyson didn't even want to go where William was taking him. Tyson's mood was starting to feel more like the weather.

"What about your mother?"

"Nah, not going to happen." Tyson hoped the bluntness would stop the questions.

"I'm sorry. I'm not pushing you. I'm glad at least you've chosen to talk to me. That's someone. I couldn't convince you to come in on Saturday, still?"

"Nah."

"You sure? It's a very friendly atmosphere. It may help to be around other people. It's certainly not like a bar. There's not that many people there. I know you don't like crowds. It would just be a few friends for a coffee."

"Nah, man."

Tyson could hear the resignation in William's voice, but he didn't push it further. "Well, the offer is always there. I am there pretty much every week. Maybe give it some thought."

"Sure." Tyson didn't feel in the mood to talk much longer. Between the idea he might never be with Marc, and bringing up his father, a pall had dropped on him. "Look, I got to go. Work."

"Okay. Well, thanks for calling again, Tyson. I hope we can talk again soon."

Tyson hung up, and leaned against the wall of the phone box

for a while after. He knew his mood wasn't going to lift any time soon. In fact, given how things were going anyway, it was only a matter of time before he felt this shit again. No biggie. All he could think of was Marc's big arms, his broad chest. Being slowly folded in against him. He remembered where he had tucked away Marc's business card, yet still felt the fright of the idea of calling him.

Tyson stared out at the rain and wondered why it was always up to him to make things get better. Nothing ever came easy. He thought how he would do anything for a chance with Marc.

Tyson took the plunge and dialed Marc's number.

CHAPTER FOURTEEN

Tyson stood in the shelter of an abandoned booth. He guessed that it had been some sort of parking booth, where you paid for your ticket on the way out. It was barely recognisable from its previous life, having long since been destroyed by time and taggers. Tyson had known where the place was but had never been here. As he waited he gazed at the large field of potholes and cracked concrete. Beyond it was an ancient edifice, equally abandoned. The place seemed to have a wild air to it, wind blowing heavily through the bush that lined it. The sun was still a while from coming up and the area was all long shadows and dark places.

Tyson's stomach was arguing with him again, twisting with nerves. He kept his hands shoved deep in the pockets of Rawiri's long jacket, wearing two hoods up. He wasn't even listening to his iPod at the moment. It had taken him about all his nuts to call Marc, and the call itself had been hellish. A garbled accident of words, nothing like he had spent so long planning and practicing.

This was different. This time it really was just him and Marc. Nothing else to get in the way. This time felt dangerously intimate.

Tyson was keeping his eye on the streets so closely that he picked out Marc's big form in the darkness a way off. He was wearing his usual sagging pants and sloppy hoodie, both black. His T-shirt was black this time as well, blending him well with the night, if not for the whiteness of his face and the slight shine of his thick silver chain. He walked with the same wide, confident swagger. Tyson was losing his own confidence the closer Marc got.

"Hey, my man," Marc said. He gave Tyson one of those one-armed hugs, and Tyson relished it despite how brief it was. "What's new?"

"Nothing really. Hope this is cool."

"Sure. Would have said something if it wasn't. I just been organizing some shit for another event, plastering the place up." Marc started to walk towards the car park, stepping around potholes and muddy puddles. "What you think of the battle?"

Tyson fell in close, but the terrain made it hard to stick too close. "It was cool."

"You bugged out pretty early. There wasn't any problems, right?"

"Nah," Tyson replied. It was mostly true. "Crowds were getting to me a bit, that's all."

Marc laughed. "Fuck, you like hip hop, right?"

"Hell yeah. I love hip hop. Think I've got about everything that's been released local." Tyson meant it, and there was a passion in his voice that made it unmistakable. "Why?"

"You love hip hop so much, and you don't even turn up to the gigs."

Tyson frowned. He didn't like having his love questioned like that. Truth was his music was there for him like no one else. Some days it felt like breathing. "Like I said, I just don't like crowds that much."

"I'm just fucking with you, mate. Would have been a good experience for you anyway. Probably gonna end up making a pretty sweet graffiti artist, seems you such a loner!"

Tyson nodded, thinking on that. It was disarming hearing Marc putting it that bluntly. But he found part of it refreshing as well. "You really think I would make a good graff artist?"

Marc shrugged his big shoulders. "If you put in the work, yeah. You catch up with Loot?"

"How? I don't even know where he lives."

"He lives in the same hood as you. Ain't like he or his crew is hiding. Get off your ass and go talk to him. He'll teach you a thing or two about graffiti, get you started."

Tyson switched off. Even though he had been introduced to Loot, it didn't seem right to just walk up to him on the street. Tyson stared at the long fence line they were walking towards. It was graffiti-blackened corrugated iron, running the length of something that looked like a stadium. The place looked beyond wrecked. Tyson was surprised it hadn't been ripped down.

"How good are you at climbing?" Marc asked, smiling back at him. "Better yet, how good are you at avoiding getting your ass all scratched up in barbed wire?"

Tyson put the pieces together fairly quickly as they moved along the fence. Rusting iron gave way to tall chain link, and he could see the stadium beyond it. He had seen rubbish dumps in better condition. Tyson was starting to feel his nerves sinking in deep. "This ain't legal, man."

"Nah, it ain't. Neither's graffiti. That ain't gonna stop you, is it?"

"What about cops?"

Marc laughed. "It look like the police hang out anywhere near here? Come on, soldier. I'll give you a leg up."

"I can climb it okay." Tyson didn't much like the look of the barbed wire at the top. Tall fences were there for a reason. Marc and Tyson were that reason.

"Cool, my man. C'mon. Over there. See where the barbed wire's broken a bit?"

"You come here much, man?"

"A bit. Just felt like finding some place quiet to chill. Just you and me."

Hearing those words from Marc steeled Tyson's resolve. Hell, he would do the climb twice, with cops hanging around, if that's the way it was going to be. Tyson gauged the fence and then after a moment's surveying threw himself up onto it. He climbed quickly, the fence rattling in protest. He hit the ground a little harder than he had wanted, looking back to see Marc already climbing the fence with gusto.

Tyson couldn't help being impressed. Marc moved pretty quick for a guy his size. Tyson's mind lapsed into the fantasies again, wondering at what sort of strength he had beneath those baggy clothes.

Marc smiled when he got down on the other side, and the tenseness of the situation kept Tyson silent. He'd never broken the law before. There was something thrilling, something that kids half his age would be doing. Between that and his hormones, fueled by Marc's last words, Tyson let the quiet between them linger.

They were standing in what used to be a stadium. Even in the bad light and deep shadows lent by the yawning void that was the field, Tyson could see the graffiti. It looked as if every spare space had been tagged up. Tyson could see why the place had been abandoned. It wasn't much of a stadium, just a field, fenced off, and one large grandstand for seating. Eden Park was countless times larger.

Tyson stayed quiet and followed Marc. He thought how he wanted to be alone with Marc, and how he couldn't get more alone than this. Despite the city, towering and shining behind them, the spot seemed isolated. The relative calm was disturbed by the sound of a train behind the thick line of trees on the hill. Marc was heading towards the grandstand, mounting the first steps quickly, and taking them two at a time.

Marc was right. It wasn't like cops hung out near places like this. The giddy thrill of breaking in mixed with the rush of getting away with it. It felt like there was no one for miles. Tyson noticed the amount of rubbish and spray cans scattered along the rows on the way up.

"You cool, my man?"

"Yeah, bro."

Marc sat down at the top row and Tyson joined him, thankful for the rest. He shoved his hands into the pockets of his jacket, checking the place out. Tyson didn't care where they had ended up, it was the company he cared about.

"You been doing that stuff long?" Tyson asked, eventually. "I mean, your work."

"Guerrilla Advertising? Yeah. Few years now. Why? You want a job?"

Tyson considered that, but shook his head. He pulled his jacket about him in the cold. This high up, the wind bit. "Nah, just wondered. Don't think I could ever do that. I mean start up a company for myself."

"You want something bad enough, my man, you gotta take it. Life isn't gonna give you anything. In fact, life probably gonna shit on you before it gives you a break. I wanted to make it on my own, so I did. What the fuck you got to lose, just from trying?"

Tyson nodded, looking over at Marc. He could see the determination in his expression as he spoke, and heard it in the tone of his voice. "You seem like you doing a good job. You dress pretty good." Tyson didn't want to seem like he was hitting on him. Marc didn't appear to notice, just shrugging dismissively.

"You want something, just take it, Tyson. Life ain't gonna give you nothing for free." Marc smiled a bit and looked as if he remembered something. His tone was less harsh when he spoke again, fishing his pockets. "Well, except maybe for now. But it's different between mates."

Tyson tried to hide his frown when he saw the blunt Marc produced. Marc put the blunt between his lips and lighted it up with a cheap-looking lighter. The heavy winds didn't do too much to tug away that unmistakable smell. It reached Tyson's nostrils all the same. The end of the blunt flared brilliant red in the dimness of night as Marc took a few heavy puffs and handed it over.

Tyson hesitated, only out of habit. Then it hit him. Marc smoked. He didn't want to have Marc think less of him because he didn't. He took the blunt carefully between two fingers, treating it like it might shatter if he held it too tight.

Tyson took to it with the enthusiasm that he had taken the fence, wanting to impress Marc. He felt the suffocating smoke fill his throat and lungs in one tight suck. The heat of it swept through him, before he started coughing heavily, billowing out clouds of the stuff. Marc was laughing, but his hand was rubbing and thumping at his back. Tyson couldn't stop coughing.

"Fuck, man, haven't you ever smoked before?"

"No," Tyson wheezed when finally he could get a word out. The smoke coated him on the inside. It felt rough. Marc starting laughing again. Tyson saw the funny side. He didn't figure he would have with anyone else. He grinned back, still coughing occasionally.

"Suck it in slow. Don't swallow. Just hold the smoke in you for a bit and then let it out. Just don't swallow."

Tyson was eager to try it again. He took a cautious puff, could feel the smoke flowing into him like water.

"That's it, my man. Now breathe out."

Tyson did. Marc's hand was still on his back. His cheeks grew hot, as well as his chest, as the smoke issued out of his lips. He coughed again, thumping at his chest. Tyson scowled at himself, muttering as best he could, "Fuck, I thought I did it right."

"Yeah, you did better. Just got to remember you haven't done weed before. It's good shit. It's gonna make you cough."

Tyson stayed quiet, pulling on the blunt again. Filling his lungs before exhaling it and watching the wind drag the plumes of smoke away. He heard Marc chuckling next to him. His hand was still slowly rubbing his back. Tyson couldn't help grinning as his head swam. He felt a warm glow at Marc's attention.

"Now you're going for gold," Marc said. "This is the bit where you pass it back, mate."

Tyson was still holding on to the blunt and did just that. He watched as Marc puffed away on it, looking like a seasoned veteran, smoking like a house on fire. Tyson was sorry Marc's hand wasn't on his back any more. His throat still felt a bit raw and his mouth tasted like sticky smoke. He waited patiently, telling himself that he would start up another conversation and turn down the blunt if he offered it again.

He didn't.

By the time they had burnt it down to just a small end which Marc pinched expertly in his fingers, Tyson was feeling strangely heavy and light. He had slouched down on the row, unintentionally leaned up against Marc's big frame. He felt bad, but his lanky form didn't seem to have the strength to move anywhere else. All he could do was watch the city. It was all shining jewels that were slowly winking out as light began to come to the sky's cheeks.

"It's good getting away and just fucking chilling alone sometimes," said Marc, out of the blue. Tyson liked how he felt against Marc's body.

"Yeah…I get that plenty, though…"

Tyson heard a quiet, husky chuckle. "I pretty well fucked you up, my man. Been a big morning for you. Getting your first puff of weed. Damn, you *are* fucked up. Here."

Tyson couldn't move for himself, feeling Marc pushed him upright. He couldn't stop smiling, as he felt Marc's big arm around him. Tyson could feel another part of him was starting to come up. He didn't feel the urge to take things any further. He just rested his head in against Marc's shoulder. Even that was a huge effort. His whole world became blissful and light as he heard Marc's voice lingering on the edge of his senses.

"Yeah, that's cool, mate. Just rest there, no need to stress about shit. Probably going to take you a while to come down off it anyway. I'll look out for you."

Tyson smiled. He stared down at himself, seeing the way his loose jeans jutted. He couldn't help but dwell on those words as he felt Marc's protective arm about him.

I'll look out for you.

CHAPTER FIFTEEN

By the time Tyson headed back to Britomart, he was feeling great about himself. He knew he was down off the weed but he still felt like he was flying. He couldn't stop smiling. He had watched longer than he should have as Marc headed off his own way, hands shoved into the pockets of his hoodie, hood up. He walked with that usual swagger, not giving a fuck what anyone thought.

Tyson stopped at a store in Britomart to buy food. He had an overwhelming urge for potato chips, and downed two packets waiting for the train. He felt happy about the fact that Marc had brought up meeting again. He told Marc where he worked and Marc had told him that if he was free and in town on Fridays around that time, he would meet him there. If he wasn't, no stress. Tyson had his number if he wanted to meet up. Marc said he was happy for the chance to have a sesh alone with him, given all the time he had to deal with people.

For once it seemed as if there was life outside his life. It was like things were slightly more bearable and that he could see a wider perspective.

When Tyson headed back into his street, the sun was already starting to climb. It was pale, given the overcast clouds. Tyson wasn't all that surprised to see Rawiri sitting on his front fence. He greeted his friend with a bit of stupid grin, nodding staunchly.

"Fuck, what sorta time you call this, cuz?"

"What? I was just taking care of something." Tyson stopped up short, seeing the way Rawiri was staring up at him. He had shaved but it hadn't made much difference. His hair was tied back in a black T-shirt.

"Fuckin' that girl, more like." Rawiri gave a dismissive shrug. "I don't care if you fuckin' her, man, you oughta just say, though. I thought we didn't keep shit from each other?"

"We don't, man." Tyson was hurt. "It's not that. I'm not hitting any ass. Wish I was."

Rawiri surrendered a bit of a smile and Tyson replied in kind. He helped Rawiri up as he started struggling slowly to his feet. His big solid shoulder slammed playfully against him, Tyson staggering a few steps in surprise.

"You're too fuckin' old to be a virgin, cuz," Rawiri muttered.

"When I lose it, man, you'll be the first person I tell."

"Better."

Tyson smiled, feeling a bit strange as he remembered how Rawiri had been last time he had seen him. It looked as if he was dealing with it somehow. He couldn't remember the last time Rawiri and he had just pissed around and had fun.

"I better get some sleep," Tyson said. Rawiri watched him with that slow, constant stare. Tyson waited to see if he would back off, but when he didn't he gave up on the subject. "You can come up, bro, but serious, I got to sleep. I'm fucked."

"Even starting to swear like you had your dick in something." Rawiri groped at Tyson's chest a moment, Tyson squirming, backing off. "Startin' to grow some fuckin' chest hair, huh?"

"Man, cut it out. You coming or what?"

Tyson headed inside, noticing that the door was already unlocked. He could hear the sound of morning cartoons from the lounge, knowing that his two brothers would be glued to the screen. He smiled at his mother as he headed into the kitchen, getting a strange look from behind her own smile.

"Hey, Mrs Rua…"

"Rawiri's just going to crash with me a while. I got to get some sleep."

"Off you go, then," she said, keeping at the dishes. Tyson felt a pang of guilt, having left his share from the previous night. He quickly mounted the stairs, slowing down so as to not leave Rawiri too far behind.

Tyson dumped his stuff, going through his routine. Maybe it was the weed, but he wanted to tell Rawiri about what he'd just done. He took in Rawiri's harsh expression as he awkwardly tried to pull out the mattress from under his bed. Tyson went to help him.

Rawiri dropping himself down and pulling up the leg of his jeans to get his brace off. Making himself more comfortable. It was a sure sign Rawiri was going to be in for the long haul. Tyson wondered if it was possible things could finally be going right. Maybe Marc was wrong, maybe life did give you a break now and then. Things seemed happy enough right now.

Tyson shucked his T-shirt and self-consciously got himself another, rather than be all that bare around Rawiri. He tossed the old one into his washing basket and excused himself as he took it downstairs. His mother was still busy with dishes. Tyson ran back upstairs, two steps at a time, slowing when he heard his mother's shout. Rawiri was looking through one of his black books when he got back to his room.

"Fuck, cuz…when did you start drawin' guys' dicks?"

Tyson froze, going red as he stood stunned at the door. He remembered tossing the book out of his satchel when he had finished it, getting himself another. But not putting it away. Rawiri was looking at him with a vaguely bemused expression. Tyson broke from his silence as he propelled himself across the room, making a grab for the book. Rawiri held it aside, out of his reach.

"Fuck you, Rawiri, give me that shit back!"

"Cuz…"

Tyson struggled with him. Rawiri wasn't able to move but he

certainly had him beat on strength. Tyson shoved Rawiri hard in the chest, making a sudden twist and pulling the black book off him. Tyson was shaking as he pulled off his friend. Rawiri's expression was nothing short of annoyed.

"Quit going through my fucking stuff! That's private!"

Tyson half expected the taunts and calls that would follow, but Rawiri said nothing, looking pissed off. Tyson didn't care. Fuck Rawiri. Tyson knew he shouldn't have been so stupid as to leave the book out. He crossed the room and shoved it into his wardrobe. The bedroom was deathly quiet.

Tyson didn't know what to do. He headed to his bed and lay down, turning his back on Rawiri. Any thoughts of opening up to Rawiri about it all were gone. He couldn't believe that he had even considered it. Rawiri stayed thankfully quiet. Tyson panicked silently before fatigue finally took him into sleep.

❖

The room was as quiet when Tyson woke up. Nothing was as blunt as the isolation and guilt that he felt knowing Rawiri wasn't there. The bedroom looked as though he had never been there. The mattress was shoved back in and in the darkness his local rappers gazed down from the walls. Tyson checked his clock for the time.

Tonight was K-1 night. Tyson wondered how he could have fucked that up.

Getting up, Tyson walked over to the window. Next door was dark behind the heavy sweep of trees. He could go next door and find Rawiri. The fights were long since over, though. He just wanted to try and work out if Rawiri knew, if he suspected the truth.

Why the fuck couldn't he just tell him and have everything be cool? Why couldn't he and Rawiri be chilling up here now? Whatever high Tyson had been feeling had been crushed. He thought about Marc. He felt like smoking again, remembering the release it had given. In the end he ended up scribbling in his latest book, drawing big graffiti versions of Rawiri. He worked on a large sprawling work of text, indistinguishable in its twists and turns.

I'm sorry.

It wasn't unusual that Tyson didn't see Rawiri for nights at stretch. By the time he got towards the end of the week, all Tyson was thinking about was meeting up with Marc and having a quiet smoke with him. He was surprised when he walked out of work Friday morning and saw Marc standing across the road, his hoodie making him look shifty. Tyson was worried.

"'Sup, my man?" Marc gave him one of those half hugs. Tyson figured he could get used to this.

"What you doing here, bro?"

Marc grinned. "What? Why you looking so surprised?"

"It's not Saturday morning."

"Nah, but it's about that," Marc replied. Tyson's heart sank. "I got to go down to H-Town for the week. I was in the area so I figured I'd try catch you and let you know I can't make tomorrow."

Tyson nodded but he knew he did a piss-poor job of keeping the disappointment off his face. Marc piped up before things lingered into an uncomfortable silence.

"I'll be back next week, though. Should be able to catch you Saturday."

Marc unshouldered a rather expensive-looking black pack and fished about in one of its front pockets. He pulled out a tin and opened it up, brazen and unworried. Tyson glanced about nervously, willing Marc to put it back away as he plucked out a blunt from among the grass and other smoking things. He shoved the tin back away and offered the blunt to Tyson.

"Man, I dunno..."

"Take it. No reason why you can't have one for me."

"Nah, bro..." Somehow it seemed different when Marc wasn't there smoking and offering it to him. Marc shoved his hand into one of the pockets of Tyson's jacket, slipping it away.

"There. Don't turn down free weed, mate. It's bad manners."

Marc swung his pack back over his shoulder and zipped up his hoodie. "I'll catch you next Saturday. Don't do nothing I wouldn't do, my man." He pulled Tyson in for departing hug, then swaggered off with as much notice as he had arrived. Tyson felt the sharp absence already, not looking forward to even a week without Marc around.

The day dragged painfully. Tyson dreaded going into work that night. He still hadn't seen Rawiri and was starting to wonder if he even would come Saturday. Rawiri had been right about the swearing, he didn't usually do it. And then he had all but turned on him when he had seen those pictures. Why couldn't he have come across the ones he had drawn last night?

Tyson's feelings were harsh and sorry for himself by the time he went into work. When he found himself pressed to make the call, or just let it drop, he acted on impulse. He welcomed the sound of William's warm tones when he answered the phone.

"It's Tyson again...I was just wondering about when you guys meet up on Saturday."

CHAPTER SIXTEEN

Tyson found himself back at the stadium once work was done. The alternative was to stay in town another twelve hours. The wind was still heavy and rain threatened. He lingered around outside, listening to the distant rumble of passing trains.

Tyson considered breaking in again, like they had last week. He could smoke up in Marc's absence, smoke one for him, like he had asked. He felt paranoid. Didn't cops look out for guys like him to be carrying around weed in their pockets? Young, brown, and a head full of dreadlocks? He dumped himself down against the corrugated-iron fence and stared up at the dark clouds racing overhead.

Tyson had to get his shit sorted. He hoped that meeting William would sort it all out. Maybe there might be other guys like him there. Maybe after tonight he might not have to keep on thinking how he had to tell Rawiri or Zadie about this shit.

Night faded into day, hours dragged on into hours, and by the time afternoon came he was raw and exhausted from staying up. He worried about Rawiri, but figured after what happened they probably weren't going to talk any time soon.

It was hard enough trying to pass the time. Each hour seemed to go slower than the last. Tyson eventually made his way up to Ponsonby Road. He had an idea where the place was. He bought himself something to eat long before he got there. His iPod had long since run out of battery by the time he approached the café. It was near seven and he was shot, but wide awake from having stayed up so long.

Tyson tried to push down the fear as he lingered near the place. He watched it from across the road, but it looked like every other well-to-do café on Ponsonby Road. It was still nothing much next to Epicurious. Large glass windows opened it out onto the sidewalk, which was busy with extra seating and freestanding overhead heaters. The name "Quartet" was done in stylish letters and backlit, giving it a pale purple halo.

Tyson pensively entertained just leaving, but it occurred to him that he had no better place to be. Quartet reminded him of the sort of life he had seen in the gay newspaper. He thought how there seemed to be nothing he had in common with it. He crossed the road and remembered to shove off the hood of his jacket and hoodie as he approached the front door like some masked villain.

Now or never, before he lost the nerve.

It occurred to Tyson as he stepped inside that he didn't even know who to look for. William had described himself, but what if Tyson didn't recognize him? He stuck out as much as he did in the front of Epicurious. He scanned the place nervously, having to step in to let through a loud couple wanting in behind him.

The place had a comfortable feel to it despite the up-tempo, throwaway jazz. The tables, what few there were of them, were engaged elbow to elbow. Well-to-do and the casually occupied come in from the weather to sip lattes and share war stories of late nights and last dates. The counter that doubled as a salad bar was just as cramped, and Tyson wondered how the staff managed to work behind it. He panicked a bit as he noticed a stairwell in back, where the loud couple were heading. He couldn't remember if William had mentioned an upstairs.

Pushing on and too tired not to sit down for a while, Tyson followed. The narrow climb to the top presented an area as small as downstairs, except the presence of jazz was replaced by a few kitsch paintings on the wall. Some of the tables towards the far end had been pushed together haphazardly, near a window that overlooked the street. Tyson hesitated, taking in the youngish crowd that had taken up residence and looked to have taken over the top area with their boisterous conversation.

An older man looked over in his direction, white haired and well weathered. He looked like he had spent his life on the sea, not helped by a close-knit turtleneck that made Tyson think of some sort of sea captain. The short mustache and almost angular beard only lent to the image. He looked over at Tyson as he lingered near the stairs. It was starting to unnerve Tyson, before the man smiled and got up.

"Tyson?"

"Yeah," Tyson replied, sharply uncomfortable.

"I'm William." His handshake was firm. "I'm glad you could make it. There's a decent turnout of people here today, we're usually not this many. Let me introduce you to everyone."

Tyson held back a moment. It was weird enough coming here in the first place, let alone meeting someone who knew he liked guys. He felt like William was about to brand him with a label right in front of everyone. Tyson scanned them quickly. He was hopeful when he noticed a brown face, but then noticed that he seemed to be sitting outside the tables where the group had camped out.

William started to introduce them, but Tyson forgot the names almost the instant William said them. He couldn't concentrate on them, lending a thin smile of sorts, looking at the gathered. How many of them were as fucked up as he was? Tyson thought they looked as if they had their stuff sorted out. They looked young, comfortable with who they were. Tyson felt like he was wearing someone else's skin being here.

"You want a coffee? I usually buy the newcomers a coffee," William said. His warm smile did something to put Tyson at ease. "I guess a sort of reward for having the courage to come in. It's always a big step."

"I don't really drink coffee."

William nodded and waved at a lady who was clearing up the table where the loud couple had just sat down. "A hot chocolate? I have to buy you something. It's the rule, after all." William repeated the order to the lady. "Sit down, it's okay."

Tyson had a sudden fear as he sat that maybe brown people weren't gay. Maybe only white people were gay. The guy across the table where William was sitting was looking at him in a way that made Tyson feel like he was on show. He looked about Marc's age, early twenties, and looked like he had come straight out of the pages of *Express*. His hugging white tee showed off his physique, and his hair had a look about it that he had spent hours making it look like he had just run his hand through it once before heading out the door.

"Tyson, huh?" His voice seemed a hint effeminate. "Like the boxer Mike Tyson? He's a big one." Tyson grimaced a little at the insinuation that lurked beneath that remark.

"My dad was into boxing," Tyson replied, his automatic response to that stupid question.

"Don't see many brown boys in here, you'll be pretty popular."

"Come on, Robert, let's not be treating him like he's fresh meat. He's not on the party scene or anything. We've been talking on the line for a while now. I think it was a pretty brave move coming in here." William slapped Robert on the arm when Robert rolled his eyes a bit. "Not everyone's a show queen like you."

"Oh, that can be changed. You can learn." Robert gave Tyson a light glance before reassuring him in a tone that didn't. "It's okay, Tyson. I don't really go for boys your build anyway. I like a bit of meat on them."

Tyson frowned. It wasn't bad enough that Robert was confirming maybe he wouldn't find anyone like himself here, but now he wasn't even his type? Tyson wondered why it mattered so much in the first place, but it still felt rough. It didn't help that he felt so tired.

"Ignore him, Tyson. Robert's just a bit of a shark." William had that look about him that was gentle and sincere; it seemed like Tyson's one place of refuge. William was regarding him with a look of wistful familiarity. "Thanks for coming in, though. Like I said on the phone, it gets easier from here."

"Oh, he's always saying that." Robert played with the straw in his bottle. "But I guess it's true. I've just been queer too long to know any different."

"When did you know?"

"That I was queer? Probably when I started trying to hit on the guy doing our lawns when I was a teenager. If I had known any better, I probably would have been bonking a hell of long time before that."

Tyson tried not to look at him like he was some sort of alien. He didn't seem to care that anyone knew. Tyson wondered briefly what that would be like. Too much like Siege and the Barge Bar, this was a million miles away from a life of washing dishes and catching trains. Tyson could smell the warm scent of cologne from Robert.

"You been with a guy?" Robert asked, as he regarded him with that same easy look.

"Hell no." Tyson grimaced. It reminded him of how sharply he had replied to Zadie, and he tried to take it back. "No. Just...dunno if it's my thing."

"Don't worry, just because I wouldn't get with you doesn't mean you won't have plenty of white boys lining up at your door begging for it."

"Or you can just ignore the whole scene and just be comfortable with who you are, like me," William said. "Not everyone who's gay is like Robert, Tyson."

"Thank God for that," replied Robert.

Tyson smiled a bit as the waitress put down his hot chocolate. He found himself somewhat lost between the two as they talked, and he paid more attention to his hot chocolate. William was tapping him on the arm and motioning towards Robert, breaking him out of his tired mindlessness.

"I said are you coming out after this? Me and some of the others are heading out to K Road. Bit early, but there's a few more cafés we're heading to before we hit the clubs."

Tyson shook his head. "No. I need to get home soon anyway."

"You can help me keep the seats warm here if you want, Tyson. I'll buy you a second."

Tyson nodded to William. He felt like there was no way he was opening up with all these people here. It was bad enough they knew he liked guys. Tyson was relieved when Robert pulled himself up from his seat and a few of the others from the tables nearby got up to join him. The place started to feel a bit empty once they had left. Tyson scooted about to the other side of the table.

"Don't mind Robert. Not everyone comes across as strongly as him. He's a bit of a character."

"Is everyone who likes guys as…gay as him?" Tyson couldn't think of any other way to put it. The question had been brewing on his mind almost since he had started talking with Robert. William chuckled warmly.

"Do I seem that way to you?"

"I guess not."

"No, not every gay guy wants to jump in bed with you at the drop of a hat," William reassured him, sipping again on his coffee. "You don't have to take anything other than what you want from all this."

"Is it true not many Māori guys come here?"

"Not a lot, no. There are a few, though." William gave a little of a wry smile. "I thought you weren't looking. How's things going with that friend of yours?"

Tyson felt the fatigue dragging down on his mood like a weight. For a moment he wasn't sure if William was talking about Marc or Rawiri, or if he had even told him about Rawiri. He assumed Marc, and remarked over his wide cup of hot chocolate, "He's out of town for a bit."

"And how's things going with him?"

"Good," Tyson replied, trying not to make it just sound like pleasant conversation. It made him think about Marc again. "I really like him."

"I'm sure you do. Just because you feel like this about one guy, though, doesn't make you gay, you realize."

Tyson shook his head, trying to explain, "It's not just him. I think I've always had feelings about guys...I dunno...just felt different with him."

"Because you have stronger feelings," William replied. He gave another of those wry smiles. "There's nothing wrong with that, of course. You should still play things safe. Get to know him as a friend before you try to jump into bed with him."

"I don't want to do that!" Tyson paused, wondering for a moment. He toyed with his cup under William's easy smile. He considered trying to explain it all, but William put a hand on his a moment.

"Even if you don't, take your time. You don't need to rush into everything you see. Not like Robert. If there's one thing I've learnt growing older, it's patience."

Tyson nodded, looking back across the table at William. It felt strange talking about this stuff with anyone, let alone an adult. There was something about William's manner that seemed trustworthy to him. He nodded again and took another sip of his hot chocolate.

"I wish it wasn't this hard..."

"I know."

Out the window, a glimpse of rain. The city beyond Ponsonby was starting to sparkle. "I wish it was as easy to get a guy as it is to get a girl. And having no one to talk to...and hiding it from my friends."

"My experience is that if you have known them long enough, then chances are they may already know."

Tyson glanced back at William, studying that aged face. He wondered if it was true, that maybe Rawiri already knew he had these feelings. It sent a chill through him when he thought about the picture that Rawiri had seen. He murmured quietly, "I don't want to lose my friend Rawiri…"

"I'm sure you won't. Friends can be very enduring like that."

"I known him since I was a kid. We grew up together," Tyson said. William was watching him with a warm smile, just listening. "We used to get in all sorts of trouble together. It was fun. Then… well…" Tyson thought better of mentioning Rawiri's accident. He clammed up like he knew how to do so well.

"I doubt you'll lose him," said William. "And if it's a guy you want, you will get one in time. You don't need to rush things, even if it feels like you don't have all the time in the world."

"Where's Robert and those other guys going?" Tyson asked, out of interest. "I mean, K Road."

"Oh, the clubs?"

"What are they like?"

"Same as any other clubs, I guess. Loud and sweaty." Tyson smiled at that description. Didn't sound too much different from the Barge Bar. "And a lot of rather horny guys. Which is nice, if you're looking for the same thing they are."

Tyson brooded a moment. Maybe he wasn't like them. He finished up his hot chocolate and drank another. He liked the fact that he didn't have to keep talking. William seemed about as happy with the silence as Tyson looked out the window. It wasn't much longer before he decided he should get home.

"You want me to drop you home? Or at least nearer home?"

"It's okay," Tyson replied. "I like catching the train."

"I'll drop you off at the station, then. And you had better learn not to turn down offers of help!"

Tyson managed a smile again. He thought better of saying no to the lift to Britomart. When they had got there, and Tyson had made his farewells, ready to get on the train and get home. He couldn't help sleeping most of the way there. Back to familiar ground.

CHAPTER SEVENTEEN

Tyson woke up late afternoon feeling worse for wear. It took him a while to realize where he was, and what time it was. Weak sunlight cut in through aged fishnet curtains. Outside he could hear the sounds of a neighborhood one only heard during the day. Somewhere in his street a mower was droning.

Tyson got ready for work, already feeling the grind again. Every new thing he did felt as if it was taking something out of work. Every weekend that he had done something, it felt slightly harder to go back to washing dishes. Work felt longer and harder. It didn't take him long to realize that he was off his usual schedule. He decided to shower and get ready. He would take his things with him and head into work early.

First he wanted to catch up with Rawiri and find out if he was okay.

Tyson dwelled on it as he showered and then dressed. All he had to do was open his mouth and somehow find the strength inside to say those few short words. They could be as few as two.

I'm gay.

The idea seemed worse for what might happen afterwards. Everything told him it was just easier to do like he had always done. Keep quiet. Don't rock the boat. Maybe saying it to Marc would be easier, and then he wouldn't have to.

Tyson shouldered up his satchel, checked everything over once, and slipped into Rawiri's jacket. He had become all too comfortable wearing it these days. Heading out of a quiet house, he psyched himself up for tracking down Rawiri. He hoped that it would be as easy as finding him in the sleep-out. He didn't much like the idea of going inside his friend's house again.

Tyson slipped through the fence and across the backyard, which had turned into a mud bath since the last downpour. He avoided the worst of the mud, jumping this way and that until he got to the garage door. Maybe Rawiri would be asleep. Or maybe he would be working out. Tyson found himself on edge at the idea of seeing Rawiri straining at the weights. His light features flushed as he knocked on the door. He wasn't surprised that there was no answer.

The door swung open under his knocks, and Tyson went in to check if Rawiri was inside anyway. He lurked, all too aware of how totally silent it was. There was a dead calm in the sleep-out, brought down further by the dim light. Tyson picked a path through the mattresses and clutter. He looked over the aged gym equipment, vaguely entertaining what it might be like to use them himself.

Tyson frowned. It wasn't like he hadn't wished he was more Rawiri's size. He saw the towel draped over the crossbars, smelt the strong, acrid smell of sweat. He had images of Rawiri's big arms, those solid shoulders he had seen when he had come over to watch K-1. Tyson looked at the thin white boxes dumped down next to the gym equipment. A few tabs had slipped out.

Tyson reached down to grab the package, intending to put the tabs back inside. His heart thumped when he read the labels. For a moment Tyson wasn't sure if he was really looking at what he thought he was.

"Cuz."

Tyson glanced back behind him, seeing Rawiri at the door. There was a frank look of recognition on Rawiri's solid features, which dawned into a frown.

"Bro. Are these steroids?" Tyson asked. Rawiri stood at the door for a long moment before closing it behind him.

"Put that shit back, cuz."

"Man, this stuff isn't safe. Why you taking steroids for?"

Rawiri ambled his way over mattresses as he made a line towards Tyson. He grabbed the box out of Tyson's hand with a force that startled him. Tyson watched him as he sat on the gym equipment and started gathering up the few other boxes there. Tyson could see the tension along the line of his jaw. His tone was harsh, yet still as quiet as he always spoke.

"Guess we even now, cuz. You goin' through my shit too."

"This is different," Tyson said, giving Rawiri a bit of room. "This isn't drawings in a book. You're fucking yourself up!"

Rawiri didn't respond, getting up with some effort. Tyson stared at him as he crossed over to the workbench that lined one side of the sleep-out. Rawiri shoved the boxes into the first drawer he could find that had room, slamming it away. Tyson felt a steel resolve building inside him, fueled by a strange anger that he couldn't understand.

"I'm not going to let you take that shit any more," Tyson decided.

Tyson went for the drawer, moving to get the boxes out. He just wanted to save Rawiri somehow. The mate he knew wouldn't do this shit. He pulled the drawer open, and then felt Rawiri's hand heavy on his arm.

"Leave it alone, Tyson."

"Bro," Tyson said, hard. "Why you doing this shit to yourself? When did you start taking drugs, man?" He made a push again for the drawer, but this time Rawiri shoved and moved in front of it. Tyson staggered back, surprised that his friend would put his hands on him.

"I said fuckin' leave it alone, Tyson!"

Tyson moved in again, reaching around Rawiri to the drawer. This time Rawiri grabbed him, and it hurt. He fought a moment, seeing the dark rage growing in Rawiri's eyes. Tyson hit the ground as Rawiri shoved him back. He felt a pain in his arm as he struck the side of the home gym. Tyson looked back up at Rawiri, scared for himself.

"You got no fuckin' idea, so just keep out of my fuckin' business, okay, cuz?"

"You hurt me!"

"Well, maybe you won't stick your fuckin' nose in other people's shit, then!"

Tyson held his arm, pulling himself up from the floor. Everything told him to just split and get out. Rawiri was raising his voice. Fuck that, Rawiri had *hurt* him. He felt his throat turn raw as he kept back the tears. Rawiri was like a thick-built tower of shadowy fury of over him.

"You think you know how shit is for me, Tyson?" Rawiri demanded. Tyson was already backing away. "You think you know how fucked up my life is, cuz?"

"Why didn't you talk to me?" asked Tyson, his voice hoarse. "I thought we didn't keep stuff from each other?"

"Maybe you have your dad belt you a few times, and you see how much you wanna talk about it!"

"At least you got one!"

"Fuck you, Tyson! You want my fuckin' father? Maybe I'll give you a fuckin' taste of what I get!"

Tyson bolted for the door. Even as close as he was with Rawiri, he didn't want to stick around and find out. The sound of Rawiri's voice was ringing in his ears as he shot out of the sleep-out, cutting around the side of his house and back out onto the street. Tyson didn't stop running until he was halfway to the park. He dumped himself down against the iron fence, squatting down in the broken glass and rubbish, and cried.

❖

Tyson felt like the world was closing in around him. He felt the weight of it on his shoulders. His hood had always looked like shit to him, but now it looked worse. Cold winds threatened to rip the tears from him. The glass under his feet felt like his insides, all sharp and broken. He'd lost track of time, but when he realized where he was again, he was back in the park. Too close to where Rawiri and him chilled, he noticed.

Home felt hollow. Tyson didn't want to go back there. Even worse, given he couldn't go next door. His best mate hated him. He'd hit him. The images of it had been playing back in his mind over and over.

All too much. Too fucking hard to cope with. Not a life without his mate.

I got to tell him I'm sorry. I got to tell him I'm gay. Fuck this.

Tyson came to again wandering on the far side of the park. The weight of his satchel hurt his back, even though it wasn't heavier than usual. He was still wearing Rawiri's big jacket. Should he give it back? Tyson thought in a curiously mundane way that he was going to be late for work. It would be easier going the long way out the back of the park.

Even his music wouldn't give him a break. Tyson felt like crying all over again when he started it up and heard Nesian Mystik singing about brotherhood. He let himself wallow in it, sinking in deep. Let it all just swallow him up. He walked hunched and more like a zombie to the world. He glared dead and raw hate at the homeboys he saw swaggering into the park.

Just keep walking.

Tyson felt a hand on his shoulder, reacting sharply. He was scared maybe he'd pissed someone off, the way he was looking. He pulled back and saw the concerned expression staring back. That and those strange grey eyes. High cheekbones. Ihaia's thick hair was tied back in a black T-shirt this time, and he was cutting a sharp-looking figure in a heavy red hoodie and black Dickies.

"You cool?"

Tyson dragged off his headphones, hearing the tinny sound of the music from around his neck. It took him a while longer to find the button to turn it off. He managed a nod, that vast empty feeling still inside him. He couldn't talk.

"Saw you walking around the park, uso. I just live over there," Ihaia said, pointing back towards the park. Tyson missed where. "You remember me from the Southstyle Freestyle Battle, right?"

"Yeah."

"Hey, you sure you okay, uso?" Ihaia looked concerned.

"Yeah."

Ihaia didn't look fooled at all, but at least he let it drop. "Shot, then."

Tyson kept walking, the streets sounding all too quiet now neither of them were talking. It was an uncomfortable silence that Tyson couldn't fill with words. "I gotta go. Work."

"Nah, that's sweet. I got to make a run to the shops. You going to the station, right?"

Tyson wanted to say no, but it was a lie he couldn't cover. He just nodded. Ihaia's voice was soft, that with his smoky tone sounded rather cool. "I'm not gonna push you or nothing, uso, but if you want to talk, you got me."

Tyson couldn't help but wonder why. Who was he to Ihaia? He just shrugged it off, dismissed it. He found that he was still shaking, noticing again for the first time where he was. His mind kept going back to Rawiri, and it hurt, deep inside. No one should care about him, he couldn't even look out for his best mate.

"So you work nights?" Ihaia asked finally. They were walking through the same mindless maze of squat housing that Tyson lived in on the other side of the park.

"Yeah."

"When you start?"

"Eight."

Ihaia checked his watch, then shoved his hands back into the front of his hoodie. "You got a while yet, uso. Should come chill with us guys."

"I dunno. I mean, Siege don't seem to like me."

"Siege don't like anyone he doesn't know." Ihaia managed a smile. "But if Marc vouches for you, then you're okay."

Tyson fought down the hardness that risked escaping to his voice, "Marc doesn't...I mean, I'm not really as good as he says I am." He didn't want to badmouth Marc, his feelings ran too deep to do that. But it was obvious Marc was mistaken. "I just copy down shit in my black book. I haven't even touched a can." Ihaia seemed unaffected, although Tyson was hoping it would make him back off.

"You like it, though? Doing that stuff?"

"'Course."

"Then you got what it takes. You love hip hop?"

Tyson scowled. He didn't like the b-boy him asking that question. Maybe it was how he acted in the club, how he didn't hang with a crew. "'Course I love hip hop. It's my life."

"Then you got what it takes."

Tyson fell quiet, watching the way Ihaia's smooth smile crossed his handsome features. He kept looking at the guy's strange eyes and then finding somewhere else to look. Every time he looked, Ihaia was looking back, warm and supportive.

"I love hip hop too," remarked Ihaia as they crossed the street. "Been dancing as long as I can remember. My mum said that I was dancing before I could walk. If you got that sorta passion, uso, then that's all that matters."

"I don't even go to clubs."

"Sweet as. You don't need to. Hip hop's more than the club scene. Easier to meet hip hop heads that way, though." Ihaia shrugged. "Don't mean nothing, though."

Tyson fell silent again, finding himself stuck and distracted. On one hand, Ihaia made him think of things other than what had just gone down. But on the other, he couldn't think straight to try and set Ihaia straight on the matter. He kept thinking of Rawiri. He thought about going back but was scared of what Rawiri was. He wondered how he couldn't know his best mate to miss something like that.

"Life is sorta shit right now," Tyson managed. He tried to stop his voice from choking up. Inside, his mind was screaming not to say anything. He didn't even know this guy.

"Yeah. Life *is* shit sometimes."

Tyson couldn't bring the rest of it out. He felt the cold breeze against his face, pushing past the hood of his jacket. His neck was starting to cramp a bit from the headphones around it. He was tired and sore all over. Ihaia didn't push, just spoke quiet and supportive.

"I got your back, uso."

Tyson just nodded. They were closer to the shops now, and the station wasn't too far off. The roads were heavy with after-work traffic, kids still in uniform, shirts loose and disarrayed. Tyson hated the sight of the shops, especially now. A tired TAB, next to a bottle store, the only thing open longer hours. A line of greasy Chinese takeaways. He watched himself on the pavement; it got more cracked and misplaced around the corner. It felt like he was stepping through a sea of cigarette butts sometimes.

Tyson spotted Siege, standing out a mile with his size. He was hanging out with a few others, near the bottle store on the far end. Tyson slowed, then felt Ihaia's hand on his shoulder.

"Come and chill, uso."

"Nah. Work."

"You still got a while yet," Ihaia said, in a quiet, concerned tone. "Plus, better you come hang and distract yourself from life. Come on."

Tyson found himself drawn both ways. He wanted to be alone, but the thought of hanging with guys he had admired from afar seemed appealing. Better than thinking about Rawiri. Ihaia was right. If he went to work now, he'd only end up wandering around in town, thinking about all this shit more.

"Come on. Think there's a few others from Dodgee you ain't met, uso."

Tyson nodded, distracted by the way that it made Ihaia smile. He kept his hands dug deep into the pockets of his jacket as he walked shotgun with Ihaia. The breaker was all smiles and staunch nods as they approached. The look Siege gave him made Tyson feel like the outsider he was.

"Look who I found wandering by the park," Ihaia announced. Tyson felt the eyes. Worse was Siege's shark gaze. "Dodgee's next big name."

"I still don't know this bitch."

"Now's your chance, then. You going to speak bad of Marc, uso?"

Siege just grunted, the sort of thing Tyson expected from the big guy. He tried to stow that feeling of attraction, lust and danger a potent mix. Siege was the sort of guy who would beat him down if he knew the truth. It just made Tyson want to back off all the quicker. Dark secrets and dangerous rappers didn't mix. He gave a hint of a nod to Loot. Tyson didn't recognize the few others.

"Good work on the Freestyle Battle." Tyson spoke as confidently as he could. "I mean, taking it out. Did good."

"Ain't no surprise there. Fuckin' load of pansies."

Tyson nodded, staring up the street towards the petrol station. It was packed this time of day. Siege cut through his idle thoughts. "What makes you think you Dodgee material? I don't know you from dog shit."

"Ease up, Siege," Ihaia said. "You know we need to get our numbers up with Sam going down south."

"I'm just saying. Fuckin' run this crew like a business, else how we gonna make our mark? What makes you think you good enough? We ain't looking to sign with no one like Dawn Raid. We doing for ourselves."

Tyson forced down the urge to cuss Siege out, even if he did get a beat-down. He dragged his black book out of his satchel and thrust it out. Loot took it, starting to page through it with respect.

"This some good shit."

Tyson felt a flush of gratitude. Loot looked at each page with a discerning eye, like an art critic going through some Newmarket gallery. The others were gathering around, checking it out on interest. Ihaia stuck by his side. Tyson caught the smile the breaker gave him, smooth and assured.

"Marc's right on this homeboy's shit," Loot said. He handed the book over to Siege, who looked at it begrudgingly. Tyson saw the respect that escaped onto the guy's face. The look of someone who knew he could work it in his advantage. Loot asked, "Graff's more than shit in a book, though, son. How good you with a can?"

Tyson was shaking again, wondering if he should push Marc's lie. He shrugged. "Do most my stuff that way. Ain't really done much with a can." He waited for the worst.

"You gotta celly?" Tyson shook his head, and Loot pulled out a thick marker. "Cool if I write my number down here, then? I'm going out in the weekend. Call me up. We'll run."

Tyson nodded, still shaking, some from the acceptance. Things were moving too fast, and already he wondered how far he could go without having even touched a can of paint. Briefly, he had images of him graffing up walls. He thought of all the stuff he'd seen, Phat1, Askew, and fantasized about his work next to theirs. Something about it made sense. He wondered why he'd never thought about trying it sooner.

"Mostly just copies," Tyson said, mumbling. Loot shook his head and passed the book back.

"Plenty shit in there I haven't seen on the street. Recognize a lot of it from the line, though. You got a good eye for it."

"That's all that matters, uso," Ihaia added. He put a rough and playful arm about Tyson's shoulder, shaking him a little. "Got you the hook up. You'll be Dodgee before too long."

Tyson gazed up at Siege, expecting a response to that, but the guy was too busy checking out someone across the street. Siege had that edgy look about him, like someone ready to pull something. Wasn't too much longer before the rest of the crew was looking in the same direction. Tyson saw the guy, feeling himself flush a bit with embarrassment. Even from across the road, he could see the guy's effeminate manner.

"Yo!" Siege boomed, throwing his hands up. The guy kept walking, a few nervous glances in the rapper's direction. "Yeah, you better keep walkin', faggot! Fuckin' child molester! Why don't you come over here so I can put my fuckin' foot up your ass!"

Tyson wanted to melt into the background, thankful for the hood of his jacket. The sound of Siege's voice was overwhelming, what he was saying more so. He felt himself burning under Siege's profane tirade, like every word was directed at him. Tyson found himself walking away, shaking, hearing Ihaia's voice, then Siege's.

"What's his fuckin' problem?"

"Hey, uso!"

Tyson kept walking as the world closed in on him again, shoving his black book away. Ihaia was at his side by the time he was back to the corner. He avoided the gaze of those grey eyes, searching under the hood.

"Work. Gotta go."

Ihaia looked at him like he wanted to say something. Tyson hoped he didn't, suddenly thinking how maybe he did a shit job hiding he was a faggot too. Ihaia just smiled, albeit one frosted with concern.

"We gotta chill sometime. I mean, hook up. When you get off work?"

"I gotta go," Tyson said, pushing on. He felt like he could still feel Siege's presence, his dead stare. "Later."

Tyson crossed the road and Ihaia didn't follow. Tyson didn't look back as he headed off towards the station.

CHAPTER EIGHTEEN

Friday came. Tyson hoped to see Marc waiting for him when he left work. He gathered his things and left by the front door, feeling the weight lift off his shoulders when he saw that familiar, solid figure across the road. Tyson couldn't help but smile a little. Marc looked so good, not just because he looked all shifty in his off-the-shelf hoodie, but because Tyson knew things would be better now.

Tyson crossed the road feeling like he was running to salvation. There were so many things he wanted to say to Marc. He wanted to know everything would be cool, and to lie under the homeboy's arm like he had those few weeks back. He felt giddy, unable to hide the grin that was etched on his face. Tyson greeted him like he had been gone for years. It felt like it.

"Hey, my man. Glad to see you too."

Tyson threw his arm up around him, lingering longer than staunch allowed.

"Something up?"

"Nah," lied Tyson. "Just been a long week. Good to see you back, bro."

"Good to be back."

Tyson kept his hood up, although the early-morning weather was relatively calm for once. He fell in step beside Marc, willing to forget everything for a while. This was his and Marc's time. It was like the rest of the world didn't exist. Tyson kept stealing glances, like he was seeing his homeboy again for the first time. He couldn't believe it had only been a couple of weeks.

"You got anything important tomorrow?" Marc asked, walking with his usual swagger. "I mean, I was thinking of bouncing. Going back to my place. You can crash there if you ain't got anything better to do."

Tyson tried to stifle his grin, "Nah, I'm free. Would be sweet." He didn't want to go home anyway. He had dreaded it every morning. It made him think of Rawiri. Saturday night would be worse.

"Cool. We'll catch the ferry if we go quick."

"You live on Waiheke?" Tyson asked. He followed Marc's casual, swaggered pace as they stepped off the curb.

"Nah, mate. Live over at Devonport."

Tyson tried to hide his surprise. "Devonport? Isn't that expensive?"

"I just rent," Marc replied. Tyson noticed something in the tone of the homeboy's voice. "Rent off my parents. Left home a long time ago, though. I make my own way with Guerrilla Advertising."

"I can't get over that, bro. You twenty?"

"Twenty-five." That in itself was a surprise.

"And you renting in Devonport?" Tyson tried to put all the pieces together, but it was like it wouldn't fit. Marc was shrugging it off like it was nothing, seeming rather distant and aloof.

"It's nothing, my man. Just taking care of business." Marc changed the subject, something that wasn't lost on Tyson. "You catch up with Loot?"

"Yeah, how did you know?"

"I was talking to them, Loot said you ran into them out South."

Tyson wondered if that was all that was said, especially when he had walked off when Siege had started getting all homophobic. Tyson wondered if it made them suspect something. His reply was more subdued. "Yeah…ran into that guy Crunch."

"Fucking good breaker. Should be him going to Germany and winning World Champs. Fucking lunatic."

"What you mean?"

"The shit he does," Marc explained. "If you know him well enough, then you know he's called Crunch because he smashed his shoulder once. Trying to get all suicidal with his moves. Breaking like he does, you either get better or end up in hospital. He got better."

Tyson tried to picture that, but it made sense. He nodded absently as they headed towards Britomart. He had never been to the ferry terminals before despite the fact he went by the building's clock every morning to catch the train. Tyson broke the silence as they headed past Britomart, through the dregs of late night revelers wobbling and swaying in search of the nearest taxis.

"Is Dodgee Dozen that good?"

"Most of them, yeah."

Tyson risked it, remembering what he had seen of Siege in the short time he had known him. "That Siege guy seems like a bit of an asshole…"

Marc laughed. "Yeah, he is. He's every fucking way an asshole. If he's not getting all worked up about white guys, then it's rich people, or gays. Thinks the world owes him something."

Tyson frowned when Marc mentioned gays. So it wasn't just him; maybe Siege *was* that bad. He decided not to ask too much about that, in case Marc suspected something. "If he hates white guys, how come you promote them?"

"I go through Loot, few other guys too. Ignoring Siege, there's at least another Dodgee eight to work with. Plus, it's money, my man. You don't turn down money."

"I guess not."

"Haul your ass, mate." Marc started picking up the pace. "Gonna miss the ferry."

Tyson quickened his step, smelling the strong smell of the

harbor being swept in by the wind. It hadn't picked up all that much, but what breeze there was cut. Tyson pulled his coat tighter about him, heading into the terminal. He heard the bubbling rumble of the ferry, revving up, Marc hitting a slight jog as they headed to the entrance. Tyson worried a moment about tickets before Marc pulled out a card.

"Two."

"Thanks, bro."

"No problem."

The ferry felt unstable under Tyson's feet as they headed inside. He hadn't been on a ferry before but didn't want to seem that green to Marc. He saw how Marc was smiling at him as Tyson did his best not to want to grab for something. He heard bells, and the ferry vibrated under them as the attendants started preparing to get them under way.

Tyson wasn't even sure if the few number of people sitting here or there was normal for this time of the morning. Marc swaggered over to a row of seats and took up the centre. He looked like he could have anything he wanted. Tyson took up a seat next to Marc as they started to head away. Tyson hoped he wouldn't get sick.

"Dodgee Dozen is cool, my man. If you want to get somewhere, then it wouldn't hurt hooking up with those guys."

"You love local hip hop too?" Tyson asked, thinking it was a given. He didn't listen to anything else, really. Marc chuckled.

"Fuck, no. Can't just love it all blindly. The best local shit, you don't even really hear about."

Tyson frowned, shaking his head, "You hate local stuff? I thought you said Dodgee Dozen were good."

"I don't hate *all* local stuff, I just hate bullshit artists who think they can drop a few tracks and think they are all that. This game takes work."

Tyson sat in silence for a moment, thinking over the drone of the engine. He looked at Marc under that hood of his. There was all that passion in his voice, but he didn't seem all that affected by it in terms of how he looked. Tyson was still trying to understand how he could hate something so good.

"Is there anyone you like, then?" he asked, cautiously. Marc looked like he had to think about that. His hands were deep in the pockets of his hoodie, pulling down. It stretched his already oversized hoodie tight.

"DLT was cool. He worked with overseas rappers way before anyone." Marc shrugged his solid shoulders dismissively. "Ever heard of Native Dialogue?" When Tyson shook his head, Marc continued. "Yeah, I like them. They from up north somewhere. Heard one of their mix CDs they sent me."

"Can't believe you hate local hip hop."

Marc smiled and shoved Tyson in the shoulder. "I don't hate it. I just hate bullshit."

"You make your money off it, though," said Tyson, searching Marc's expression.

"I make money off advertising for people, my man. There's a real difference there."

"Oughta nickname you Ruthless, bro."

Marc shrugged again. It looked as if none of it even fazed him. Tyson wished he could be like that, not bothered by anything or what anyone thought of him. Marc looked like he could take on the whole world and still win. Tyson caught himself staring at Marc's chest again, the way his black T-shirt pulled tight across it. He started thinking less about hip hop and more about sex. Even then, he tried to push the thoughts aside. Marc yawned widely and openly.

Tyson watched the way that the harbor swayed and then decided it was better to watch Marc instead, the lesser of two evils. Tyson wished that his mind would stay quiet. It seemed like everything that he saw or happened twisted inside his mind and kept coming up time and time again, like the way the ferry rolled and rocked on the water. Staring at Marc filled him with a hot thrill but only made him think of everything else that came from it.

Was he really like Robert? Or like William? Either option only filled Tyson with a deep loneliness. He thought about the café he had gone to. He wondered if it was any different in the clubs Robert went to. Tyson felt a sinking feeling inside when he wondered if maybe what he always thought was true.

Māori guys ain't gay.

Tyson stared at Marc, not needing to hide it as much now, given Marc was starting to nod off. Maybe Tyson could work up the nuts somehow and tell Marc everything. Marc wasn't Māori, and as much as he seemed not to like hip hop, everything about him was. Tyson tried to work out if it really was love he felt staring at him all the time.

Marc woke up about the same time the ferry pulled into the harbor. The two of them got off and already Tyson was noticing the differences. Even working on High Street every night, with its gleaming shopfronts and assuming customers, didn't seem much next to Devonport. As they headed out onto the street, Tyson noticed houses lit by a newly rising day. Nothing was out of place here. If anything was, it was him. Even the air seemed to smell different somehow.

Every house they passed, walking along the waterfront, Tyson had to wonder if Marc was going to walk up one of those spotless drives. Old wooden villas that looked like they had just been built but had probably been there years sat nestled between ultramodern, starkly square models of architecture. No graffiti. No cars up on blocks. Not even any suspicious groups of youths hanging out on the corners.

Just past one of the stately villas, Marc stepped off the footpath. Tyson followed him across a front yard that looked better kept than a golf green. Tyson felt like they were breaking in as Marc pushed open a tall side gate beside the garage and headed down the path there. The back area was spacious, despite the look from the front. Automatic lights flushed the path in clear light. There was a small place out back that looked almost as expensive as the house despite its size.

"This is my place." Marc unlocked the door, his key chain catching the lights. He headed inside and Tyson followed.

Tyson felt like he had stepped into some sort of rap video. It was little more than a single large room, kitchen on one side behind a counter, big double bed on the other, with a couch and lounge in the middle ground between. The windows didn't have curtains, rather they had blinds. The widescreen TV and the subtle glow of the stereo's lights and dials made Tyson think of a pimped-out ride. PlayStation controllers were dumped on a coffee table between the TV and couch. It had the look of someone sloppy and hip hop, from the clothes left out and hip hop posters, but the wealth of it shined about as bright as the white walls.

Marc was digging around in the stuff near his bed before he came out with a familiar-looking tin. Tyson remembered it from when he had given him the blunt, except this time Marc had a bong with him as well.

"You scared you going to get the carpet dirty or something?"

"Uh, yeah. Actually I am. You *live* here?"

"Sleep mostly, but yeah. Why?"

"I couldn't afford this if I worked for the rest of my life."

Marc looked as unaffected as always, but his tone hinted at something harder. "Mate, it's no big deal. Get your ass over here, and let's get blazed, okay? I just want to smoke up."

Tyson shucked his jacket and then pulled himself free of his headphones and satchel before sitting down carefully on the edge of the couch. It was taking longer than he expected for it all to sink in. Tyson guessed that he really didn't know much about Marc in the first place anyway. Marc dumped himself down, taking his hoodie off.

Tyson couldn't take his eyes off the partly opened wardrobe, where Marc had been rummaging around. He could make out lines of basketball jerseys. "I never seen you wear any of those…"

"Why, you want one?"

"You serious?"

"Yeah, go on. Go grab you some. You're right, my man. I don't wear them as much as I could. They just going to hang in there for who knows how long."

Tyson frowned. He felt like he would be pissing on Marc going through his clothes, like some rat going through other people's stuff. Tyson looked at him, seeing a glance that made him realize he was serious. He pulled himself up from the couch as Marc started packing the bong.

Tyson wished he had even half the money that bought all this stuff. He pushed his way through the jerseys, feeling more buzz than he had the few times he had ventured into the urban clothing stores near his work.

He felt an uncomfortable flush to his cheeks as he stopped pushing through the jerseys. He stared at the one that he had seen Marc wearing before on the street. It was the plain black and white Los Angeles one. It made his dick jump a bit to think Marc had been in it.

"This one okay?"

"Sure. You want to get you another one? Put it on."

"Nah, this one's cool," Tyson mumbled. He pulled it off the clothes hanger and held it like it was something sacred. When he pulled his hoodie off and slipped the jersey over his head, it fell over his body and all but swam on his lighter frame. He heard Marc chuckle.

"You look pretty styling. I know what to buy you for your birthday. Get you all skuxed up like some those homeboys." Marc checked his handiwork with the bong before nodding Tyson over. "Come get you some of this."

Tyson wandered back towards the couch, glad that the jersey was long enough to hide what was heavy between his thighs. Marc was already smoking, the bowl filling with the warm, grey smoke, bubbling madly before he sucked it away. Tyson took the bong when Marc passed it to him. He vaguely thought how he was getting a habit, and how he had turned down even Rawiri all those times he offered.

Tyson worried about Rawiri.

Marc coughed a little as he exhaled, and instructed him on how to use the bong. Tyson figured he did a little better than he had when he had first tried smoking on the blunt. The weed hit his head, making him flush warm in those familiar, comforting sensations. Nothing mattered but being here. But he still found himself with a willingness to talk.

"You want to watch something while we smoke?" Marc sorted through the remotes on the coffee table. "You heard of Akira Kurosawa?"

Tyson shook his head but Marc was already turning on the stereo. It looked like it was what a nuclear reactor would be like firing up, all those lights and gauges working away. Tyson held on to the bong, deciding to give it another try while Marc was busy.

"I'll put on some Frontline instead," said Marc. He smiled as he put the CD changer through its paces. "I don't hate Frontline. I think Con Psy had some balls putting out that track about his brother."

Tyson smiled a little, getting a chance to pass the bong back. Any more and he would be high before he gave it back. "I just like local stuff," Tyson said, slouching back. "It's better than overseas shit."

"For sure. Can't stand all that fucking 50 Cent posing shit. I see people over here wearing G-Unit crap and I want to go slog them."

Tyson nodded, but he wasn't so sure that he agreed. He mused on it, his thoughts coming back all too muddled. He settled for watching Marc, watching those lips as he sucked away hard on the bong. That pale expression, and those big solid shoulders. His white T-shirt, oversized and flawlessly clean as always, fell down over that broad chest. It reminded Tyson that he was still partly aroused. This was the first time he had seen Marc's forearms, or him in anything less than a hoodie.

Tyson tried not to look like he was staring, but he figured that Marc had half a clue, by the way he kept looking back at him and smiling. The weed made Tyson grin it off. He was starting to care less and less if Marc worked it out. Everything felt warm and mellow and peaceful. In his mind, Marc would work out what was up and they would hold each other again like they had at the stadium, or maybe even closer.

Tyson kept working on the bong every time Marc passed it until Marc put it aside, smiling widely to himself. Tyson felt pretty much the same way, everything seeming to sway and dance in front of him to Con Psy's flows. Tyson felt too weak to move again, like his body had turned to jelly against him. He heard Marc's husky voice and a quiet chuckle.

"Wish I could be like you, my man."

"Why?" Tyson looked over at the grin Marc had on his face, noticing those reddened eyes.

"This shit hits you harder and better if you don't smoke it so often…"

"I'll smoke every Friday with you, bro. Fuck, I'll smoke whenever you want." Tyson felt like he might be babbling.

Marc laughed. "Yeah, that's my lil soldier! Turn you into a full-blown stoner yet, my man. You pretty fucked up."

"Always…"

Tyson tried to move, partly on purpose. He knew that Marc would try and catch him, and he did. He loved that Marc seemed to be there for him. Marc had always been there for him, and it was just taking him this long to work it out. Marc had put him onto the Dodgee Dozen and pushed his talents, even if he hadn't believed in himself. He had gone out his way to smoke with him. And when he said he would be gone for a week and would be back the next, he was. Tyson felt warm and drifting, feeling as if he had worked everything out.

Tyson leaned in on Marc, feeling himself get harder as the homeboy settled him against the curve of his body. The courage came easily to put his arms around him as he rested his dreadlocked head on Marc's chest.

"You comfortable, then, Dred?"

"I like it when you call me that, bro."

"What? Dred?"

"Yeah, that's the name you gave me for my graffiti. When I get famous and I'm rolling in the cash like you are, I'm going to tell everyone you got me there."

Tyson felt the chuckle rumbling in Marc's chest, just under his cheek. Marc's slow, gentle breathing and his strong arm put Tyson into a more restful state than he could remember. It was everything he had dreamed of, being here in Marc's arms, and more than ever it felt like nothing could ever touch him. Marc's voice was quiet, but in their own private world, Tyson heard it easily.

"You don't have to do that, my man. You're a cool guy. Worked that out pretty quickly. I'm just being a good mate, that's all."

"You're pretty cool too, Marc."

"Thanks."

"I'd do anything for you, bro."

Marc chuckled again, Tyson liking how that felt against him. There was such a big presence to Marc, physically and otherwise. "That's just the weed talking, my man."

"Nah, it's true," Tyson replied, feeling his cheeks really starting to burn. "I really like you."

"I like you too."

Tyson stayed silent a moment, wondering if that meant what he thought it did. Con Psy filled the silence between them until Tyson spoke again. He wanted to be sure. Tyson felt his cheeks burning as he found the courage, not caring where it came from. He uttered the words.

"I'm gay."

CHAPTER NINETEEN

All the times that Tyson had wondered how it would all turn out, all the times he had played it through in his mind, it had never been like this. The silence that had fallen over the two of them was slowly crushing Tyson like a vise. Under him, it felt as if Marc had stopped breathing. He heard Marc clear his throat, replying at a murmur.

"That's cool…but I don't swing that way, my man."

Tyson felt the overwhelming pain of emotions sweep over him. It had been easy to say after all that. But now that it was said, he wished that he could take it back. Tyson tried to hold back the tears, but they were choking and swallowing him. He did his best to try and get up, despite the weed's hold on him.

"I'm sorry, bro," Tyson managed, barely at a choke. It was all he could manage to pull himself from under Marc's heavy arm. The absence felt worse than anything he had ever felt. He tried to get up from the couch. He didn't want anyone to see the tears that were ripping him up inside.

"Where you going?"

Tyson didn't answer, trying to get his things together before he started crying. It was bad enough with the emotions swelling up inside him, more difficult because he was high. Marc did a better job than him of standing up. Everything was swaying around him, threatening to pull him off his feet.

"Tyson, where you going?"

Tyson couldn't hold back the tears any longer as Marc's arms came up around him. He tried to pull away. He knew for certain now that Marc wasn't into guys. Marc wasn't like him. No one was like him. Tyson felt so incredibly alone as his body was wracked with sobs. Marc was the only reason he was still standing up. Marc held him until it hurt to cry any more.

"Sit down with me, mate. You're not going anywhere while you stoned," Marc insisted. Tyson felt him pulling him back down. "Probably knocked the high out of you, anyway."

"I'm sorry, bro."

"Nothing to be sorry about, my man."

"I'm so sorry."

"Quiet, man."

Marc kept his arms tightly around him, but it didn't feel the same. Tyson still tried to pull away but Marc wouldn't let him go. He held Tyson until he stopped fighting, and then until he stopped crying. By the time Tyson was done, he felt sick, like everything had been stripped out of him. Con Psy continued rapping, unapologetic at being a visitor to Tyson's horrible situation.

"I dunno why shit has to be so hard, bro."

"That's just life, my man," Marc said, still holding on to him. Tyson pulled up, and this time Marc didn't stop him. Marc's words stung, even as he qualified them. "You just got to keep strong."

"I can't."

"Then you ain't going to make it. But you made it this far, so I'm guessing you ain't the sort to give up easy."

Tyson wondered how Marc could know anything about being gay. He had nothing but hard feelings inside. The grief of saying it and coming down had left him as raw as the tears. He couldn't believe he had been stupid enough to say it!

"You got balls, Tyson. I wouldn't admit what you just did to anyone…if it was me."

Tyson shrugged it off, it sure didn't feel like a good thing at the moment. He lay back against the couch, the weed making him feel sick rather than high.

"You got it easy, bro. You got everything. You rich, you good-looking. You got everything." Tyson regretted saying it almost as soon as he had, seeing the look on Marc's face. It reminded him of how Rawiri had looked when he had spoken out against him. Marc's reply was hard, but he was too in control to ever need to raise his voice.

"Fuck that, mate. You think because I've got money that I've got it easy. I still have problems."

"You got two parents, bro. More than I got."

"I might as well have none, my man, the amount I see them in my life." Marc's husky voice had that powerful confidence he always had. "Don't go talking yourself down, Tyson. You can either be a victim to your shit or you can deal with it. You don't have any more problems than anyone else."

Tyson felt like crying again but there weren't any more tears to call on. He had exhausted them all, and himself in the process.

"Everyone's got problems, my man," Marc continued, softer. "But you can't let life fuck you over. You got to deal with your shit head-on, man. Don't expect anyone else to be there for you. That's how I've learnt to deal with it. Because if you wait for something to change, it's not going to happen. You have to change it yourself."

The words stunned Tyson, but the conviction behind them drove them deep. He still felt shell-shocked from what had happened. He wanted Marc to cave in and hold him, like he had imagined he would do in his fantasies. To hold him and say everything would be okay. It seemed more like Marc, the way he was reacting now.

"Does anyone else know?"

"Nah." Tyson considered telling him about Robert and William, but that wasn't really the same. Marc was the first person he had really *told*.

"You got balls, my man. I like that sort of courage."

"Why you stuck there with me all this time, bro?" asked Tyson.

Marc shook his head, like he had heard this question enough times already. "You *got* to have more confidence in yourself, Tyson. I don't know. Because you seem like a cool guy. I just had a feeling about you. I can't explain it." Marc stared at the blank TV in front of them, as if searching for the answers. "Maybe it was fate or some shit. Maybe we were meant to run into each other so that you could do what you just did. I don't know."

Tyson worked out there didn't seem to be any easy answer to that question, one that Marc could give that would convince him. It all kept coming back to him. Maybe Marc was right, somehow. He had to be.

"Things are really rough right now," he said quietly. "It's more than just this…I found out my best mate is doing heavy drugs."

"Hard."

Tyson nodded in agreement. Marc was frowning. Despite his heavy way of dealing with things, Tyson could see the sympathy there. The emotions were starting to choke him up again. "I had an argument with him, when I tried to take them off him. I don't think I'm going to see him again…"

"Why not?"

"He almost hit me."

"If he's your best mate, my man, then you'll see him again," replied Marc. Tyson felt Marc looking at him, and felt Marc's hand on his shoulder. "You all dealing with telling me you're gay and you got feelings for me and now you going off about your mate? He know about this shit?"

"No. I wouldn't tell him that, bro."

"Why the hell not? You'll tell me and you won't tell your best mate? How's that work?"

"You're different," Tyson started, quickly cutting himself off. *Because I have feelings for you, I want to be with you.*

"Nah, I'm not. You shouldn't be dealing with this shit alone, you either tell him or you tell someone who can help you. Because I don't know how to, my man. I don't know anything about this stuff."

"I can't believe we're not talking, we tell each other everything, bro. I wish things weren't so fucked up for him. He was in an accident when he was a kid. His father was driving drunk and he crashed, smashed up my mate's leg…he was going to be an All Black, bro, how does that shit work?"

"I don't know. You should be there for him. And I know he would be there for you."

Tyson glanced back up at Marc, trying to find an expression or emotion that wasn't there. "How can you be so cool about this? I told you I was gay. I told you that I liked you."

"I got no problem with gay guys. And I like you too, you're a good mate. It's just that you like me in a different sort of way. I like that you have the nuts to do what you did, though." Marc held his gaze, despite the fact Tyson wanted to cry again. He didn't know why he just kept wanting to cry. "I hope this shit don't mean we stop being mates."

"You still want to be mates?"

"Yeah. Why?"

Tyson didn't know. He had never thought of Marc as anything other than the love of his life. He didn't know if he could keep seeing Marc and not having those feelings that warmed him everywhere. He shook his head, only because he wasn't sure enough of the answer to give a real reply. Marc's hand was rubbing at his shoulder, but the contact felt wrong.

"Cool, my man. Because mates are there for each other."

"Thanks," Tyson managed to mumble. He was feeling more tired than he was used to, and strangely dead inside.

"What you want to do? Smoke up some more? Just chill? You can have a sleep on my bed if you want, I'll take the couch."

Tyson didn't feel like doing any of them. He was surprised that

Marc wanted him around still. His eyes fell on the bong that was still sitting on the coffee table. He managed to get the words out, despite how ill he was feeling.

"I wanna blaze."

"Fucking soldier, my man. We'll blaze, then."

Tyson couldn't remember falling asleep, or how much he had ended up smoking. By the time he woke up in the morning he was feeling raw all over, finding himself lying on the couch. His throat felt like he had been puffing exhaust fumes. On the widescreen TV, a black-and-white movie was playing still, shadowy, depressing shots of a samurai guy outnumbered on a cold road. Marc was asleep on the end of his bed.

Tyson didn't want to wake him. He got up and slipped out of Marc's jersey, leaving it draped carefully over the back of the couch. Gathering his things, he headed quietly out into the light. The cool breeze slapped him awake.

❖

"What fucking hour do you call this to come in? You think those dishes are just going to wash themselves?"

Tyson was already pulling his apron on about him, keeping his head down. He wanted to be shorter somehow, anything to avoid Faye's notice. Tyson was aware of things enough to notice the way the other workers in the kitchen were staring at him. Tyson was starting to care less what Faye thought about him and his dishes. He murmured something of an answer.

"What the hell did you say?"

"No, chef. Getting right on it, chef."

Shove it up your fucking ass, chef.

Tyson ignored the tirade that Faye rained down, especially on anyone who had delayed in their work to watch Tyson get the raw end of things. Tyson started filling the sink, moving the piles of plates carefully out of another, where they had been stacked because of a lack of space. He ignored the glances that Zadie was giving him. Tyson just wanted to keep his head down in a pile of dishes.

By the time he was due his first break, Zadie was pulling him aside. He resisted at first, but she shot him a warning glance. The alley outside was almost too cold to stand in but Tyson welcomed it. There was something entirely bracing about the way it cut across his skin.

"Since when do you turn up late to work?"

"I don't know." Tyson watched Zadie spark up a cigarette. He wondered where he could get him some weed. "Since tonight, I guess."

"Something's up with you, and don't bother trying to give me those usual lines you give about everything being okay, Tyson. What happened to our Saturday-morning coffees?"

Getting into work after coming back from Marc's had been a struggle. It was getting harder and harder to care about work.

"Just leave me alone, okay? I had things to deal with. I've had a heap of shit to deal with last while."

Zadie fell silent, and Tyson thought he could almost hear the sound of her cigarette flaring and burning down as she sucked on it. Tyson felt like he was only half there, but he knew he wasn't going to get him rest any time soon. When Zadie spoke again, there was a firm caution in her voice.

"I know that you're dealing with stuff, Tyson. You're shit poor at hiding that. The last month you've been all over the place. And now turning up to work late."

"I can deal with it, okay?"

Zadie was staring back at him when Tyson looked up. The concern he saw did little to soften him. Tyson felt long past wanting to let anything get to him. "I hope so. Just don't forget that you have people who care about you."

"I got dishes to wash."

"Okay then," replied Zadie. She wasn't even partway through her smoke, which meant in her opinion the same of her break, Tyson had learnt. "Just promise me that this Friday after work we do coffee again. Even if you don't want to talk. Just coffee."

"Sure."

Tyson pushed himself up and headed back inside. He knew that if there was one thing he could count on, it was that there would always be dishes to bury himself in. He ignored life through work, and come early morning when he finally got off work, he pulled his headphones on and ignored the world that way instead.

CHAPTER TWENTY

Tyson looked up at the sky through the scrawny branches of the trees. His hoods were up but he could still feel the bracing cold of the wind. When he closed his eyes, there was nothing, just that empty, hollow feeling. Beyond it were the pain of crying until there were no tears and the reality that he could never tell anyone.

He could smell the oil and the rubbish over the scent of grass. He could hear the rumbling of the distant trains, and the Morse code hiss of the spray can as it worked.

Tyson didn't know what he was doing here. Not just lying in the grass along some part of the train tracks, after calling Loot's cell phone to hang out. Here. It didn't feel as if there was much worth sticking around for. Not life after Marc. Everything that mattered was crushed, and Tyson couldn't work out how he had never seen that Marc wouldn't be like him. No one was.

"Still sweet, uso?"

Tyson glanced over, still hiding under his hood. Ihaia was sitting further along the bank, a respectful distance away. Tyson put up the same mask Rawiri always wore and maybe Ihaia saw the same thing Tyson always did. He gave the breaker a token nod.

"You really should go over there. Let some of that stuff out on the wall, uso. You and Loot ain't too different." That piqued Tyson's interest and Ihaia obviously saw the look, smiling. "Strong silent type. Putting all their stuff into their art."

"I never even touched a can."

Marc had said that he had. Marc had called him Dred. Given him his name. Marc was gone.

Tyson looked across the track at where Loot was working. There wasn't much more than random broad lines of grey that seemed to make no sense at all. Siege was sitting on an old crate, one of those old jobs that beer used to come in. It was a wonder it held his weight. He looked like a soldier in full urban camos, his thick braids sticking out at strange angles like snakes.

"Always a first time, uso."

Tyson looked at the way that Siege was smoking his weed. That made Tyson think of Marc too. Smoking weed. He watched the way the wind carried away the smoke and it reminded him of that morning in the park. Tyson jumped when he felt Ihaia's hand on his shoulder and then saw the way the breaker was looking down at him.

"You want me to come over with you?"

"Nah."

"Good stuff, uso. Get at it."

It took everything to get back up on his feet, but Ihaia helped push him up. Tyson glanced down the long length of track. No train. It felt like it took the same balls it did to approach Marc to cross the tracks to where Loot was working. Tyson tried not to look at Siege. Loot was lost in concentration, his dark features shadowed by the towel draped over his head. Tyson thought how the guy's height must be good for reaching up higher.

"You wanna grab one them cans?"

"Don't know what I'm doing."

"Yeah, well, that's where I come in, right?" Loot looked down at Tyson, expectant. Tyson glanced around and saw his pack open, revealing the cache of spray cans inside. "You learn can control better if you come from tagging, but you got good concept work. Just got to take it from the paper."

Tyson felt Siege's dead stare again but it didn't have the same harsh edge to it that it had when they first met. He thought about his black book and what it had opened up. What Marc had opened up. Tyson took up the first can he found.

"You know this shit?"

Tyson looked up across the wall. "Basic throw up."

"Yeah." Loot's voice was deep but quiet. "So the center's going to be purple? You do that shit, then you can redo the outline. Stay in the lines, son."

Loot was smiling, a slight, almost sardonic expression, but Tyson could see it was all good-natured. He gave Siege a glance. The rapper was watching him like a hawk. Tyson shook the can up, pulled the cap, and threw himself into his work. There was the same thrill he had with Marc. He was doing something wrong, something illegal. Most of him didn't care.

"You ain't graffed before?"

"Nah."

"You watched people graff?" Loot asked.

Tyson nodded, watching the way the paint turned the brick purple. "Yeah. A few times. Hip hop summit."

Loot nodded in respect. "You got decent can control there. No drips. Maybe you *are* a natural."

"Just seems right." Tyson shook the can up again. When he looked back, he saw Ihaia watching him with a warm smile. He looked too well dressed in his Dickies to be lying there against the bank, hood up.

"Get some this in you, homeboy."

Tyson glanced over at Siege, who had pulled himself up from the crate. The guy was towering over him, solid as a fridge and about as wide. He was handing him a joint. Tyson could feel the rapper's full presence, the heat of him, his weight. He thought of

Marc again, how he was the only reason he had started smoking in the first place.

"Nah. Don't smoke."

"Didn't ask if you smoked," Siege said, bluntly. He gave him a look, put out the joint again.

Tyson took it. He toked up and felt the burn of it straight down into his lungs. He tried not to cough it all back up, ready to pass it back, but Siege had gone. The rapper was swaggering further down the wall. Tyson tried not to gawk as he unzipped his pants and started pissing against the wall. Tyson's hands shook when he noticed a hint of flesh.

"Think he might like you." Loot took the joint. "He don't share his weed."

"True."

"Fuckin' Dodgee all the way, motherfucker! Pissin' on the fuckin' world!"

Loot grinned as Siege bellowed out. He pulled Tyson's attention away from the rapper, motioning back towards the wall. "Get this all done up, we'll hit further up the tracks. It's just throw up, so it don't have to be perfect."

"Nah. I want it perfect."

"Good shit."

Tyson kept at it, his hands still shaking as he thought about everything. Maybe he would give up trying to be gay. Maybe it was all a mistake somehow, a one-time thing. Now that Marc was gone, what did it matter? Tyson fantasized about being a graff artist, being down with Dodgee. Maybe Siege did like him. If all that was true, then there was no place for him being a faggot.

"Good shit, homeboy." Tyson staggered, leaped in surprise as he felt a crushing weight about his shoulder. Siege was patting him heavy, mussing his dreads as his hoods fell off. "You fuckin' family now. Fuckin' Dodgee. Now where's my joint?"

Tyson motioned over towards Loot, who gave the joint back.

He wasn't sure if this was homophobic Siege's way of being affectionate, or if he was beating him down. His hands were all overpowering and heavy. Once he'd got himself free of the stoned rapper, Tyson went back to work. He had to think carefully a while. He felt the questions on his lips but it was a while yet before he managed to get them free.

"What's up with you and Dodgee?" The question felt as meek as Tyson did.

"What you wanna know?"

"Why you do it? Rap."

"Any other fuckin' way out of this shithole?" Siege asked. He sat back down on the ground, like he'd forgotten there was a crate just a little way up. Clouds of skunky-smelling weed filled the air.

Tyson blurted it, regretting it instantly, "Get a job?"

"What the fuck you think I can do for work? Gonna get my way out of this shit by doin' what I do best."

"Rap," Tyson said, redundantly. Loot was smiling beside him.

"Rap gets you the bitches. Rap gets you the green. Rap gets you out of the fuckin' ghetto. Better believe I'm goin' all the way, homeboy. You all just lucky you in for the ride. Who else is gonna get me out this shit?"

Tyson shut his mouth, feeling the dead stare again. He felt the question he wanted to ask, dead in his throat. Not that he would ever have the nuts to ask it, even though he had run all the way up to it.

You hate gay guys, Siege? You hate me? Bet you would if you knew I thought about sucking your dick.

"You gonna outline that shit now?"

Tyson stood back, looking at his work. One big bubble-lettered "dodgee." He saw Ihaia looking on, pulling himself up from the grass. It didn't look half-bad, Tyson figured.

"You fuckin' family now."

Tyson wondered how Siege treated his family, all things given. He ignored it, thoughts of Marc saturating his head again. He thought about how Marc would look at him, what words he would say seeing his first graff piece. Tyson grabbed up a new can and started spraying out the outline. By the time he was done, and the crew was ready to move to a new spot, Tyson felt the dark shadow of depression.

He did something like an approximation of a tag: "Dred1."

"We still got to hang, uso," Ihaia said. Siege was already halfway up the line, towards the tunnel. "But it was cool you chilling with us."

Tyson nodded blankly, pulling his hoods back up as his dreads tangled, messed like bramble. He choked back the urge to cry, hating it and wondering why he couldn't control himself. Ihaia looked at him with those grey eyes. Tyson regarded his cheekbones, envying his strong features. It was all he could do to stop himself from crying when Ihaia pulled him in for a hug, both arms.

"Stay chill. Catch you up."

Tyson nodded and wandered in the opposite direction from the crew. It had felt good having Ihaia hold him. All Tyson could think about was how Marc had held him those few times, and how it would never happen again.

CHAPTER TWENTY-ONE

"A h, Tyson. I didn't expect to see you here."
Tyson pulled up a chair, seeing the looks he got from people he remembered from last time. Tyson noticed with a hardness that there were a few new faces, but none were brown. William looked surprised, but it quickly faded to the same warm appreciation that Tyson had learnt to expect from him.

"Sit down. Do you want me to get you a drink?" William was already starting to pull himself up. "A hot chocolate, was it?"

"It's okay," Tyson replied, already slouching back in his chair. "I can buy it this time. I thought you only got a free one on your first visit?"

"Rightly so. I thought I might hear from you on the phone before I saw you here again, but it's a pleasant surprise."

Tyson nodded a little in greeting to Robert, who was sitting across the table but busy talking over his shoulder in whispers filled with too much expression to a few tight-looking guys. They looked all too comfortable with themselves, smiling and happy. Tyson thought how he hated those smiles.

"So how have things been?" William was making motions to the waitress to bring Tyson a hot chocolate. Tyson shot a glance at Robert but he looked all too consumed with his own conversations.

"Shit. I told Marc I'm gay."

"The guy that you really like?" William seemed cautious, hanging on Tyson's response. "And how did that go?"

"He doesn't like me like that."

"You mean he's not gay?"

Tyson nodded to the question, keeping his attention split between Robert and William. He didn't know why he cared if Robert heard. William was easing back into his chair, as if gauging the situation. Outside it was bucketing down, the rain beating against the window as if trying to get in. Tyson had managed to avoid the worst of the weather, hiding out after he had slipped away from work. He was wired from lack of sleep.

"I'm sorry to hear that. I thought it might be a bit tough on you if it turned out that way."

"No big deal."

"How did he respond? Was he okay with it?"

"Yeah." Tyson shrugged. "He was cool. He just doesn't like me like that."

"There will be other guys, Tyson," said William. Tyson didn't have any time for the sympathy he saw in that gaze and heard in his voice. What the hell was it with everyone feeling sorry for him? "It might not seem like it, but you're not the only one. You have to stay focused on taking things one day at a time."

"I don't know if I can be bothered with all this shit," he replied bluntly. Robert and the two guys at the next table broke into loud laughs that slapped at the air. Tyson looked at them a moment before staring back at the little cup of sugar sachets on the table top.

"I find that the more you are bothered with it, the less easy it comes. It's like sinking in quicksand. If you struggle, you end up sinking faster." Tyson could appreciate how fatal that analogy was. William continued talking, his total attention on Tyson. "What are you really looking for? If you're looking for a man, Tyson, that will come in time. You should slow down and try and deal with who you are."

Tyson gave a vague nod to the waitress as she put the hot chocolate down. He fished about in his pocket for loose change from the train to pay for it. Tyson looked at the cup and tried to think what he wanted. All he wanted was Marc. It was the first and only thing that came to him. Outside that, he didn't give a damn. But now he knew that he would never feel Marc's protective arms around him. Now he didn't really care about anything.

"It's hard finding out that someone doesn't have the same feelings for you." William reached over and put a hand on Tyson's. "It can leave you feeling fairly burnt. You won't feel like this forever, though."

"I don't want to hear it, man. I just wanted someone around who was going to make shit a little easier to deal with. I thought it was going to be him, if I had the guts to tell him. And now I have, things are still shit, but worse."

Tyson saw the look in William's eyes. He half expected him to give him some answer, try and make things better by explaining things more, but he didn't. There was just a silence between them, and that soft look of sympathy.

"I just want to know I'm not the only one like me," Tyson explained, his voice quiet. "I guess guys like me ain't gay."

"When you say guys like you, you mean Māori guys?"

Tyson scowled at that, but refused to pick at that particular sore. He shrugged, fighting to find the words to explain it. He hated having to explain himself. "I mean guys like me. Guys who like the stuff I do, and yeah…brown guys too. Like I said, I guess guys like me ain't gay."

William chuckled, and there was nothing mean about it. "You aren't the only one like you. You're probably just the only one like you who has the courage to try and do something about it. For every guy your age who decides to come in here and take a chance to discover something about themselves, there are another ten or twenty or even more who don't. They hide away and hope that something might change."

Tyson toyed with his cup, and glanced out the window. The skies were still open, the downpour drowning the city in rain and shadows of grey and concrete.

"There are guys like you out there, Tyson. It might just take a while to find them. Not all of them come to the sort of understandings you do by the same path. Look how far you have come, though. It wasn't too long ago that you were Wiremu, talking to me on the phone."

Tyson saw the wry smile and shook his head. "I don't feel like I understand things any better. I just feel messed up."

"I know you don't want to hear it, but it will take time. But not as long as you think."

Tyson shrugged again. He didn't want to have to think of things without being able to think about Marc. Now it was just that same empty feeling inside, and no hope. It made him hard, in a way that he didn't care to try and change. Tyson glanced back over at Robert, who was still talking with the guys at the next table.

"They going out to the clubs tonight?"

"I'm not sure. Perhaps you should ask them. Why? Are you feeling a little adventurous?"

He had nothing to lose. Maybe he might find someone like Marc at the clubs. Maybe guys like him just didn't come to cafés. He knew he wouldn't usually be caught dead in a place like this, and he figured the same went for guys like Crunch or Loot. Tyson considered he might just be looking in all the wrong places.

"Robert," William called, having to try a few times before he got the guy's attention. "You feel like chaperoning Tyson here tonight? He might be up for going out on the town tonight."

Tyson shrank a little as Robert looked over at him, almost as in a totally new light. His eyes stayed fixed on Tyson for a time before he nodded, smiling. "Sure. We were thinking of hitting some of the clubs along K Road. There's a new place that's opened up that I wanted to have a look at."

Tyson started feeling the uncertainty almost immediately,

wondering if he was making the right choice. That same fatalistic mood pushed him forward, blinding him to much other than the hard feelings inside. Robert was starting to pay him more attention now.

"You sure that you can keep an eye on him?" William asked. "We don't want him ending up anywhere that he doesn't want to go."

"Strange men's beds aren't out of the question, then?" replied Robert. He smiled in a suggestive way that made Tyson think of a shark. He felt more than ready to protect himself, especially with how he was feeling lately.

"Just keep him safe. And remember that it's his first time out in this sort of atmosphere. You know how it can be sometimes, a little overwhelming."

Robert looked Tyson over in a more discerning way. "You're going to go dressed like that?"

"Is that a problem?"

Robert gave a rather dismissive shrug, almost rolling his eyes. "No, it's fine. I'm sure we can get you into the clubs. If not, I'll just have a talk to the bouncers. I know most of them."

"When you going?"

"Eager." This time Robert's smile smiled genuine. "The clubs really don't start happening until later tonight, so we're probably going to end up café-hopping and catching up with some of Jason's mates." He nodded over towards one of the two guys at the next table.

"Sweet."

"I'm serious when I said to look after him," William said firmly. He looked at Tyson again. "You sure you want to go out?"

"Yeah. I'm up for it."

Tyson figured that he would be able to hang on until then, even though he had stayed up the whole Saturday after work. His mind was starting to swim by the time they left the café. Tyson dwelled a moment on the long look that William gave him when finally Robert gathered up his things to leave. He seemed in no rush to move, but when he did it was in a whirlwind of action with entirely too much fuss. Tyson shared the quiet glances between William and him, finally pulling up his hood as they headed back downstairs.

Robert made mention of a car over the winds and driving rain, and disappeared, leaving Tyson with the two that had been at the other table. They exchanged introductions: Jason, who Robert had already mentioned, and John. Tyson kept his hands shoved deep in his jacket pockets as the two tittered on in conversation while waiting. Jason was short and seemed almost unable to stay still, all bright eyes and wide expressions, easily excitable. John was almost the opposite. Tyson couldn't help reflecting how they both seemed like carbon copies of Robert. He wondered for a moment if all gay people were like them, but then maybe all brown guys seemed alike to them.

They made the dash through the rain to Robert's car when he pulled up. Tyson piled into the back seat with Jason, who quickly continued conversations with Robert and John in the front seat. It was hard enough to hear, even over the loud music. As they pulled away along Ponsonby Road, Robert made the loud announcement back to Tyson that they were going to stop at Jason's house to get ready and then hit the clubs from there.

Jason's house turned out to be an apartment over one of the stores along K Road. The rain had let up a little by the time they piled out and headed up. The place was up a narrow stairway above a scungy 4-Square and turned out to be equally aged. Most of it was a single room that stretched out towards windows that looked down on the street. The place looked like it was halfway through being painted, but after the first impressions Tyson figured an artist of some sort lived here.

Madonna's throbbing beats filled the loft and Tyson weaved his way around the various artworks, looking at boards and canvases on easels. He forgot about the noisy trio, turning down an offer of a drink when it came, as he looked at the various half-painted and finished paintings. They were faces and people, cut in blacks and greys. They sat in parks and cafés, eyes staring distantly. Tyson wondered why they all looked so sad. He came across one that was of just a window, and saw the inspiration was directly behind it.

"You doing okay? This isn't all overwhelming?" Jason asked. Everything about him seemed tight and highlighted something of his form, whether it was his jeans or T-shirt. Tyson blushed over the words emblazoned across his chest, wondering how he had missed them: "No, fuck *you*."

"No, I'm sweet."

"You don't want a drink of something? I've got rum, or whiskey, or maybe you're a beer sort of guy?" Jason put a hand on his hip, pointing, with a curious expression on his face. "You don't play rugby, do you? I have this friend who hangs out with this guy who sounds like he fits your description."

Tyson shrugged. He was still wearing his jacket and satchel. He sat down at the window seat, feeling the cold breeze that whistled through its loose fittings. It was made of a solid wood that looked as if it had warped shut in the wet.

"Oh well. You wanted a drink, didn't you? Beer?"

"No, I don't drink. I'm fine."

Jason drifted off, obviously to get drinks for the others. Tyson rested his head against the window frame and let the cold draught keep him awake. He figured either tonight was a bad idea and he would drop from lack of sleep, or maybe he might end up meeting another homeboy like him. Either way, he figured he didn't have anything to lose now. Maybe he might even get laid. For some reason that prospect terrified him.

Tyson thought about Rawiri again. In his exhausted state he worried and apologized. He knew that Marc was right about that, if nothing else. Tyson had to think of some way to talk with Rawiri again and make up. Maybe he might even have the guts to tell him he was gay.

When had they started keeping shit from each other?

Tyson rubbed at his face, feeling worse and worse. For some

reason the cool breeze reminded him of when Rawiri and he had played rugby in the park. Well, Rawiri had played, he had just thrown that ball back. All that movement and activity, and then suddenly to be crippled. Tyson had never thought about it like that. Rawiri's dreams had died then. No more rugby, and no more All Blacks. Tyson thought of the drugs and wondered what it would be like to be that strong and suddenly end up so fucked up.

"You look like shit. You sure you should be coming out with us tonight?" It was Jason, who was nursing a bright blue bottle of something Tyson didn't recognize. "You can crash here if you want. I don't mind. The other flatmates wouldn't even notice."

"I'll be cool," Tyson said, not sure what was driving him on. He felt like he could sit here all night and be happy. "Where's Robert?" Tyson resisted remarking that he was meant to be "looking after" him.

"Oh, John's showing him some photos from an overseas trip. You're one of those rap kids, aren't you?"

Tyson frowned more than he already was. "What do you mean?"

"You lot always dress with your pants hanging off your asses." Jason smiled, but Tyson wasn't sure whether he should be offended or not. "Not that there's anything *wrong* with that, I happen to like it."

Tyson wondered if he was being hit on, and changed the subject. "Who does the paintings?"

"That's me."

Tyson seemed surprised, Jason didn't seem to be the type. "Why you paint that stuff, you don't look depressed."

"It is a little dark, I guess. It's just those sort of people that stand out to me, I don't know why." Jason looked at him with a careful eye, almost as if sizing him up for a painting himself. "You look like one of those sorts. It's like the whole world is on their shoulders and you wonder what's going on inside their heads."

"You ever asked them?"

Jason chuckled over a sip from his bottle, "Of course, silly. Nothing more than what's going on in everyone else's. I guess it just shows different in them." Jason paused a moment before asking, "Can I ask what you're looking for tonight?"

Tyson knuckled up again. Time to avoid getting hit on. Was that all these faggots ever did? Something of the question tugged at him. "I don't know…"

"Just going for a look, I guess. Your sort are pretty popular in the clubs. Robert's probably going to be spending the night doing what he always does, so I'll keep an eye on you."

"What sort?"

"Homeboys," Jason replied, with a smile. "Oh, they go crazy over a nice-looking Māori guy looking all rough like you do. It's probably because you lot are so masculine, and straight acting. They're happy to get them a homie or a rugby player. And you know what they say about brown boys."

Tyson noticed the coy look, and figured he knew, but played dumb all the same. "What?"

"Hung like horses!"

Tyson flushed a bit, shrugging. "I wouldn't know. Never been with one." He tried to sound offhanded. "Many go to the clubs?"

"No, not many, that's why they'll be all over you. Most of them stay away. Not their scene, I guess."

Tyson felt his spirits sink lower, if that was possible. He had known the answer before it came. He wondered again why he was going out. Jason gave him a playful shove.

"It's okay if it's just going for a look. I'll protect you. I certainly won't hit on you unless you want it. You're safe with me."

Tyson looked back over at Jason and managed to find it within himself to believe him. It occurred to him that someone who created paintings like he did couldn't be half-bad.

Chapter Twenty-two

The night skies had opened up again by the time they hit the streets. Jason had managed to coax a bottle of V into Tyson, which he had felt better for. He wanted to ask Jason about his paintings and bring up the subject of graffiti, but by the time he had mustered the courage and energy they were out the door in a torrent of loud shouts and calls of challenge to the night.

Tyson couldn't believe three people could be so loud. It only added to his disorientation, along with the dazzling sight of K Road late at night. Older couples shared the footpaths with streetwalkers and larger-than-life queens that scared the hell out of Tyson with their boldness. There seemed to be an obvious mix of straight and gay, without any concern for it. As if it was normal and accepted. The entire town looked to have come out, despite the weather that thrashed down on the streets.

Robert, Jason, and John had all changed a few times during the night, finally settling on attire that seemed to Tyson the same as what they had started with. Tyson felt out of place in his usual sagging jeans, black T-shirt, this one a 4 Corners one, and Rawiri's big jacket, furred around the hood. John had remarked that he looked like the hired DJ with his battered satchel and headphones, and that maybe he could get them into some of the places quicker if they had lines. Tyson hadn't had time to dwell on the remark long before Jason slipped something in his jacket pocket.

"Just in case," he said, with another of those private smiles. "I know you're not looking, but it's no fun if you're caught without."

Tyson had felt it out by touch, the sharp, square wrapping, and the almost gel-like, squishy centre. He knew what condoms looked like enough to work it out.

They moved from place to place along the street. At times they waited at length for the rain to stop before making a dash between streets, then other times hardly waited around for someone they met by chance while they bought cigarettes. Tyson found the flighty nature unnerving. He was too tired to resist as Robert led them quickly along the currents of humanity.

When they finally settled on a club, Tyson found himself lingering about behind the others. There was a tight grip of people hanging around outside a large set of doors, over which was set a bold sign proclaiming "Stairway to Heaven." Tyson felt nerves pinching at his gut, listening to the steady thump of music inside. Those coming and going almost looked like a rather normal bunch, he thought. Although some looked like Robert and Jason, others seemed normal enough.

Jason tucked an arm under his and Tyson didn't find himself quick enough to resist. "Just stick close to me, hon. I'll take care of you."

Before Tyson could give it any more thought, he was taken inside the club. He briefly looked at the bouncer, wondering if he would be questioned. The burly islander acted as if nothing was out of the ordinary. The dark, loud heat of the club quickly swallowed them. It was like riding a roller coaster, entirely out of his control, as they plunged over the dip.

It was the sound more than anything that overwhelmed Tyson. Then the sights. So many men packed into such a small area. The club was cavernous in front of him, a number of levels up, with a big, sweeping staircase leading up to the first floor. Tyson felt a fright that someone might somehow know him.

Robert was shouting to Jason beside him but Tyson couldn't

hear what they were saying. The music was drowning out everything, suffocating as it throbbed and beat around him. Tyson just let Jason pull him gently, threading them between groups along the dance floor. Nothing of this place was anything like the Barge Bar. Not even the number of people.

Tyson was overwhelmed by the number of people, the different sorts of people. The scene was surreal, bare flesh, tight leather, people who looked like they'd come straight from the office. People he wouldn't even guess were gay, talking with queens large and proud. He watch two men kissing like they were the only two people in the world. Seeing it, Tyson wondered at what it would be like to try it.

Drinks were bought at the bar and Tyson managed to understand enough of Jason's shouts to work out that he was asking him what he wanted. He replied "nothing," and Jason brought him back another bottle of V, never straying too far from his side. Robert pounced on a table as soon as it was vacated by two stern, cut-looking men. It wasn't so much a table as it was a perch to rest drinks, a few stools in front, and a long seat lining the wall behind.

"You dance?" Jason shouted into his ear. Tyson shook his head. Almost as soon as they had sat down, Robert was off again, exuberantly greeting a group of tall queens. He vanished into the throng with them, as Jason shouted to Tyson again.

"What do you think?"

Tyson shrugged his shoulders, and tried to shout back, "Loud." Jason laughed, the music moving his body despite the fact he was sitting.

Tyson opened his bottle of V and drank on it nervously for lack of anything else to do. Just sitting there watching was overwhelming. Everything was so shameless. Near the bar, a few tables up from where he and Jason were sitting, a couple of guys were the in process of making out. More than just kissing, it involve touching in all the most private places, lingering on obscene.

"Is it always like this?" Tyson managed.

Jason dipped in closer. "Yeah. Loud, isn't it?"

Tyson ignored the answer, drinking on his bottle, the V giving a raw edge to his fatigue. The sharp taste of the drink colored his mouth. Tyson wondered if it was because he was tired, but as he continued to stare he felt his mood dipping.

It was like looking though the magazine. How long ago had that been? The pages seemed to catch all too accurately the sort of life that was playing out in front of him. Tyson wondered why it was any different from going to the Barge Bar. Here was a place where he was meant to belong. Wasn't this what it was like to be gay? Tyson tried to find anyone who wasn't so pale, the search still proving fruitless.

The dance floor was packed, and even above in the balcony levels more were watching. The more Tyson looked, the harder his mood became. So many people, and no one that looked remotely like him. Tyson started to notice an older guy at the bar staring at him, rather openly. When he noticed Tyson had spotted him, he smiled openly. Tyson figured that the guy would be scared off by the expression on his face. He probably looked like a criminal.

Tyson was being dragged off by Jason again, who was saying something that he couldn't hear above the thump of the music. It was a sound that Tyson could feel in his chest, making his heartbeat pale in comparison. Jason tugged him through the crowds as he tucked his bottle into the pocket of his jacket. He almost stumbled on the first couple of stairs as they headed up to the next level.

"Old men gawking at you?"

"Yeah." Tyson scowled. He appreciated that Jason had noticed.

"Told you. Homeboy."

"Where's Robert?"

Jason shrugged, his only answer, and easier than saying something. Jason had tucked his arm under Tyson's. The closeness felt strange, the weight of Jason against him as he tussled him up the stairs. He was close enough that Tyson could smell his aftershave and the scents of him. It was hot enough that Tyson was long since considering taking his jacket off, sweat making his T-shirt cling.

Jason took him along the crowded balcony until they found a free spot. He dived at the gap and squeezed himself in, pulling Tyson with him. Despite having to move, Tyson was impressed by the view. A dance floor full of writhing, dancing bodies. Short, muscular Asian boys or tightly dressed European twenty-somethings, pressed tight with beefy, gruff-looking men in leather pants and little else. Tyson dwelled on the floor below a while, thinking that he spotted Robert among the throngs. So much for looking after him.

Tyson started noticing the attention he was getting again. He looked at Jason, but he looked happy, drinking on his neon pink bottle. Tyson nudged Jason and shouted in his ear.

"Why is everyone fucking staring at me?"

Jason laughed, like he tended to, and put an arm about Tyson's shoulders. Tyson didn't mind it. That was ironic given he couldn't stand the stares from others. He had only known Jason a while longer. "Because you're a rap kid. You're all straight acting and hard looking. They want you."

"I don't want them." Tyson glared at a nearby guy. "They're looking at me like I'm meat."

Jason nodded, his expression seeming somewhat sympathetic. "That's clubs for you."

Tyson slouched forward on the rail, staring down. The noise and the constant thump was getting to him. Below, a huge billow of smoke from a smoke machine near the DJ's booth issued into the crowd. Tyson glanced at the DJ, thinking that he could make out a brown face from the shine off his equipment. He felt a tapping on his shoulder, already to react to it harshly, but feeling Jason lean in against him.

"That what you're looking for?"

Tyson looked where Jason was pointing. The guy stood out because he was brown, looking all tall and solid. He had the same tight build as Ihaia, even if his dress sense was less street. He wore a plain, button-down shirt and brown coat, contrasting with the lighter brown of his pants. Tyson stared a moment, his face flushed as he thought that the guy had to be gay. He seemed like the sort of person Tyson would pass on the street. How the hell was he meant to tell him apart from anyone else?

Jason smiled and said something, but Tyson missed it as he watched the guy weave his way towards the bar. He seemed to linger there as Tyson's gaze lingered on him. He was easy to pick out, even despite the low light, distance, and now growing haze of smoke. Tyson felt hot, and a sense of hope. He thought forlornly of Marc for a moment, brooding. He remembered the times he had stayed awake in bed wanting Marc to be his first.

Tyson slurped on his V, watching. The guy looked popular, if the number of people who were talking to him was any indication. Tyson felt tapping on his arm again and Jason's voice hot against his ear. "Why don't you go talk to him?"

Tyson clammed up almost instantly. "Nah…it's cool."

"You obviously have a hard-on for him!"

Tyson frowned, but it was hard to be angry at Jason. It helped that he was only telling the truth. Tyson stared still, feeling Jason pull at his arm again. He resisted, but only a bit. Wasn't this what he wanted?

Tyson was sweaty as they pushed back down the stairs. His mind felt numb, letting Jason guide his movements. He wouldn't have been able to move otherwise. Jason muscled his way through the crowds and shoved them up to the bar a few people away from the guy. Tyson found himself staring now they were closer. The guy looked good.

He definitely had the look of a rugby player about him, something a little more refined than Rawiri. Rawiri was provincial strength, this guy was tall and tailored touch skill. Tyson dreamed briefly what his legs must look like inside those pants. He felt himself feeling the effect in his own, scowling at himself but humming with the exuberance of the situation.

When the guy beside him moved, Jason shoved him helpfully up to fill the gap. Tyson felt small next to the guy. He had no idea where he plucked the courage, but tapped the guy on the shoulder, trembling somewhat. He looked like an islander. The guy gave him a brief nod, barely acknowledging him. The look of disinterest was lost in Tyson's nervousness.

"What's up?"

The islander frowned, and Tyson repeated himself. Eventually, he leaned in closer and Tyson saw the look of recognition. The guy shifted his shoulders, still leaning against the bar. Tyson couldn't help but notice how big the guy's back was. Still charged on the moment, Tyson leaned in again and shouted over the music.

"My name's Tyson."

"Cool."

Tyson wondered how this sort of thing was done and went with the first thing that came into his head. "You want me to buy you a drink?"

"I don't do brown."

"What?" Maybe it had been lost in the music. It was pissing Tyson off.

"I don't fuck brown guys."

"What sort of bullshit is that?" shot back Tyson. The guy looked decidedly ambivalent, turning his back again. Tyson trembled, but more with anger as the surprise turned inwards. "What does that shit mean?"

Jason was pulling on his arm again, ready to whisk him away. The guy wasn't paying Tyson any attention at all. The anger boiled and burned, turning quickly into a self-pity that weighed heavy along with the fatigue of the night. He was still trying to work out what the islander had meant as Jason pulled him back towards one of the tables. They had emptied somewhat, as people took to the dance floor. Jason gave him a few uncomfortable glances.

"Some guys are assholes," Jason said.

"What does he mean he doesn't get with brown guys?"

Jason pressed him down onto one of the seats, but Tyson's anger had already pushed past being dangerous. He felt the perspiration beading down his back, under his layers. Jason pushed in close again and said something about needing to use the bathroom. Tyson just nodded, thinking about leaving anyway. He was shaken, thinking of Marc again.

Tyson was left alone with his thoughts for the moment, feeling the stares again. The crowds felt as if they were pressing in on him. It had been hard enough going to the Barge Bar, but here things felt worse. Here there were crowds, and people who made him feel like meat. Tyson didn't know that he could feel that cheap just by the way someone looked at him. When Jason returned, he was already on his feet.

"I'm going."

"You sure?"

"Yeah."

"Let's go outside."

Tyson pulled his jacket about him, watching the islander at the bar, who was laughing with a few older white guys. He wanted to run up to him and smack him in the side of the head. Or worse. Jason kept him on path as they squeezed out through the crowds. Tyson wondered where Robert had got to. He wanted to kick Robert's ass too. Fuck him for not looking out for him.

The cold air hit him like a blast as he stepped out and the sweat on his skin started feeling more uncomfortable. Jason was close, still wearing that look of concern. Tyson wondered why he bothered to care. What was Tyson to him? Just some stupid Māori kid.

"You okay?"

"Yeah."

"You sure? You need a lift home or something? I can borrow Robert's car and drop you off if you want."

Tyson shot back at the suffocating concern, "No, man. I don't need a lift. I can take care of myself. And wasn't Robert meant to be taking care of me? Where the fuck did he end up?"

"Robert's like that sometimes."

Tyson watched the people lining up and moving along the footpath. Beyond, the streets were still wet, but it had stopped raining. Everything was shining, hard and chrome. He watched as an old car moved with the slow line of traffic. Tyson could hear the bass over the thump of the club's music. It almost sounded like PNC. One of the darkened back windows wound down.

It took Tyson a slow moment to see Siege. As if in a dream. And then the moment drew longer as Siege stared back with a face frowned in recognition. Tyson thought he could almost see the cogs slowly slipping into place inside Siege's mind. Tyson remembered where he was, standing out in front of a gay club.

"I got to go," Tyson said, tossing his hoods up over his head. He glanced back, seeing the car moving as slowly. Siege was still watching, but saying nothing. "I'll just catch the train home. Thanks."

"Tyson!" called Jason after him.

Tyson pushed his way into the foot traffic. Maybe there was some chance that Siege hadn't seen him. Seeing him had charged Tyson into a paranoid fear, sharpening his senses. *He didn't see me*, Tyson started repeating in his head. The nervous sweat lingered long as he made his way along K Road. *He didn't see me.*

CHAPTER TWENTY-THREE

Everything was a distant memory by the time Tyson got back to his neighborhood. The cold kept him awake and he had forgotten about listening to his iPod. Tyson was scared, long since past cursing himself for being stupid. Stupid for opening up to Marc and stupid for having run off to some gay bar to find someone who would look after him. Tyson thought on what William and him had talked about. What he was really looking for?

The streets were all too quiet and the air was too crisp and cool, almost electric. Tyson was near collapsing by the time he headed up the path along the side of his house. He was too bitter and too tired for tears, just that raw and empty feeling inside. It had been stupid going to the club, even worse now that Siege probably knew what was up. Somehow in one evening he had managed to fuck up absolutely everything. He wondered how long he could avoid the Dodgee Dozen.

"Ty."

The soft call made Tyson leap, too tied up in his thoughts to have noticed the dark shadow hanging out in the car among the trees. Tyson looked into the dark, remembering how he had fucked up his friendship with Rawiri too. But for some reason he was sitting there, where he always sat, waiting for Tyson. It was like none of this had even happened. Somehow he had never met Marc or wondered what it was like to be with a guy. It was like things had always been.

"Rawiri...bro...I'm sorry, man..."

"It's forgotten, cuz."

Tyson hesitated, his heart starting to drop as Rawiri stayed in the car. The fright started to grip him tighter than the cold, and for a brief moment he was scared, feeling all the old fears creeping over him like the weeds that had crept over the husk of the car.

"Bro? You okay."

"I think I need some help, cuz…"

Tyson was in to help Rawiri in a second, fearing what he would see, but still there anyway. Rawiri was dressed as he always was, the hood of his blue overcoat pulled up over his head. Tyson begged to whatever gods would listen that it wasn't how he thought it was. He helped Rawiri out of the car, feeling his friend's weight almost pull him back in with him. He caught a glance from Rawiri, trying not to show his shock when he saw the deep, unnatural shadows of his face.

"Fuck, bro…"

"I just wanna go inside, cuz. It's cool if I stay over your place a few days, right? Just till I get straight?"

Rawiri's voice was all too calm and quiet. Tyson felt the emotions tearing at him. The fatigue hit him all too hard, "Fuck, bro…"

"Just get me inside, cuz."

Tyson put an arm up about Rawiri, feeling the weight as his friend slung a big arm up about his shoulders. If he hadn't been out at a gay bar trying to get with guys he could have been back here with his best friend, stopping this from happening.

Tyson was busy fussing as he got Rawiri upstairs. He didn't bother pulling the mattress out this time, like he always had. The room was dark and inky as he guided Rawiri over to his bed, easing his weight down. Rawiri sat himself back against the wall, letting out a long breath. He sat in silence, Tyson just staring. From the brief light from the window, he could see the state of Rawiri's face.

"My dad bashed me," he said, as if needing to confirm it somehow. Tyson stood stony silent in front of Rawiri. For the moment, neither of them could seem to say anything. Tyson had seen it before, but it didn't make it any easier to deal with.

"You're staying here, bro. You ain't going back. I'm not going to let you. Not this time."

"It's my home, Ty. It's not like I got anywhere else to go."

Tyson's voice was hard, and his words looked to take Rawiri off guard, "Fuck that. You can stay here. It's not like we're kids any more. Your dad's belting you up, man."

Rawiri hung his head. Tyson couldn't handle how quiet he was, despite what he had been through. Tyson felt a building anger.

"I thought I could take care this shit, cuz," Rawiri explained. His bottom lip was thicker than usual, split on one side. "I figured if I bulked up I could take care myself. I can't fuckin' move fast enough. My fuckin' leg…"

Tyson melted inside as he saw Rawiri starting to choke up. For some reason he still hesitated when inside everything was screaming to do something. He saw how Rawiri tried to wipe his bruised and bulging eye, and how it hurt him almost instantly.

"I'm gonna take care myself, Ty. I'm gonna fuckin' take care myself. I ain't a fuckin' kid any more. What sorta man lets his fuckin' father bash him?"

Tyson felt frozen inside, standing and staring, as sobs starting to shake Rawiri's big shoulders. He was fumbling in his coat pocket. Tyson's eyes widened as the light from outside glinted off metal. His chest felt like it was crushing him as he stared at the pistol Rawiri was pulling out.

"I'm gonna fuckin' kill him."

"Rawiri! Fuck!"

Tyson moved quickly, surprising even himself as his limbs sprang to motion. He snatched the gun, shoving it away from them both. It came away from his friend's hand all too easily and the look of surprise told him that Rawiri hadn't been expecting him to grab for it. Tyson trembled as he held it, his eyes locked with his friend's.

He saw a pain he thought only he had felt, one that cut too deep inside. One eye bloated and purpled, the other far too filled with emotion.

The pain started flowing out from Rawiri in torrents. Tyson tossed the gun aside, making a grab for his big shoulders, pulling him in close. Rawiri cried into his chest and shoulder, great sobs shaking in his body. Tyson held him, shocked into silence. He couldn't think of anything to say, holding on to him as if he was the last person in the world.

"Why the fuck this shit gotta be so damn hard, Ty…"

Tyson heard the words come quiet as he kept Rawiri close. It stunned him hearing them come from Rawiri. He wondered how fucked up he had been thinking that *his* problems were bad when Rawiri had been going through all this. Tyson stumbled for an answer to give him, but none came. He rubbed at Rawiri's big back, murmuring quietly.

"It's cool, bro. I'm here for you. I'm not going anyway now. Things going to be different…"

"Fuck, cuz…"

"It's going to be cool, Rawiri."

Tyson didn't let him go, despite the resistance that he felt. Rawiri wouldn't be stupid enough to do something like kill himself? Tyson felt a harsh emptiness inside. How much did he really know Rawiri, when there were things about him that even Rawiri didn't know? Tyson wanted to get rid of the gun. He could feel Rawiri's exhaustion within his arms, in how his weight was heavy against him.

"I'm sorry I hit you, cuz. I didn't mean for shit to get like that."

"It's okay, bro, it's forgotten," Tyson replied, stony.

"I figured if I could get like I used to be I could take care myself."

Tyson stared down at Rawiri's hooded head. "Bro, you never

been as big as this, what you mean? You the strongest person I know anyway…and I don't just mean because you're buff. I mean you been through all this shit, and you still here, bro."

"I'm sorry I lied to you, cuz…"

Tyson sat stunned for a moment, feeling his heart thumping in his chest, his cheeks starting to flush red. He replied hesitantly, "What you mean?"

"About my leg. It didn't get fucked up in the accident…my dad fucked it up. It got broken up worse after the accident. He bashed me up a few times after the accident. Said it was my fault."

Tyson didn't know how to reply. Rawiri felt warm against him. He had always wanted someone to hold him like he held Rawiri now, to take away all the pain and hurt. Tyson never anticipated he'd be the one comforting his best friend, someone he never believed was weak.

"My dad fucked my leg up, cuz. He's fucked up everything in my life."

"You don't have to go back there, Rawiri. You can live here. I'll take care of things." The words felt all too easy to say, but their weight came heavy on Tyson's shoulders. There was never anyone else to take care of things.

"I don't need to be fuckin' blubberin' on your shoulder, Ty," Rawiri replied. He pulled himself up, the swollen bruises only adding menace to his look. "I gotta fuckin' harden up."

"Nah, bro. Don't do that. Don't hold that shit inside." Tyson looked at Rawiri's face, feeling the hurt that it held, wondering how he could stand how it must feel. "This is the most we really talked for in years. If we been doing this before, then none of this shit would have happened. Neither of us would be as fucked up as we are."

Rawiri looked at him, and instantly Tyson wished he hadn't said it quite like that. "What you mean? How you so fucked up?" The words had venom.

"I just been going through some hard stuff," Tyson replied,

picking his words too carefully. He changed the subject. "It's cool now, bro. I'll take care of it. You can live here. I know my mum would be okay with it."

"What hard stuff?"

Tyson looked at Rawiri again, but only saw that dead stare from his friend. Tyson started thinking when either of them had last slept. Rawiri's eyes didn't give up, blunt and demanding answers. Tyson trembled. He thought of what Marc had said and found somewhere else to look. Anywhere but his friend.

"Bro...I think I'm gay..."

The silence was anything but easy as it crushed down between them. Tyson knew he was probably going to lose Rawiri as well, after having lost Marc and fucking everything up for himself. He wanted to start crying. It was too late. He should have kept his mouth shut.

"Why didn't you fuckin' tell me?" Rawiri murmured.

"I'm sorry, bro. I didn't know how to say it..." Tyson dared to look at Rawiri, seeing the surprise on his friend's downcast face, and the dull acceptance.

"You should have fuckin' told me. Friends don't keep shit from each other, cuz."

"It's not like that," Tyson said. "I didn't want to risk losing you, bro. You all I got. I know we shouldn't be keeping shit from each other, but..." Tyson took a deep breath, scrambling to try and make things right with words. He tried to see rejection in Rawiri's eyes, expecting it. His good eye was all too sharp for the damage in his other. Tyson struggled to see much more than Rawiri's bashed exterior, wishing instead that he was full of emotion and weak with tears again.

"Is it cool?"

"What? You being gay?"

Tyson took a slow breath, venturing carefully, "Yeah. I know I should have told you, bro. I just been trying to deal with it myself is all. Sort of like how you been dealing with your stuff. But I guess maybe we should be dealing with this shit together…I mean…that's if you still want to be mates."

"I known you since you was a kid, cuz. You pervin' at guys instead of girls don't change that shit."

Tyson felt the waves of relief. Rawiri's look still seemed guarded, and cautious. The two of them looked at each other, Tyson wondering how it was he could not find that face so frightful the way it was right now. All he could see was his friend, battered and bruised. He saw the concern, melting again. Tyson ignored everything and held Rawiri again.

"Thanks, man," Tyson said. The emotion was starting to overwhelming him. He joked quietly through it, "How is it that we can be such good mates and let things get this messed up?"

"I dunno, cuz."

Tyson kept hold of Rawiri's big body, relieved all over again that he was holding him as close. It felt good, enough that he was wondering if it should feel as good as it was. He thought of Marc and all the things he wanted to do with him. Rawiri was back to being quiet and withdrawn. Tyson wanted to hold him all night, even if nothing else.

"I'll talk to my mother in the morning, bro."

"What about your work?"

"I'll call in sick. This is more important."

"Chur, cuz."

Tyson reluctantly broke the embrace, pulling back a bit. He took a slow, long breath, only just noticing he was still wearing his jacket, satchel, and headphones. He stood up slowly. "I'm going to go get us a drink, okay?"

"Sweet."

Tyson headed over towards the door. "Things will be all good from now on, bro. I promise. I'll make sure nothing happens to you." Rawiri nodded, pulling his jacket off, the shadows of the room falling deep over him. By the time Tyson got back upstairs with the drinks, Rawiri was fast asleep.

❖

The light hurt Tyson's eyes enough that he wondered if there was ever a time when he had kept the same routine as normal people. He sat hunched over the kitchen table, watching as his mother fussed with breakfast. He stayed silent, just watching as she moved this way and that. Tyson rubbed at his eyes, still feeling exhausted. He had hardly even slept, and he had done so on the floor.

"His dad has been beating him up for a long time." Tyson found it difficult bringing it all up again. "I just want to do something about it this time."

"It's okay if he stays here, you know that. Things aren't too hard that we can't let him stay in your bedroom."

"I'm sure he can help pay his way a little," Tyson said. His mother stopped beside the table, holding his face a moment. She looked far too worn.

"I know that money is tight sometimes, but we can manage."

Tyson frowned, looking down, despite her touch. She stood there, and her fingers lingered along his jawline.

"With us both working, it will be cool. We can run things when we're both working."

Tyson didn't miss the rather loud sigh from his mother. She stood with her hands on her hips, wet tea towel draped over one shoulder. Tyson felt how quiet the house was and how long it had been since they had both had the chance to sit down together.

"You're just like your father," she said. Tyson felt those words strike deep inside. "You know that it should be *me*, not us. Why don't you let me take care of us?"

"Someone has to take of things." Tyson felt his tone coming across begrudging. "You can't take care of things all by yourself. Plus, I can help out. That's why I am. You won't notice Rawiri's here." He tried not to make him sound like a stray pet he had brought home.

"It's not a problem. And the money is fine."

Tyson watched her as she headed back into the kitchen. He could smell sausages grilling in the oven. The toast popped up with a metallic bang. He watched as she checked on the food. Tyson couldn't help smile, despite everything, and how tired he was. His mother was too much like him. Or maybe it was the other way around. Pigheaded.

"We don't get to talk enough," Tyson said, carefully. "Or see each other enough."

His mother put down the butter knife she had just got out, leaning on the counter a bit. Tyson lowered his head, not really wanting to see the way that she was looking at him. It was knowing and regretful. She spoke softly.

"I know. I promise we will find some way to change that. We both work such crazy hours. I think I'm pretty close to getting promoted to team leader. That might let me move things around a bit."

Tyson knew too well that him working nights helped less. His mother worked normal enough hours, and looked after his brothers. All he could see were the unending piles of dishes. She broke his train of thought. "Did you ever get anywhere with that chef's apprenticeship?"

"No…"

"What's stopping you?"

Tyson frowned. He knew the answer. "Nothing, I guess. We need the money."

"We! There we go again with the 'we'! I swear you're just like your father." She rounded the counter and sat down at the table. Tyson wondered if he was going to look that run-down when he got to her age. The thought suddenly scared him. He was worried for both of them. She was smiling back at him.

"I wish he was still around…things would be easier."

"Maybe so, Tyson. But that's in the past."

"Do you still think about him?" Tyson watched as she gazed out the window. Her eyes looked distant.

"I do."

"I do too. I wish he were still around."

"I know," she replied. She took Tyson's hand, resting it there on the table top. There was a tone in her voice that lifted Tyson's chin. "You father would have been proud of you. I know it's hard for you not to try and be what he was and not feel like you have to take care of everything. You don't have to stop. Just remember to be there for yourself a little too. Let me take care of things as well."

Tyson pulled a strange face as he thought on that. Thinking about his father seemed to come up at the funniest of times. Sometimes he wouldn't think about it for months and then suddenly it hit him at odd times. He wondered what his father would think about him liking guys. He wondered what his mother would think. Tyson hesitated, biting his lower lip as he looked up at his mother. He held the words inside. He just wanted to sleep.

"Is he asleep?"

"Rawiri? Yeah. I was going to call work and then sleep. I think he's going to sleep a while too. I'm going to set up the mattress on the other side of the room, out of the way. I can sleep there."

"I'll keep something in the oven for you two when you wake up. I'll be over at your grandparents' this afternoon if you need to call."

Tyson nodded and pulled himself up from his chair. He felt his mother's touch lingering on his hand, like she didn't want to let go. There was a lump in his throat as he thought about what he had told Rawiri and what he was still keeping back from her. Finally, he stepped away from the table. Her voice paused him at the foot of the stairs.

"Even though we don't get to talk and see each other as much as we want, don't ever forget that I love you, Tyson."

"I love you too, Mum."

CHAPTER TWENTY-FOUR

Tyson almost shit himself seeing Ihaia waiting for him when he stepped off the train. He kept his head down. He couldn't see any sign of Loot. No sign of Siege either. Just Ihaia. The b-boy spotted him and pushed up from the wall where he had been waiting. Tyson shook, thinking up a bevy of excuses why he was coming out of a gay club. Anything to fix the damage Siege had probably done.

"Marc told me you catch this train home, I ain't stalking you."

"Could have fooled me." Tyson had to admit, Ihaia looked good. Snug blue jeans, a blue satin NY Yankees jacket, and a matching cap that made him think of how Misfits of Science used to dress. Ihaia fell in step, smiling.

"Nah, serious. I just come from my girl's place. Had to go check on my baby son. Then was passing by here and figured I'd try my luck."

Tyson didn't know why hearing Ihaia had a girl spiked him with jealousy. It put an edge on his mood. *Everyone gets someone but me* was all he could feel shifting through his brain. He snuck glances at Ihaia, seeing the guy in the dim light of the streets. He figured Ihaia's girl was pretty damn lucky.

"You talked to Siege?" There. He said it. Tyson was sick with worry at the answer.

"No? Why, uso?"

"No reason, I guess," Tyson replied. He'd dodged that bullet, but it was only a matter of time. He figured this was the last time he was going to be hanging with anyone from Dodgee.

"Looked like you had a good time hanging with him and Loot, though. All that graff stuff. I admire you guys."

"Why? I think you breakers are more impressive than us, bro." It felt strange saying "us." A graffiti artist by implication. "Never going to see a graff artist bust their shoulder."

"You want to see the scar, uso?" Ihaia laughed. He looked serious, but Tyson kept his head down. He started heading down the main drag towards his part of town, and Ihaia was still following.

"I gotta go home. Why you wait around for me, anyway?"

The breaker hesitated, glanced down the street. "You want to come check something out?"

"What?"

"Just something to show you why I think you graff guys are better than us breakers."

Tyson tried to see the motives behind Ihaia's smooth features. All this was going to change once Siege started spreading the fact one of their own was gay. A paranoid thought crossed his mind, that Ihaia knew and was leading him somewhere for a beat-down. Ihaia smiled back, eyes dancing with mischief.

"You so damn hard to convince of anything, uso. Come chill with me for a bit. You waiting for a reason?"

You won't be so friendly when you know the truth, bro.

Tyson shrugged, mumbling something of a reply. Ihaia motioned them back towards the town, the industrial parts where the trains ran. He remembered the thrill of rolling with Marc. Time healed some of the wounds, but the emotions were still there. Occasionally they came scratching to the surface again.

"You pretty cool," Tyson admitted. He toyed with the idea of beating Siege to the chase, then remembered where they were going. Big industrial sheds that cast shadows as heavy as the mood.

"Yeah, you pretty cool too, uso."

"What's that mean? Uso."

"Brother," Ihaia explained. Tyson thought he could get used to how the breaker stuck to his side. "It's Samoan."

"You…"

"Yeah, and Māori."

"Mean."

"Yeah, my mum's Samoan. My dad's Māori."

"You speak it?" Tyson asked out of interest. He thought about how he wished he had a skin tone like Ihaia's. That was how a real Māori should look, that smooth shade of brown. Not as light as him.

"Yeah. Both. Got no choice around the house. Else my mum gives me the jandal." Ihaia let out a laugh. "Straight-up island styles."

"Bet you got tats too."

"Me? Nah. Too chicken." Tyson frowned, trying to see the breaker who was cool with busting a shoulder, but didn't want to go under the needle. Ihaia added, "Bet you got some nice ink, though."

"Why you think that, bro?"

"Dunno. Just think you'd look pretty sweet with some Māori styles. Figured you already did."

"Not me."

Tyson let the conversation lapse into silence, as they headed into a wide, empty yard. Overhead spots cast a harsh light that Ihaia walked about to avoid and Tyson stayed close. Tyson kept thinking about opening up. Marc was meant to be that, though. Marc was the guy who was going to save him from all this shit. Stupid romantic bullshit. He toyed with the idea of giving everything up. Now it was just him and Rawiri, like it had always been. It was dumb to try for anything else.

"It's up through this way," Ihaia said as they came through the back of the block.

It looked like some sort of packing yard and smelt like forest.

They pushed through a broken chain-link fence, then they were ankle-deep in rubbish that Tyson didn't want to look at. The two-day-old stubble lent a deep shadow to Ihaia's face. This place was darker. Tyson could see the twin shines of tracks, though, back out by the trains. He listened to the distant sounds of the city, ever present. The sound of their feet on gravel.

"Life been pretty shit for you lately?"

Tyson wondered about opening up again, but thought better of it. What came out was at least a half truth. "My best mate's been through the wars. Just trying to keep on top of it."

"Mean."

"Yeah. Why you want to know?" That came out sounding far too harsh.

"I got plenty of family. I can tell when they going through trouble. It's usually me who's cracking them outta it."

Tyson looked at Ihaia a moment, and wondered what it would be like being brother to a guy as cool as him. He let himself think that it was all like Ihaia said it was, brotherly concern. It seemed strange to think that someone was showing him concern. In his family it was definitely Tyson for himself.

"It true what Siege said?" Tyson asked, quickly changing the subject. He didn't want to lie about the rest. Ihaia was too nice a guy for that. "That he wants to use rap to get out of here?"

Ihaia nodded, straightening his cap about a little. "Yeah. Hangs with us to keep away from the beer at his family's place and keeps his head down in his rhymes to stay out of the way of the gangs."

Tyson muttered quietly, "He's not too nice a guy, though, right, bro?"

"What you mean? The way he acts? He seems cool with you. Better than a lot of people that have tried to hang."

"I mean he's pretty full on."

"At least he ain't on the beer. Seen him lay out five guys when he's been drunk. He talks crap but at least it's kept him off the beer."

Tyson shuddered to think what Siege would be like drunk knowing what he knew now. He looked down at his sneakers, stepping over trash. He wondered how much of this crap could come off trains.

"You got dreams?"

Ihaia smiled, chuckling in a warm way. "Where do I start, uso? Like maybe I want to join Blackout or the Disruptiv Allstars and go to the world champs, if Dodgee don't take me there. Or maybe I want to be a carver and do all those sweet Māori carvings. Then I think about just picking up and sailing the Pacific like our ancestors did. Just me and the stars."

"You for real?"

"Yeah, why not?" Ihaia asked. "What's your dreams? Go visit NYC, see where all this graffiti stuff started?"

Tyson smiled a bit at that. "I never even thought about real graff until I met Marc." Ouch. It still hurt, Tyson realized, and he fell silent a while. He admitted quietly, "I don't have dreams."

"Just got to let yourself dream."

I wish I could meet a guy half as cool as you and we could be together forever, bro.

Tyson looked at Ihaia, watching the breaker as he searched the other side of the tracks. Their pace slowed up a bit and it just gave Tyson the time he wanted to just stand and stare. He didn't even want to go there, not so soon after Marc. Not with another straight guy. This time around he would pick them apart.

"Maybe take care of my mate," Tyson settled for. He was starting to feel the heavy weight of everything again. It never fully disappeared. "My family. That's about it."

"That's some pretty sweet stuff," said Ihaia. "Your friend is pretty lucky, having a mate like you. Always good to have someone in your corner when things get hard." Tyson brooded on that remark, but Ihaia interrupted the thoughts. "Well, you got me now, uso. I mean, if we cool."

"Yeah. We cool, bro."

Ihaia stopped and looked at Tyson for a moment. In the silence Tyson could hear the trains again, distant thunder. Somewhere out there was the rumble of traffic. He found himself staring back at Ihaia, looking at the guy's lips. They weren't like Marc's, but Ihaia was nice in other ways, he realized. Those gentle eyes and the way he was easy with a smile. Tyson found himself wondering if he would ever see Ihaia shirtless.

Not after Siege started talking. Best he savor these few last moments being a member of the Dodgee Dozen. Come morning all this shit was over, Tyson thought.

"What?" Tyson found himself unnerved by the looks, uncomfortable in the silence. Ihaia nodded past him, and Tyson realized he wasn't looking at him. He was looking at the wall behind him.

"Oh. Mean."

The shine of light off it caught Tyson by surprise, the lazy arc of industrial-strength light from the yards opposite illuminating the piece. It was high up the warehouse wall, enough that Tyson wondered how the hell someone could have got up there to do it. It took a good few seconds to take it all in, and even then it was impressive. Cut in 3D shades of blue, arrowhead fonts crossed in and out of each other. Tyson tried to make out the letters, but couldn't, only making out two or three at best.

"What does it say?"

"No idea," Ihaia said, putting an elbow on Tyson's shoulder. Tyson didn't mind the weight. He liked the closeness of it. "But it's pretty sweet, huh? Who knows what it says. Just the guy who did it. Could say anything."

Tyson kept staring, tracing the passage of the lines, trying to decipher the script. Looking at it was almost hypnotizing. He frowned as he looked around the sides of the art. "Who would do something like that and not sign it?"

"Pretty mean, though."

Tyson took a few steps back. He wanted to take out his black book and get it all down. It was different standing in front of it rather than watching it from a train. He didn't want to commit this one to memory and copy it down later.

"I want to do shit like this," Tyson admitted, half to himself. He felt Ihaia's arm around his shoulder, gripping him close.

"Yeah, thought you might like seeing this, uso. Thought you might."

"Thanks."

"No problem. That's what I'm here for."

It took a while longer before Tyson gave up looking at it. He shrugged himself carefully out of Ihaia's embrace and took a step back. He saw the look of concern on the breaker's face, probably from the way Tyson was looking at him. Tyson mustered up the courage to talk, but it still came out as a murmur.

"Promise me something, bro."

"Anything."

"No matter what happens, you'll show me some your breaking moves."

Ihaia frowned, the mask of concern. "'Course, uso. Any time. Why? What's going to happen?"

"Just promise."

"'Course. I promise. Anything, uso."

This time it was Tyson who pulled Ihaia in close. He didn't bother with savoring the feelings of Ihaia's form, only just realizing how solid the breaker felt in his arms. Ihaia held him back, just as tight, and it was a long few moments of heavy breaths before Tyson let him go. Tyson thought how good it would do him to keep a mate like Ihaia. He just wondered if he would still be a mate after the shit came out.

Chapter Twenty-five

There was something comforting about having Rawiri as his roommate, on more than a few levels. Other than knowing where Rawiri was all the time, considering he barely left the room, it was cool knowing that he would be there when Tyson got back from work. The room had started to smell sharp, the smell of sweat, given that Rawiri had brought some of his weights over, along with a backpack of his clothes and closest gear. Tyson didn't mind the smell so much, although he kept worrying about the drugs.

Rawiri was asleep by the time that Tyson got home early Saturday morning. He tried to be as quiet as he could be coming in, despite discovering Rawiri was a heavy sleeper. He watched Rawiri sleeping for a time before he put his things away, finding that he was comfortable enough around Rawiri now to strip down to his boxers before going to bed.

Tyson's mind was a muddle of graffiti and sketches that he had done on the train back. He couldn't sleep, thinking of what Ihaia had said about dreams, and thinking about his own. More than a few times he found himself waking to thoughts of Marc or Ihaia, finding his hand inside his boxers. He stared at the dark shape on his bed and brought himself pleasure thinking about Rawiri.

When Tyson woke up, the low afternoon sun was blocked by the trees outside. He saw Rawiri sitting over on his bed still, reading a magazine. Tyson glanced quickly at it from where he lay. Rawiri seemed like the sort who would have stacks of porn magazines. Tyson rather half wished that it was. It was a fitness magazine instead.

For some reason Rawiri seemed cool with Tyson being gay, and still dressing as lightly as he did. Rawiri was usually in boxers and a tank top that showed off his large chest, shoulders, and arms. Tyson almost always stared and tried to make it not seem obvious.

"Took your fuckin' time, cuz."

"Sorry, bro, I didn't sleep that good."

"Yeah, I know."

Tyson raised an eyebrow, mussing his dreadlocks. They were almost due for tightening up again. Rawiri answered his question before he could ask it. "You toss a lot in your sleep."

"I don't talk, do I?"

"Why? There somethin' you don't want me to hear you sayin', cuz?"

Tyson grunted, pulling himself up out of the tangle of sheets he had managed to get himself into. Rawiri was shadowed from the brief spot of sun that cut through the curtains, but his face was healing fast. He didn't look half as bad as he had, and his mood was back to its usual self.

"You got any weed on you?" Tyson asked, changing the subject. Rawiri gave him a sort of gaping look. "What?"

"Why? What you gonna do with it?"

"What do you usually do with weed?"

"Fuck, cuz. Fuckin' wake an' bake. Since when do you smoke?"

Tyson rubbed at his shoulder and found himself a T-shirt to slip into, even though he was only going to shower in a moment. He frowned a little, as the answer made him think of Marc. He didn't know why it was taking so long to get over him. "I sort of met someone and started smoking with them."

"You fuckin' smokin' with a stranger and you never smoked

with me?" Rawiri asked. Tyson half expected some sort of retaliation, but instead there was the hint of a smile on Rawiri's thick lips. "At least you come around to the right way of thinkin', cuz."

"This guy was different."

Tyson considered talking about it, but from the look he saw from Rawiri, he didn't push it. Rawiri wasn't going to ask, if he didn't explain it. There was an uncomfortable stillness. Tyson pointed towards the door.

"I'm going to take a shower. You want to do anything before we watch K-1 tonight? Go out to the park or something?"

"Not unless you sweet with smokin' up here in your room, cuz. Can keep the window open. Get ourselves blazed before the program comes on."

Tyson left to take a shower, finding that it got rid of some of the fatigue that last night's sleep hadn't. His thoughts kept coming back to Marc, and then what Ihaia had said about dreams. How could everything be as simple as Ihaia seemed to make out it was? Tyson remembered asking Rawiri about his dreams, and how he had had none. After Marc, it seemed like dreams weren't really worth having.

Tyson showered, dried, and dressed himself in the bathroom, despite how casual Rawiri seemed about himself. Tyson still hadn't made the full leap to being as casual with himself around his best friend. Rawiri was stretched out on the bed as scantily dressed as before. Tyson did his best not to stare, especially given that Rawiri knew he was into guys.

Rawiri was already rolling up a joint from what little he had brought over with him. Dumping his towel, Tyson pulled the window up with some effort, feeling it protest under his shoves. The cool afternoon air flooded the room, tugging at the aged curtains. He pulled his desk chair over next to it, watching the looks he was getting from Rawiri. Tyson managed a smile.

"This might sound pretty stupid, but I'm sort of looking forward to this."

"Shit, cuz, you that much of a stoner already? How much shit you smoke with this guy?"

Tyson shrugged and dumped himself down on the chair, feeling the breeze cut at his bare forearms. "Not a lot…I guess I was just sort of getting used to smoking with him. Don't know if it was him or the smoking, though…"

"Bit of both." Rawiri struggled with sitting up on the bed and passed the joint over with a lighter. Tyson glanced down at Rawiri's leg, the skin around his knee mangled and scarred without the brace. "You can do the honors, then."

Tyson sparked up the joint and took a few tokes before blowing the smoke out the window. It came back almost as quickly, curling about him, and filling his senses again with its thick smell. He was about to pass it to Rawiri, noticing that he was getting up. Rawiri moved himself over to the window, and Tyson got up to give him the chair and then the joint.

"I been thinking, bro," Tyson said, as he leaned up against the window frame. "Just about stuff for the future…"

Rawiri was looking distant, but Tyson wondered if he was just too preoccupied with smoking. He pushed on, all the same, wanting to broach the subject but not sure how best to do it.

"It's sort of cool having you over here, bro. And smoking with you."

"Smokin' is always cool, cuz. How long has it taken you to work that shit out? I been tryin' to get you to smoke for years."

Tyson tried not to stare at Rawiri's big shoulders. His singlet was snug on him and he seemed to bulge a lot larger than he had before. He definitely hadn't had all those veins before. His thick black hair was hanging ruggedly about all that hard muscle. Tyson noticed Rawiri looking back at him, expectant, holding out the joint. He took it and toked again, feeling his head start to swim.

"You haven't thought about what I asked you before? I mean, if you have any dreams?"

"Nah. When you ask me that?"

"We were in the park, you were smoking up. I asked if you had any dreams."

Rawiri just shrugged those big shoulders. Tyson stared out the window instead, looking down on the ragged tree line and hints of Rawiri's backyard beyond that. Rawiri's tone was dark and all too quiet.

"You know me and that shit, Ty."

"Was just thinking about things, and thinking maybe how it might be sort of cool if we got a place together. You know. Place of our own." Tyson swore at himself silently, thinking how that sounded like a seedy come-on line. He risked a glance back at Rawiri, wondering if he had taken it that way, covering himself all too quickly with more words.

"I mean, my mum's probably sweet with you staying here a while, and I've lived here all my life. Just thought that if I was going to move out, it would be pretty sweet to get a place with my best mate."

"Guess so."

Tyson sat down on the floor under the window. Rawiri was passing the joint back and Tyson toked, feeling the warmth spread all too easily around his body, like smooth butter on bread. He tried to blow it up so it would go out the window.

"And maybe I could get a better job. So we could have our own place, and I could still help out my mum…"

"How's your mum so hard up she can't pay for this place herself?" Rawiri asked, rubbing slowly at his thigh. "Ain't she gettin' benefits?"

"Yeah…but…you know. It's rough running a place when you only got one income."

Rawiri shot him a stare. "You sayin' you would want me to get some job or some shit? No reason me gettin' a job when I'm gettin' the dole. Like I'm good enough at anything."

"You could find something, bro…"

"Not with my leg, cuz. No shit a Māori is good at other than buildin' and makin' fuckin' roads. No way I'm doin' that shit on my leg."

"I'm sure there's other stuff," Tyson said. He found the tone of the conversation was making it difficult to relax with his buzz. He didn't want to push Rawiri. The dream of it almost sounded rather good. "But you think all this is a good idea? Even if you do stay on the dole? Getting a place with me somehow? You think it's a good dream?"

"Guess so."

"I think it would be sweet living with my best mate." Tyson hoped again that didn't sound like he was hitting on Rawiri. He kept stealing tight, cautious glances, trying to make sure his mate wasn't taking it that way.

"Just you and me, huh?"

"Yeah, bro. Ain't it been that way all our lives anyway?"

Rawiri didn't answer, and Tyson watched as his friend stared out the window. His dark gaze seemed distant, as if fixed on something far away. Rawiri had his thick forearm rested lightly on the window sill, the wind tugging the smoke away from the joint he was still holding between two fingers. For some reason, seeing Rawiri like that made Tyson feel sad. As his mind swam, he tried to think of something to say to make him feel better somehow.

"You and me, bro, we always going to be mates. No matter what. I know we been through some shit..." Tyson thought that weed was meant to make it easier to say things. "And I'm real sorry I didn't tell you about me liking guys sooner...but you're my best mate, Rawiri. You always going to be my best mate...I just never want that shit to change, bro."

"It won't."

Tyson stared at Rawiri's distant expression, trying to make sense of it. He couldn't help notice that big chest rising and falling deeply, and those hard shoulders. It was like Rawiri was trying to find words outside somewhere, only to come up short.

Tyson smelt the strong funk of the joint as Rawiri finally took another deep drag on it. He tossed the remainder out the window and nodded sharply to Tyson, spreading his arms to him. Tyson struggled up and took the hug for what it was. Rawiri felt solid against him, and he noticed that Rawiri was hugging him with both arms. How good it felt radiated in his groin, Tyson feeling his cheeks flushing bright. Tyson kept his arms tight around his friend's broad body.

"Nothin's gonna change, Ty," Rawiri said. Tyson felt the heat of his breath against his neck as he spoke. "We been mates all our lives. Nothin's gonna change that…"

Tyson wanted to say something else, anything, but felt like it would just end up coming across sounding queer. It felt good holding Rawiri, even if a little awkward with him sitting there in the chair and Tyson half-standing. Tyson didn't want it to end any time soon, but when it did he found himself trying to act casual.

"Sweet, bro. You know it's all good."

"Sweet as."

Tyson glanced back up at Rawiri, frowning a little as he wondered what he had missed. Rawiri seemed to look as staunch as always. Tyson leapt as he heard a banging on the door, and his mother's voice coming muted through it.

"Oh fuck…"

"It's sweet, cuz," Rawiri said, putting a hand down to steady Tyson as he tried to struggle up from the floor again.

"She's going to smell it, bro!"

"Nah, it's sweet."

The door opened, and Tyson tried not to look so guilty as his mother poked her head in cautiously. Tyson watched her carefully, almost paranoid, frozen in place on the floor. She just gave the two of them a casual glance. Rawiri nodded staunchly in greeting.

"Hey, Mrs Rua."

"Hello, Rawiri. Tyson, I'm just going over to your grandparents' for the evening. Are you two okay to get yourself something to eat?"

"Yeah…we're cool."

Tyson couldn't move, just staring at his mother, feeling the room swaying around her. She smiled back at him warmly before making to leave. "I'll call you later on tonight, then. Love you."

"Love you, Mum."

She left almost as quickly as she had come in, Tyson sure that he saw a lingering smile on her lips. He figured it was going to be hard enough for her finding out that her son was a stoner, and then there was finding out that her son liked guys. Tyson didn't think either of those conversations were coming too soon, if he could help it.

"Told you."

"I can't have my mum finding out I smoke, bro." Tyson tried to relax.

"Your mum probably already knows. Mums know everything."

Tyson wondered if she suspected the rest of it as well. Marc and Rawiri hadn't seemed too shocked, but that was different. He didn't figure either of them had seen it coming. It wasn't like he was like Robert. Tyson wondered if that would change after he had been with a guy. The yearning for that came like the need for weed nowadays, powerful and persistent.

Tyson pulled himself up and wandered over to his bed, flopping down on it. Rawiri offered a smile.

"You want me to roll up another one now she's gone?"

"I should get the TV."

"Nah, wait up. Don't want you droppin' it. We can chill a while, then you can get the set, and I'll roll up another."

Tyson nodded, watching as Rawiri went back to staring out the window. When he finally felt right enough, he went down to get the television. He ended up watching Rawiri watching the TV. There was something cool about watching him when he was watching his programs. Tyson felt like he could see something in Rawiri that had come away from him since the accident. Something more like the kid he grew up with. K-1 seemed like one of the few things that got Rawiri excited.

Tyson dreamed about living with Rawiri. His thoughts kept coming back to Marc and sex. He tried to banish the brief thoughts of what it would be like to be with Rawiri. Tyson swore at himself silently for thinking about his best mate that way. The thought struck him sharply as he tried to figure out whether that would make living with Rawiri more difficult.

Tyson figured he needed a plan, but as the night dragged on, and he smoked more, he figured that plans could wait until tomorrow. Tonight he was happy just chilling with his best mate. He eventually drifted off to sleep, sitting back on his bed, watching Rawiri.

Tyson had no idea how long he had been out when he felt the insistent shaking and the distant sound of ringing. Rawiri was over him, looking at him serious.

"Cuz. Your phone's ringin' off the hook."

Tyson remembered that his mother said she would call. He wondered why it was so late.

CHAPTER TWENTY-SIX

Tyson felt his stomach churning, his body ragged from running. The cold air of the night kept the shock sharp and raw. Around him, everything seemed hard and bright as he ran on instinct. He knew his neighborhood like the back of his hand. The fastest route from his place to the hospital was an easy one. It just left his mind to worry himself sick as he heard the call playing over and over in his head.

"Fuck, please be okay. Please be okay."

Tyson dodged traffic as he belted his way across the street and finally up to the well-lit mammoth that was the hospital building. All he could think of was his mother dying, and then thoughts of things worse, that she was dead before he could even get here. The hospital entrance was all but abandoned as he ran inside. The receptionist looked up at him, directing him to the emergency wards when he finally managed to babble out why he was there.

Tyson felt cold inside as he followed the signs. Nothing seemed right. He was still ragged from the running and breathing so heavily. His gaze darted about the busy ward as he tried to find his mother, his mind singular in its goal.

"I'm looking for my mother! Where's my mother?"

A concerned-looking nurse approached him, in blue, with a no-nonsense appearance about her. "Calm down. What's her name?"

"Hine Rua."

"She's down this way. She's okay."

Tyson stared, feeling the fright going through him as he walked into the room where she was. She looked anything but okay, with an oxygen mask over her mouth, lying out on the sterile white bed. Tyson felt his knees going weak and he shook, just standing there, staring. Everything seemed to be falling to pieces about him.

"What the fuck happened to her?" Tyson's voice was hoarse. "My grandfather said it was an accident or something."

"You'll have to wait for the doctor."

"What happened? I'm her damn son!"

Tyson saw the expression on the nurse's face, the way that his words whipped out and struck at her. She seemed taken aback, but the growing rage only seemed to fill Tyson with a charge. He could feel it shaking through his lanky form. He felt ready to tear apart the hospital to get what he wanted.

"A drunk driver hit her while she was crossing the road."

Tyson studied the nurse's expression, but it gave little outside the firm look of her face. She was guiding him towards one of the chairs in the small room. "You need to sit down. I know this is hard."

"My mother's all I got. I got two younger brothers!" The words tumbled out of him. "I can't lose my mother!"

"She's going to be okay. It looks bad, and she's taken some serious injuries, but she's stable. It's just going to take time," the nurse said, in a slow and measured tone. Tyson wasn't in the mood to listen. He wasn't able to look away. "I'll get the doctor so that he can explain things for you."

Tyson sat down. The place felt so desperately empty and alone, despite the presence of him and his mother. The quiet sound of the respirator and the ECG were all too steady. Tyson couldn't make it work inside his mind, not able to make the connection that what he could see was his mother lying in front of him. Even with that proof, it didn't seem possible. There had to be some sort of mistake.

A young Asian man came into the room after what felt like a silent eternity in which Tyson had just sat and stared blankly. He introduced himself, but Tyson almost instantly forgot his name, even before he had finished shaking the doctor's hand. Tyson listened as the doctor explained his mother's situation, but still nothing seemed to stick. He picked up snatches of words about internal injuries and damage to her lungs. Tyson had felt too shocked for tears, but he was starting to feel them burn inside him.

"We will watch her, but her condition is stable. I feel that she is in no danger, despite her injuries. We will just have to observe her for a time."

"She can't be here." Tyson struggled to reason. "She takes care of my grandparents and my brothers. Who's meant to look after them if she's in here?"

"You might have to call on other family. She will be here for a while. She has to recover, and that will take some time," the doctor said, more firmly.

"I don't have any other family! I just told you my whole family!"

"Nothing can be done about that. You have to give her time to recover."

Tyson scowled deeply, as if the doctor was somehow causing all this. He wanted someone to blame, and the doctor seemed like the most appropriate target. "How the fuck can she get hit by a fucking car?"

"The ambulance crew told me that the driver was drunk—"

"Fuck the driver! She can't be in here!"

"Shouting isn't going to help her. You have to stay calm and quiet, for your sake and hers now."

Tyson fell silent, but inside he was anything but. He put his head in his hands, feeling his dreads as they fell through his fingers.

He heard the sound of the doctor's voice above him, and it only made him want to lash out at him.

"The best thing you can do right now is be strong and make sure that your brothers understand what has happened. Your mother will be well, in time."

Tyson didn't know when the doctor had left, or if he had said anything when he did. The room seemed dead. The loneliness gripped him deep inside, tearing open that hole within him. He thought of Marc again, and of his big, protective arms. Tyson thought how he had no one else to turn to right now. He refused to let himself cry. His expression felt etched in stone as he stared at the linoleum.

Tyson didn't want to look at his mother like this. She seemed so lifeless. She was always anything but, and yet here she was lying on a hospital bed. She had always looked run-down, but she looked as if she could still keep going, no matter what. The thing that was lying on the bed in front of him couldn't be his mother.

Tyson lost track of time, metered only by the nurses that came and went. They left him alone for the most part, sitting at the foot of the bed. Tyson woke up at one point with a sore neck. Without windows there was no sense of time, leaving him in an unending whiteness. When he registered someone coming, it was the nurse that he had first met, with a look of surprise on her face.

"Have you been here all this time?"

Tyson just nodded. He had no idea of the time other than the fact he felt sore from sitting and his stomach ached, but even that was a distant pain that he could filter out. She was standing in front of him, overbearing and matronly.

"Come on, time for you to get up. You can come back, but you can't stay here. You need your rest as much as your mother does." She looked over her glasses. "Do you have any family that can pick you up? You can come back, but it's hospital policy that you can't stay here for days at a stretch."

"My family's lying there," Tyson murmured.

"You need sleep and you need food. I'll call you a taxi. It's the best thing for you right now."

Tyson pulled himself up to his feet, the reality of how he was feeling settling in with a harshness. Her hand was on his shoulder, and Tyson barely gave the bed much more than a brief glance. The nurse spoke to him quietly.

"Go home and take a proper sleep, then you can come back if you want. I'll tell the duty nurse to look out for you. Do you want me to call you a taxi?"

Tyson shook his head and wandered back out into the ward, dazed on his feet. He showed himself out, meeting with a busier hospital than he had come into. Making his way back out into the entranceway, and back outside, Tyson was greeted by a dreary afternoon with little sympathy. He felt dead to it, wandering a little way in the wrong direction before putting himself back on the right path. It looked like it was going to rain.

Even more automatically than he had come, Tyson returned home. The door was unlocked and the house seemed unnervingly quiet. He was used to it, but with his mother where she was it seemed like there would never be any sound there again. Tyson mounted the stairs, hearing the light sound of adverts coming from his room. Rawiri was sitting on his bed, slumped and watching television. He was quickly on his feet, limping heavily towards Tyson, without his brace. Tyson fell into his arms.

Rawiri held him without saying anything, Tyson clinging to his big form. He didn't know what to say, and Rawiri seemed as unforthcoming with words. He stood with Rawiri, holding on to him, not letting the tears come. He suddenly remembered when Rawiri had clammed up after all that crying, like it was something he could turn off. Tyson tried to find the strength inside, but it came easy with the dull sensation he was feeling.

"Come and sit down, cuz."

"I need to ring work."

"Do it in a bit. Sit down for now."

Tyson stayed close with Rawiri, not wanting to let go. He could feel the heat from his friend's body, the slow, steady movement of his chest as he breathed. Everything about him seemed so real and so present, so solid. If everything else could change and disappear so quickly, without any warning at all, he begged that this could stay the same. Tyson wanted nothing else than to stay forever in Rawiri's arms.

"Come and sit down, Ty."

Tyson let himself be moved, and sat down on the bed. He lay on his side, feeling the exhaustion carry him down. Rawiri was close, lingering by him. Tyson saw the stony expression on his still partly bruised face. His shaggy hair shadowed his blunt features. Tyson wanted to say something, anything, and when it did it came out quiet and hoarse.

"My mum got hit by a drunk."

"Drunk like my fuckin' father." There was a hardness in Rawiri's face, and in his tone. "Fuckin' drunks…"

"I got to take care of everything now, bro…my mum's going to need it. My lil brothers need it. I got to get to work and get paid. I got to pay the rent now she's not here."

Tyson felt as if the world was closing in around him, but the thoughts gave him some focus. He looked up at Rawiri, hoping to see the support and advice that he needed so badly. Anyone could give it, Tyson just needed someone to make it right, tell him what he needed to do, or tell him that what he had planned was the right thing. Rawiri stood there, silent.

"I don't want to go back there, bro."

"That's your mother, Ty. You got to go back there."

"I don't want to see her like that."

"You want her to stay there alone, then?" The words came out in a way that only Rawiri seemed to manage.

"No, man, of course I don't."

"You got to man up, cuz. You got to take care of shit. You got to stay strong and not fuckin' cave in, then. A real man takes care of his problems."

Tyson stared up at Rawiri. There was something lingering behind those dark eyes, but it was lost. A brief light, disappearing behind dark clouds. Rawiri was stern. It reminded Tyson of Siege, except it came from a deeper, darker place. It left Tyson with no doubt who would win if the two went toe to toe.

"You can only count on yourself, Ty." Even with Rawiri's quiet way of speaking, the sentiment was rock. "If you don't take care of yourself in life, then life's going to fuck you up the ass. Hard. Don't just lie there and let life fuck you, cuz. That's not what a real man does."

The bluntness struck Tyson, who stared up at the ceiling, and Rawiri turned away. Tyson heard him mutter quietly under his breath.

"Fuckin' drunks."

Tyson stayed lying on his bed. With all the shit he had been through, and life had to do this to him as well? It wasn't as if he didn't have enough to deal with in the first place. He tried to tell himself that Rawiri wasn't right, that there was something better in all this. Rawiri was a cold wind, showing him that there wasn't. Tyson wondered why he even bothered to try and keep his head up.

"Take care of shit, cuz. If you're not going to go see your mother, then take care of shit. Just don't be sittin' around like you got something better to do."

"I got to keep the rent on this place somehow," Tyson murmured, numbed.

"Take care of it, cuz."

Tyson knew he had to get up and call work. There was no way he was going to make it in today. He didn't have what it took to just keep going in the face of that. Just one day, he told himself, and then he would be right enough to take things from there.

Tyson kept staring over at Rawiri, watching his friend sitting there at the window. Maybe there was one thing constant in all this. Rawiri had always been there for him. Rawiri's face was hard, scowled with a darkness that scared Tyson. It was a rumbling storm cloud like he had seen when he had tried to get the drugs off him. He saw the expression of someone who was fed up with what life kept dishing him. Tyson was scared that he was starting to feel it too.

CHAPTER TWENTY-SEVEN

Even after taking a day off and sleeping, going back to work so soon came harder than Tyson had expected. The skies were coal black with clouds that raced overhead as if trying to beat him into town. They were an easy winner, each step coming slower. At one point Tyson thought to turn back and go home. He had slept badly, thinking about his mother lying alone. It was his fault that she had no one there.

It had been bad enough calling his grandparents and talking to them. Hearing his two brothers on the other end had almost brought him to tears. When he had hung up, Tyson got ready for work, running on automatic.

His workmates were watching him as came into work. He shot back challenging glances from under his hoodie to anyone who looked his way. Tyson got a strange, urgent look from Zadie as he headed towards the break room. It almost made him pause, but the monotonous regularity of his work habits carried him where he was meant to go. He unloaded his stuff and got into his white apron.

"Tyson, I need to talk to you."

Tyson didn't give Zadie much of a look as he headed back out towards the kitchen. He felt like a stranger there, getting even stranger looks. It was starting to fade, as almost like a single entity the kitchen workers knuckled down with the tasks of the evening.

Usually the heat bothered Tyson a bit, but tonight he didn't care. Even the occasional, accidental clang of the pots didn't faze him.

"Tyson, this is important," Zadie said, urgently.

"Rua! My office. Now."

The shout carried over the bustle of the kitchen and was enough to pull Tyson out of his sluggish way. He looked at the set of stairs that headed up to the offices above the kitchen, watching as Adams disappeared up the last few steps. Now Tyson was paying attention, and he gave Zadie a brief, harsh stare. Her look back was almost apologetic as he headed after the man.

No one ever went upstairs. Tyson barely remembered what it looked like. He had been up there briefly when he was interviewed and got the job. He couldn't remember how long ago that was, it felt like years, but couldn't possibly be. The way up was narrow and the wallpaper hinted at what the building had looked like before Adams had renovated it into Epicurious. The landing at the top was dark but the glow of office lights beckoned a few doors down.

The office was large, lit only by a few muted lamps. It made the woods seem to glow, the wide desk, the line of bookcases along one side. On the other, oddly colored fish distracted Tyson as he entered, dancing within a liquid light that cast its own swelling shades upon the deep carpet. Adams was silhouetted against the bay of windows that overlooked the narrow backstreets of Auckland CBD.

"If this is about the time off, I can explain," Tyson said.

"It's not about that, son, but I was going to mention that. Sit down."

Tyson stared across the desk. Adams wasn't sitting, so Tyson just stood there, on the other side of what seemed like an acre of dark wood. Adams was a large man, but it was a size that came with age and wealth. His dark blue suit threatened to lose him in the quiet shadows of the room, but his pale features drew him back in. Tyson always thought that he looked like someone's grandfather. Some unlucky white boy's grandfather.

"I'm getting in some equipment later in the week, some large automatic dishwashers," Adams explained, turning his tall, leather-bound chair so that he could lower his weight into it. "The workers will be in tomorrow and they'll be replacing a lot of the bench space that you work at."

Tyson just stood there, starting to feel himself freeze inside. A conversation with Adams was never a good thing. He didn't like where this smelt like it was going. With all the rest of the bad news that had come, this was leaving him with a deep, sinking feeling.

"The dishes are going to be done by the new machines from now on, we won't need as many staff—"

"You're firing me?"

"I'm giving you notice."

"You're fucking firing me?"

Adams expression was less than impressed, especially the way he raised one eyebrow ever so slightly. Tyson could feel the way he was regarding him over the desk. Already he could feel the disbelief pouring though him again, adding fuel to a fire that had burnt as coals ever since he had seen his mother.

"You'll have two weeks, which is more than you're entitled to."

"I've washed dishes here for the last how many years? You can't fire me." It came out like a statement of fact. "I need this job!"

"Which is why I'm giving you the two weeks, son. I know you have worked here for a long time. That's why I'm not letting you go with a day's notice."

"You can't fucking fire me!" Tyson was very aware of the physical presence of the desk between them. "I need this job. I can't be unemployed! My mother's in hospital! How the fuck am I meant to pay the rent?"

Tyson missed the expression of sympathy that passed over Adams's rounded features. His patience seemed to be wearing more than thin. "I'm sorry to hear that, son, but I can't afford to pay two dishwashers. Not when I have the equipment to do it for me."

"So you're firing me? And you're keeping on that Fijian guy instead? Why the fuck are you firing me and keeping him?"

"Look, frankly," Adam started, terse toned. "He's been more reliable than you over the last few weeks—"

"I called in all those times I was late, and the times I was sick!"

"And he keeps his personal life separate from work, which you are obviously having difficulty with right now, Mr Rua."

Tyson scowled darkly, feeling his face flush hot, trembling with the fire building inside him. His voice sounded louder in his ears than he thought was possible. "You know what? You can't fire me. Fuck you, you white motherfucker. I fucking quit. I don't need your fucking job!"

"Leave now."

"Fuck you."

Tyson turned and headed straight to the door, finding his pace unsteady at first, before it built more straight. He was still trembling heavily, the rage rumbling inside him. Somehow Adams didn't understand how bad this was. Tyson noticed Faye lurking near the doorway, shooting him a look that withered him as he passed. Tyson felt the power of it surge through him. Damn right that they should feel scared of him, for once in his life.

Compared with the looks he had got coming in, the looks upon his arrival downstairs were starkly different. A number of staff looked to make more than an effort not to look his way. A few risked eye contact and stared away almost instantly. Tyson felt a tightness in his body, balling him up, winding tighter and tighter. He took off his apron, tossing it in the face of the person nearest him, daring him to come closer as he headed into the break room to get his stuff.

"Tyson, I tried to tell you."

Tyson noticed Zadie quickly rushing in after him. He ignored her, feeling himself almost vibrating with anger. He quickly got his jacket on and slipped his satchel over his head. Tyson hardened himself against the look of desperate sympathy he saw on her face, her wanting to help.

"I know a few friends who are in the same line of work. There's a job for junior chef going at a place they told me about," she explained. Tyson headed out, but she was still at his side, walking as quickly as she was talking. "Even if you don't get that, I know another place that's looking for kitchen hands."

"Fuck washing this place's dishes," Tyson spat. He saw Faye coming back down from upstairs, noticeably paled. The chef shouted as he reached the bottom.

"What the hell is everyone doing sitting around! We have a full sitting out there! Zadie, get back on these pots!"

Tyson shared a brief moment as he stared at Faye, reveling in the way he was looking back. It was unspoken fear. Tyson relished it before continuing towards the back exit. He expected Zadie to go back to her job, after having been ordered to. She was still at his side as he felt the cold slap of the night, the wet splats coming from above.

"Tyson, don't just walk out. There's other jobs. This isn't the end of the world."

"My mum's in hospital. She got hit by a fucking drunk driver. She's not getting out any time soon. Guess who's looking after my mum's place and my brothers?" Tyson remarked. "I don't fucking need to lose my job right now. Who you think's taking care of everything now? Yeah, you right. Me. So fucking back off, okay? I don't need your shit on top of everything else."

"Tyson…"

"Leave me the fuck alone."

Tyson stormed out into the night, ignoring the rain. All he knew was that he had to get away from work. The more he walked, the more he realized that Zadie wasn't following. It started to sink in, the severity of the situation, bearing down on him like an entire world of responsibilities. Tyson thought how he had thrown in his job when he could have worked another two weeks. Rage was draining out to pity, like the water that was rushing in the gutters beside him. It started to sink in what he had done.

How had he done it?

Tyson was trembling by the time he reached the end of the street, bracing himself against one of the lamp posts, but he was trembling from something entirely different now. He felt sick, his stomach churned over as he remembered he had sworn at his boss. He had totally lost himself. Tyson knew the way that they had looked at him, *young, brown, and angry, ready to snap*.

Tyson headed back to Britomart as soon as he felt he was able to. Everything seemed to be crushing in around him. He wanted to be anywhere else right now, just not walking out here. He wanted to be somewhere where people couldn't see him, where there was no world but him. All he could keep thinking about was his mother, and the fact he was alone and now without a job. He felt sick again as he thought about the house where he had grown up.

Everything was starting to make Tyson think of Rawiri. He wanted to get home. Maybe Rawiri would have some advice, some way to make everything work. Surely he wouldn't think the best thing to do now would just be to man up and take care of things.

The train trip home was a dazed blur of dark graffiti and local hip hop in his ears that didn't make sense. It was as if the voices he knew almost as intimately as his own were speaking a different language, totally barring him from understanding. There was no comfort in the rhymes and lyrics, or in the beats that had always been his bedrock.

Tyson locked the door when he got in, the house feeling ghostly in its stillness. He felt safer somehow with the door locked, suspicious when he didn't hear anything at all, not even the quiet sounds of the TV upstairs. He did everything he could to hold back tears now that he was away from anyone who could see. He went upstairs to his bedroom, just wanting Rawiri to be there to hold him and listen and somehow make things right.

Tyson pushed the door open on his dark and quiet bedroom.

Tyson stayed as quiet as he could, not wanting to wake Rawiri. Both the bed and the mattress were flat and made. He frowned, worried instantly in a way that hit him in the pit of his stomach. He looked out the window, watching the dark trees swaying under a heavy wind. Beyond, he saw no hint of light.

"Where the fuck are you, Rawiri?"

Tyson felt the silence, the way that things were so dead after his question. He shrugged off his satchel and dropped himself into his desk chair, feeling so exhausted. He thought for a moment how he needed a drink, how he should try and find Rawiri. Maybe he should try and get a copy of the *Herald* and see if he could find another job. All the thoughts jammed in the small space that was his hurting head, none of them able to get through into action.

Tyson stared at his satchel, for some reason thinking of the blunt that he still had stored away. It seemed as good an answer as any right now. By all rights he shouldn't even be home at this time. By all rights the house should be alive right now, with his mother, and his brothers, just ready to go to bed. There was no routine to all of this.

Tyson retrieved the blunt where he had put it, finding new strength in having something to do, anything other than just sit. He wandered back down the stairs in search of a lighter. He remembered the joke that Rawiri used to make sometimes, about the big white one in the kitchen. Tyson opened the door on room after room of dark, empty space, each one making him feel more alone. He had hoped maybe Rawiri was somewhere else in the house, but it was becoming as apparent as the fact that he couldn't find a lighter that he wasn't.

Tyson opened the door on his mother's bedroom. Even in the dark, he could make out how tidy it was inside. Everything had its place, things that looked as if they hadn't been moved in years. A small white porcelain dog that had been a present from his grandparents to his mother, sitting on a dresser. The dresser's tall, wide mirror reflected dark shadows and shapes. The double bed there seemed so huge. The room smelt damp and old.

Tyson stood at the doorway, staring in, knowing how long it had been since he had been anywhere in the house other than his bedroom. Maybe as long ago as when he was a kid. As long ago as when his dad had been around...

Tyson stepped slowly into the room, feeling as if the shadows were pressing extra weight on him. Even the smallest things were starting to pull at him now, like not being able to find a lighter. Each thing built on the last, each weighing down more on his soul. Tyson thought about his father as he stared about the room. He looked at the record player under the line of windows at the front of the room. The windows were dark, looking out on heavy shrubs that had never been cut back.

Tyson stared at the photo of his parents sitting on one of the bedside tables.

Tyson couldn't help feeling how much easier things would have been had his father still been around. He wandered over to the picture and stared at it. It was like watching an older, absent version of himself staring back at him. His father was tall and lanky. Where there were differences, like him being darker, and his dreadlocks being longer, there were unmistakable similarities in those proud features and steady eyes.

Tyson dropped himself down beside the bed and took hold of the picture on his way down. The emotion of everything overwhelmed him. He didn't bother holding back the tears, knowing just by the feel of the house how empty it was. He stared at his father, as if the harder he stared, the more he could bring his dad back. Tyson wondered what he would have done in this situation. Things felt like they were going to get more fucked up very quickly.

Tyson's gaze caught on the record player as he wiped away heavy tears, seeing the bright yellow lighter sitting on top of it. He pulled himself up long enough to snatch it away, and took little time in lighting up his blunt. Tyson sat the picture in front of him, on the long bureau that made up the player. It was an old-school player, all in one, with speakers built in and space for records to be stored away.

"Figure you and me just going to have to smoke this shit by ourselves," Tyson murmured.

He stared at his father, resting his head back against the bed as he exhaled a heavy puff of smoke. The effects hit him quick, but it failed to warm the parts of him he wanted warmed.

Tyson noticed he had nothing to knock the ash out onto, and made a careful pile on the edge of the faded wood of the player. He took in the rows of records, squeezed in tightly, casually pulling out one and then another. Ella Fitzgerald. George Benson. Nina Simone. Everything looked more than old school, names he had never even heard of.

"Bet none of this shit is hip hop, Dad." Tyson looked at the dark faces that regarded him with their still expressions. He pulled one out of the slip and started the record player, hardly expecting it to work. The room filled with a warm sound.

"Wonder if you ever got high to this shit." Tyson's father stared back at him, too much like the covers of the records. Tyson felt something crushing at his heart as he muttered, "Wonder if you ever had to deal with any of this shit. Fucking leave me here alone to deal with it by myself…"

Tyson kept puffing at the blunt, feeling his throat become more raw and the weed take tighter hold on his system. George Benson sang about the night in ways that seemed deeper than anything Tyson had heard anyone sing in local circles. In his high reverie, Tyson pulled the record off and cast it on the floor, picking out another. Everything he listened to seemed to cast the room in a weight dragged down by age, settling heavy around him.

"Fuck you, man, just staring at me like that…What the fuck you think I'm supposed to do?"

Tyson wondered if he was expecting something to happen,

almost willing it. Maybe he would hear his father's voice and it would make things better. Maybe the answer would come to him out of the blue. Part of him expected more realistically maybe he might hear something in the music, in everything that his father listened to. The large old headphones on the top of the bureau reminded him of seeing his father sitting here, listening to his music like Tyson listened to his now.

The music had always blocked everything out, Tyson thought. His love and life blocked out all the pain, and the need to deal with anything else outside of Beatrootz and Flowz and Ill Semantics.

Haunting tones dragged at him, like cold hands within the smoke that drifted around him. Tyson slouched deeper, not having the strength or will to change another record. He stared at his father, staring at him. Depressed and desperate chords eased from the speakers, surrounding him with a smell of their own, slow and seductive tendrils.

Tyson gave up his will to fight. Beyond the window, the wind pulled at unkempt shrubs within inky darkness. The music assaulted his ears as the weed continued to assault his soul. Tyson gave up. Rawiri was right. This was how life was, it was useless to dream of anything better. Life had decided to shit on him at every turn. First having to deal with liking Marc. Then being turned down by him. Then his mother. Then his job. Now losing the house…

Unlike Rawiri, Tyson decided, he wasn't strong enough to fuck life before it fucked him. It already had.

Tyson felt the same desperate moods of the song and its singer. She pleaded with life, yet already knew she was defeated. It still struggled and fought, even when it knew it was lost. Tyson almost cried as he felt the blunt burn his fingertips. He dropped it on himself, patting it quickly, in a frenzied panic. Then when he was sure that he got it, he was paranoid he hadn't got all of it. Eventually he lay exhausted and limp as the music washed over him. His eyes were sore.

This was how it was meant to be. There was no use trying to

dream outside of that. Maybe he just had to embrace the fact and do what was expected of him.

High and crushed from the inside, Tyson decided there was only one way to fix the way life had fucked him. When he had the strength, he pulled himself back to his feet and went out into the wild night. On his hands and knees in the dirt, he felt the wetness seep through his jeans as he pushed his hand in under the house to where he had hid Rawiri's gun.

Tyson gave himself up. It was easier than fighting it any more.

CHAPTER TWENTY-EIGHT

The night was demonic around him, an irony that wasn't lost on Tyson as he headed down the street. He had only given himself a few moments to linger at home and get everything he needed. He didn't bother to wonder if there was any better way. If there was, it should have come to him by now. He pushed aside all other thought, only feeling the hate as he pulled a thick woolen beanie down over his locks. Rawiri's jacket had pockets just large enough for the pistol. He shoved a black bandanna in the other.

Tyson remembered the way that the Epicurious kitchen staff had looked at him, the way that Faye had looked at him. No one would be surprised with this solution. Tyson tried to work out how long he had tried to be anything better. No, not better. Different. Living where he did, he already was that way.

The wind kept tearing at him, moisture heavy in the air. It felt as if one moment it might suddenly start raining, then at another disappear entirely, like his own moods. Tyson stared up as he crossed the road again, keeping his pace quick. He watched the dark clouds racing overhead. He had hoped that he might see even a few stars.

Everything had come to him so quickly, so straight and sharp that Tyson had wondered why it hadn't seemed like the right answer before. With everything already so lost, Tyson figured there wasn't anything worse life could do to him. It was all or nothing. Would Rawiri be proud of him that he was trying to get back at life? Tyson figured he would, wondering and worrying again as to where he had gone.

Why had Rawiri walked out and left him alone? Maybe he should go back and search his house. If Rawiri was there and there were problems, Tyson was more than ready for them now. Nothing could stop him or stand in his way. Only the thoughts slowed his pace. His heart thumped, and he felt painfully hungry all of a sudden. Tyson rushed across the street again, closer to the town centre. He'd go back after, he decided. Then he could deal with Rawiri.

The main street was still fairly busy; the lines of Chinese takeaways and liquor stores would be open until well past midnight. Out in front of them, tight groups of youths hung out, with no better place to be. Talking in hushed tones, talking each other up to try to buy beer even though they were underage. Tyson knew their sort well enough. Even now he lingered like a shadow as he passed them by. A few noisy cars idled along the cracked concrete street. Thirdhand cars souped up with exhausts too big for their engines.

Tyson felt his resolve harden, staring dead through a young Māori guy who was eying him. This whole place was shit. Next to working downtown, or even the brief time he had spent in Devonport. Neither were anything like this place. This was where garbage was thrown out on the street. Usually the garbage was people like him. Tyson thought he heard the kid call out his name. He kept his head down and his pace quick.

Tyson walked the long length of the street and pulled a right at the smoky intersection at the end. His destination cast the night streets into bright and cheerful colors, its wide forecourt relatively quiet other than a few cars pulling in and out. Tyson walked off the path and over an afterthought of a garden that had long since been stamped underfoot. Along its length were a line of trees that had done a better job of hanging on to life. Tyson shoved his way past them, and dumped himself down against one whose larger branches had been broken and forgotten.

Tyson tried to psych himself up. He pulled the bandanna out of his pocket and tried to knot it up around his face. His hands wouldn't work right, fingers shaking uncontrollably. Tyson swore at himself and tried to bring overbearing, blunt will to bear. *Concentrate. Man up. Fucking harden up, bitch. Now or never. Take care of it.*

It took longer than it should have but he managed to get the bandanna tied, even if it felt like it was sitting too loose above his nose. His breath felt ragged and raw, and his throat hurt from smoking and the brisk walk up here. Tyson slipped a hand into his pocket, feeling for steel, if only to reassure himself it was there.

Tyson sat and stared. He felt sick from nerves. Across the road, the brightly lit service station continued as if nothing was out of the ordinary. Tyson held himself, trying to think, wondering if there would be a break in the traffic long enough to get in and out. Should he have brought a bag to put the cash in? Were there two workers or one? Was that guy out the front a worker as well? His mind unravelled as quickly as the questions, drowning and struggling.

"Fuck!"

Tyson turned away and leaned up against the tree again. His hands wouldn't stop shaking as he took the pistol out. At least this way he would have enough cash to pay the rent and take care of everything like he was meant to. All he had to do was get it right. How hard would that be?

There was light enough from the station to reflect coldly and dispassionately off the gun. Tyson felt another wave of sickness washing over him as he heard the light pats of rain start to fall past the leaves of the tree. He noticed his ass was wet from sitting in the grass.

What the fuck am I doing?

"Fuck…"

Rain hit like a wave, crashing across the city. Tyson tried to will himself to move, to charge himself with the momentum to walk across the street. He saw drips of water reflecting light off the pistol. It felt heavy and foreign in his hand. The more he tried to will himself, the more he felt like he was made of concrete, like trying to push at a truck to get it to move. He dropped the gun as suddenly a wave of nausea passed through him, and he retched.

He couldn't do it.

Nothing was coming out, but his body was rebelling violently against him. Tyson fell back against the tree again, pulling at the bandanna, trying desperately now to get it off, after all the trouble he had gone putting it on. He had to breathe and feel the night's cold air in his lungs.

"Tyson?"

Tyson leapt, almost hitting himself against the fallen branch. His fingers stumbled for the pistol, trying to hide it as he saw the tall shadow silhouetted above him out on the sidewalk. He couldn't make out who it was, but he was walking over the garden and through the wet foliage to get to him. Tyson tried to hide the gun, feeling his fingers slip too easily around it now.

"Damn, Tyson."

"I'm fucked up, bro…You shouldn't be here."

Tyson stared up Ihaia, who had frozen where he was, gaze at one moment locked on the gun and then another on Tyson. His snug black hoodie was damp and looked heavy under the weight of the rain, his black sports pants shiny. Water glistened on his loose, thick puff of hair which had started to droop a little under the weather. Ihaia slipped his hands very slowly out of his hoodie's pockets.

"What you doing with that gun, uso?"

"I don't fucking know." Tyson dragged his beanie off his dreadlocked head, feeling hot. Everything was coming to the top again and he felt like throwing up again. "Fuck, bro…I'm fucked up…I can't handle this shit…"

"Give me the gun, Tyson." Ihaia knelt down, reaching out a hand. "You don't want to do this."

"I got to, bro! My mum's in hospital and I just lost my job! I got to get money somehow else we going to get chucked out of our house!"

Tyson felt like his body wasn't his own as he started sobbing. He held the gun down as suddenly Ihaia was there, holding him. All he could hear was the sound of his own crying and the rain hitting past the trees around them. Ihaia was an ungiving presence, like the ground they were sitting on, but entirely more comforting. Tyson cried himself out again, the rain only strengthening as he ran out of tears.

"It's cool, uso. We can sort this out. You don't want to go and do anything stupid."

"It's too hard, bro," Tyson managed to croak, feeling Ihaia's arms tighten about him. "I can't do all this shit by myself. Everything's so fucked up. My mum can't be in hospital…I need my job back and I fucked it up. I cussed my boss out…Shit, bro, I was going to rob that place…"

"It's cool. We can sort it out."

Tyson didn't know how that was possible and was starting to wonder what Ihaia was doing here and how he had found him. He contented himself for the moment to just sit. He kept his head down, ashamed.

"It's cool, uso," Ihaia said quietly after a long while. Tyson could see he was looking down at the gun. "Give me the gun."

"Nah. This isn't your problem, bro."

"I'm making it my problem."

Ihaia held out his hand, but Tyson shoved the pistol back in the large pocket of his jacket. Ihaia looked far from satisfied.

"This is my problem, bro. How did you find me?"

"I went over to your place. I just missed you. I was trying to catch up with you the whole way here, then I lost you when you went into the trees…"

Tyson risked a look at the b-boy. His eyes felt sore, his stomach chewing at him from the inside. Something about Ihaia looked deeply worried, a worry that made Tyson think of how he felt about Rawiri. The surprise of seeing it took Tyson off guard and he lost himself a moment in those eyes. Tyson felt bad that someone should look like they were worrying about him that much. He pulled himself out of Ihaia's arms, scared of what he might let himself feel.

"We should get you back to your place, uso. Out of this rain. Is it cool for you to go back there?"

"Yeah. 'Course. Bro, I almost fucking robbed a garage…"

"It's cool. You didn't do it. We can deal with all your problems later. You can't do much sitting here, though."

Tyson managed to crawl up to his feet, putting a hand out to steady himself. Ihaia was at his side, bracing him. Tyson tried not to share gazes again with him. The rain felt refreshing on his face as Tyson walked back across the garden and back onto the sidewalk. It was about the only brief good feeling he could take from himself, given his state. Ihaia pulled his hood tight over his head, somehow managing to contain the riot of hair he had. Tyson did the same, briefly wondering if they looked like two Māori kids up to no good. The pit of his stomach hurt now as he set back to worrying.

"Have you talked to Loot?" Tyson asked, cautious. His clothes were sagging off him, pulling heavily with the wetness.

"Yeah…"

Tyson fell quiet as Ihaia pushed the pedestrian-crossing button. He frowned a bit, not wanting to question his help, but wondering all the same. "My house is back this way."

"Yeah. So is Siege."

Tyson felt a frightening sensation pass over him. Ihaia's voice sounded so quiet and calm when he said that, but the implications were overwhelming. He looked at Ihaia again, studying his handsome features for any clue. They had the same sort of look about them of any guy acting staunch, a certain level of ambivalence that was acted, not actual.

"Siege hasn't really stopped talking the last few days."

Tyson wanted to ask him as they walked across the street. He didn't want to risk it being about what he thought it was, but then how could Ihaia be meaning anything else? He kept looking, hoping for the answers without asking for them. Ihaia gave a brief shrug of his shoulders, his hands deep in the single pocket that rounded the front of his hoodie.

"It's cool, uso. I don't really hang with Dodgee any more."

"Why not?"

"Siege is a bit of a prick," explained Ihaia. "I mean, he's usually a prick, but he's really been a prick the last few days. I'm sort of cutting loose from them. I think you should too."

Tyson felt himself coming down. He walked quietly at Ihaia's side, and somehow it felt as if they had always been mates. It took good mates to be walking out in the rain at this time of the night. He let Ihaia lead the way. Tyson figured that he was just taking a long way back. He knew his hood well enough to know that this way would avoid the main drag.

"You just don't really want to be anywhere near Siege at the moment. He's on a bit of a mish."

"When did it start?"

"Siege being an asshole? He's always been an asshole."

"No, I mean...when did he start...he's been talking about me, right?"

Tyson felt Ihaia's glance, and he hated it. He felt that crushing sensation again, and didn't want to deal with it. He didn't want anyone looking at him again, not the way that Marc had. That sort of dismissive glance, careful not to venture to far into the subject.

"Like I said, it's cool, uso."

The words made Tyson feel horribly alone again. Life kept scratching at that sore, again and again. "Is that why you tried to find me? To tell me Siege been talking about me?"

"Yeah..." Ihaia fell silent, and a fair measure of pavement passed before he found the words to speak again. "Last little while...

just all the homophobic stuff he does and says. And now this…I don't want to be part of a crew that's cool with someone doing that. That's not me, uso. That's not real."

"Thanks. I thought you were tight with Dodgee Dozen, though."

"I'm not tight with guys who say the sort of stuff Siege says, no."

Tyson was finding himself wondering what it was that Siege had said about him. How much worse could you say that someone was gay other than just saying it like that. Even "faggot" didn't seem to sting as bad as what Ihaia was implying. Tyson let it lie. Maybe he didn't want to know. Tyson didn't really care that he might never see Siege again. He hated that Loot had probably written him off, and even if he hadn't there wasn't much use trying to hang with him.

"It's cool," said Ihaia, as they headed along a dark stretch of industrial street. "I rather not be part of that sort of scene. I can always dance without the rest of them. Hip hop isn't something that's tied to a crew."

It was starting to seem like the sort of thing that Ihaia did, coming up with deep and interesting ways of saying things. Tyson wanted to believe that somehow this wasn't another bad thing. Maybe it was time to just keep his head down totally, and go back to how things used to be, getting through life day by day.

"Shit."

"What?" Tyson glanced up, but saw what Ihaia was talking about almost instantly. Among the dark, slanted shadows that the industrial buildings cast on the street was a deeper one that had just turned into the street. Tyson felt himself tense up, and Ihaia was pulling at his elbow.

"You don't need this right now, uso."

"Yo! *Faggot!*"

Ihaia was pulling, trying to get him to run, but Tyson felt himself seize up. Siege had obviously seen them, already breaking into somewhat of a run. It was like watching a great mountain falling down towards them, and Tyson's gut felt tight and sick. Ihaia's voice was rough in his ear, trying to get him to move. Tyson felt the sickness rise and knot his gut. He felt all the anger boiling back to the top, where it had been so close. He pulled harshly from Ihaia's grasp as he made out Siege's brute features, his overbearing size. Tyson didn't want to run any more.

"You got something coming to you, faggot." Siege was walking straight at Tyson. Tyson acted quicker, almost on instinct, as the pistol came up out of his pocket.

"Tyson!"

Siege stopped dead in his tracks, Tyson staring along the line of the barrel into Siege's eyes. His cheeks burned as he realized what he was doing, and how suddenly Siege had stopped. He could see the whites of Siege's eyes against his dark features. All the rage that he had seen bearing down on him had turned as quickly into fear. Tyson willed himself to hold the pistol straight. He'd never guessed that it would feel this heavy. Ihaia was at his elbow again, his voice in his ears again.

"You don't need this, uso!"

"Nah, what have I got coming to me to, Siege?" Tyson asked, drunk instantly with the power. "Maybe you oughta suck *my* cock. Get on your fucking knees!"

"Tyson!"

"What part of that don't you get? Go down!"

Tyson's whole being buzzed as he fed off the fear. It seemed impossible to think that he would ever see Siege look like this. The islander's blunt features weren't made to show such an expression of fear. Tyson stared at Siege's unblinking eyes. He realized that Siege could see his anger, and it only fueled it in himself. Tyson felt as if he was outside his body as he wondered what stopped him from pulling the trigger. But now Siege was as scared as he was, and slowly going down on his knees, his big hands up. Tyson thought he could hear the sound of a siren, somewhere past the industrial block.

"Tyson, this ain't cool! Uso!"

"You ain't gonna do this…" Siege said. Tyson could see how the big islander didn't believe his own words, how it showed in his eyes. It's all he saw, as the sirens seemed to get closer.

"Tyson!" Ihaia's words broke through Tyson's iron focus. "We got to get out of here!"

"I want to make him *pay*!" Tyson felt the anger again. He wanted to make Siege more than pay. He wanted him to hurt, hurt for all the things he had been through.

"Not now!"

Tyson heard how close the sirens were, and it got through that they might be coming this way, as impossible as it seemed. They'd see him. They'd see he had a gun. Why did it have to be now? The rage gripped Tyson's gut again as his expression screwed up tight. He lashed out at Siege, feeling the pain in his hand as his fist connected down against the islander's face. He heard a crack and felt a jarring pain, not knowing if it came from his hand or Siege's face. Ihaia was on him too quickly, pulling him back before he could get another blow in, dragging him finally into a run. He wanted to do more. He wanted Siege to hurt.

Tyson didn't look back, feeling the wind against his skin, the weight of the pistol still in his hand. He half expected to hear Siege running, taking chase. Tyson just kept his eyes focused on Ihaia, who was belting back the way they came. He darted across the street, towards one of the larger industrial blocks. Tyson felt fear grip him, and the reality of what he had done started to set in as the night seemed to fill with the sound of sirens. They were quickly running up on a chain-link fence. Ihaia leapt at it, but Tyson realized he still had the gun. He stopped and dropped it down the street drain in panic.

"Get over, uso!"

Ihaia was already on the other side of the fence. Tyson thought about Marc and the last time he had scaled a fence like this. There weren't police hot on his heels then, though. Tyson threw himself up onto the fence, scaling it and dropping down the other side with surprising ease. There was a fire in his veins, and unbelievable excitement. He felt alive as Ihaia dashed across the short car park and into the depths between the buildings. The sirens were upon them.

The shadows dappled in flashes of blues and reds as the sirens ripped the air. Tyson felt almost as if he could feel the velocity of the car as it sped past. Ahead, Ihaia was a dark shape, almost lost in the inkiness. Tyson's lungs were starting to burn, the ground unyielding under his feet. He wondered briefly where Ihaia was now that they were far back enough that everything was blackness and walls. He caught sight of Ihaia's rugged features, and a hand darted out to grab him and pull him into a doorway.

Tyson drew in deep breaths, gasping in the air, realizing now he was leaned up against the wall how out of shape he was. Then it occurred to him how hard he had been running. He stared over at Ihaia, watching as he watched him back. They both breathed heavily, panting. Tyson stared at Ihaia's eyes, drawn to them, fixed in the dark. The doorway they were hiding in had a little more room than would fit the two of them. He saw the hesitation there in Ihaia's eyes, then suddenly felt it himself. His cheeks burnt hot red. That brief spark of a moment as he realized that Ihaia was lingering forward just a little closer than he was seconds before.

Tyson closed the distance and kissed those thick lips. He felt their warmth and softness, and for the briefest moments that the kiss lasted he realized that it didn't feel wrong.

Tyson drew back almost as quickly, pressing back against the wall. It had been a stupid thing, in the heat of the moment, but Ihaia was smiling like he was drunk. He didn't say anything as he looked at Tyson, eyes suddenly drowning in those handsome features. Tyson felt the overwhelming sensation run through him, but it was Ihaia who leaned forward to kiss him this time. Tyson's arms went up about Ihaia's body and it was suddenly as if there was nothing else but him. He held Ihaia there in the dark, and didn't want to let go.

CHAPTER TWENTY-NINE

The night had lost its menace by the time they left the doorway. The clouds were a dark cauldron of movement. The rain still fell.

Tyson followed Ihaia into backstreets beyond the industry blocks. They both thought it was long enough that Siege would have left, and the place was clear of cops. It had taken almost as long to agree that they had to stop kissing each other, leave each other's arms and make a move. That had been the hardest part.

Tyson was floating as they headed back to his house. Neither of them said anything, although Tyson's mind was as tumultuous as the sky, boiling with questions. Somehow, none of them seemed to matter next to the fact that Ihaia was there. Tyson kept sharing sheepish, private grins with him as they walked. It had never felt like this with Marc. This was a bolt from the heavens, hitting him out of nowhere and leaving him dumbstruck. Tyson dared to hope it was love.

Tyson came down from his high as they rounded into his street. His heart sank as quickly as he caught the sight of the police cars that lined the front of Rawiri's house. There was something suddenly stagnant about the weather, bitter and nasty. Tyson broke into a run, hurting more than physically.

He saw the stretcher being carried out the front door. The body on it was deathly still, its face covered with blood, smothered with an oxygen mask. Raw emotion carried Tyson's legs as he sprinted the last distance, quickly being intercepted all too easily by one of the medics.

"Rawiri!"

Tyson wanted to kill, but he was too wounded inside to get the emotion to turn to rage. His eyes misted with the new tears, too raw to draw. He cursed himself for not finding Rawiri, and for being stupid enough to think he could go rob a petrol station. When all the while Rawiri had been next door, being beaten again by his father, beaten to death. He felt hands pulling at him as he tried to struggle past. Ihaia's voice was in his ears, his strong arms pulling around him from behind.

"It's Rawiri!" Tyson struggled against Ihaia. "He's my mate!"

Tyson felt the stunned shock of confusion as the stretcher moved quickly past. The body there was older, a grizzled, older cast of what Rawiri might look like. He couldn't let his eyes linger too long on that red and brown mess that was his face, but it was too old to be Rawiri. His hair was shaved short. The white sheet and stretcher was spotted by ample red. Tyson felt cold as his gaze was drawn again to the door of Rawiri's house, and this time he saw him, being brought out by police.

Tyson's gaze locked with Rawiri's as he was taken the same path as the stretcher. Tyson stopped pulling, still feeling Ihaia's arms about him, but not managing to comprehend his voice as it kept speaking in his ear. He couldn't get past the emotion in his best friend's eyes. Rawiri's face seemed almost blank, but his eyes reflected a painful relief.

Tyson thought that Rawiri finally seemed free.

Rawiri disappeared behind the wreath of police officers as he was pushed into the car, and Tyson lost gaze with him. The words in his ear were starting to make sense, even though they had barely stopped since Ihaia had grabbed him. Tyson tried to see Rawiri as the police car he was in started to pull about and head out of the street. He couldn't understand how quickly his friend was gone.

"Come on, uso, we need to get you out of here."

Tyson didn't know how he got to the door of his house, or inside when they stepped into the heavy silence within. He could hear Ihaia's voice and feel his hands moving him, and he was in the deep shadows of his parents' bedroom, where he had started the night. The heavy bushes outside the windows were still, as if the raging winds were suddenly shamed at what had happened. The whole house was impossibly still.

"Don't leave me, bro." Tyson's throat was raw. "Fuck. Rawiri…"

"I'm not going to leave you, uso. I'm here for you," replied Ihaia, pulling at his heavy jacket.

"Nah, I've got to go find Rawiri!"

"You can't do anything about that now."

Tyson was struggling again, and Ihaia's arms were about him, fighting it, holding him back. Pulling him down to the bed. Tyson let himself cry, too weak even to hold that back, feeling the way that it shuddered his body heavily against Ihaia. Ihaia felt so hard against him, as if he were the only thing left real in Tyson's world. Ihaia was holding him, rocking him slowly. It wasn't too long before Tyson had cried himself out. It was a lot longer before Ihaia started to let up in his embrace. This time Tyson couldn't fight it all, too exhausted.

"We can go down to the cops tomorrow. You been through too much shit to go through anything else. Come on." Those strong hands were guiding him again, gentle yet firm. "Lie back. You need sleep, uso."

Tyson felt sore as he lay back, falling into fitful sleep almost as soon as his head hit the pillow. He kept waking, thinking that he had fallen asleep after smoking his blunt and all this had been some sort of fucked-up dream. Then he would panic desperately, expecting to see an empty room. Ihaia was sitting on the edge of the bed, a sentinel shadow among the dark shapes of the room. Tyson had lost his hoodie and jeans, lying under the sheets in just his T-shirt and boxers.

He woke several more times, wondering how long he had been sleeping. The room was still dark, and Ihaia had moved. He was lying down next to Tyson, with his back to him. Tyson trembled as he felt his hormones burning, despite the situation. All he could think of was the brief memory that seemed like a dream now, of kissing with Ihaia in the dark. How their bodies had pressed against each other. He rolled over and chanced putting a hand down on Ihaia's muscular bare arm. Ihaia looked back over his shoulder.

"Uso. You okay?"

Tyson stared at the way Ihaia's sleeveless T-shirt pulled tight across his chest, and the way his brown arms looked so hard. He could feel it under his hand. Ihaia's light eyes gazed out from under his thick, messed puff of hair, full of concern. Tyson couldn't stop himself as he leaned in and kissed him again, quickly pulling himself back into Ihaia's arms. He felt the response to his desperate need, soft and hesitant, those hands trying to soothe deep pain. Ihaia pulled back.

"You don't want to do this?" asked Tyson. "I thought you said you weren't going to leave me, bro?"

"I won't, Tyson," Ihaia said. Tyson felt shame burning on his light features. "I didn't come over here to get in your pants. I just wanted to find you and ask you if it was true."

"What you mean?"

"I've had the hots for you since I met you back at the Barge Bar," Ihaia said, quietly. "When Siege started talking, I thought it was just his usual shit. I wanted to find out from you, just in case it was true…"

Tyson didn't know what to say, staring silently at Ihaia in the dark. It started to sink in slowly what he had said. Tyson couldn't believe a guy like Ihaia could have been staring at him all this time, wanting him. Ihaia's fingers toyed slowly with his dreadlocks, traced slowly over his cheek.

"I don't want to take advantage of you."

"We both feel the same way about each other, bro. I don't want to lose you now I found you, not after all this shit."

Ihaia's words were soft on his ears. "You're not going to lose me, uso."

Tyson saw the hesitation in his eyes, but he leaned in to kiss him again all the same. He felt Ihaia shudder against him, the hunger in his hands as they ran up under his loose T-shirt. The resistance started to fall away the more he kissed, and Ihaia's hands were like fire against him, making him tremble. He dared to let himself feel Ihaia's body, to move up closer against him. Tyson could feel the lump of Ihaia's manhood pushed against his own. When he broke the kiss, he saw the want in Ihaia's eyes, slowly shadowing the all-too-concerned friend. He saw the bashful grin.

"I didn't think just kissing would feel this good," Tyson said, sharing whispers with Ihaia. Ihaia's hands were all over his body, slow and gentle.

"You never been with a guy?"

"No," replied Tyson, wondering sharply if he should have admitted to it. Ihaia's hands didn't stop moving, stroking and feeling slowly.

"We don't have to do anything you don't want to, if this is what you want to do, uso."

Tyson felt as if he was falling too fast, but not wanting to take his hands off Ihaia now he was this close. "I know I want to do it with you, Crunch."

"That's it, then," Ihaia said, kissing softly again. "Let's just be together."

Tyson didn't need any more encouragement, and didn't see the hesitation that he had seen in Ihaia's light eyes. He started shaking more and more as Ihaia pulled his T-shirt off, his hardness rendering his boxers almost useless as they were. He tried to do the same for Ihaia, struggling at first with his snug T-shirt. Ihaia sat up enough to get his pants off, then pulled himself free of his shirt. Tyson couldn't help but stare, lost in love of his friend's body. He saw how Ihaia had got his nickname, as he let a shaky hand run down slowly over his stomach. They tensed under his touch. Ihaia was close enough that he could feel the heat beating off his body.

"You want to get naked?"

"Yeah," Tyson replied, hot-breathed. He tried not to stare at Ihaia's hardness as he struggled with his own boxers. Ihaia's hand came to help. There was an admiration in his voice when he spoke.

"I'm lucky I'm not packing something like that, uso. I'd end up hurting myself trying to breakdance with something like that between my legs."

Tyson was burning with embarrassment, from both the compliment and his sudden nakedness. Ihaia was pulling him back close. The kisses started again with a renewed passion as Ihaia pulled the blankets back up over them both. The fatigue that still hung in Tyson's body gave the reality an edge, and he was quickly starting to sweat from Ihaia's heat.

"You're beautiful, uso."

Tyson realized that Ihaia was talking about him, drunk on feeling and exploring. He had only guessed a few times in fantasy what Ihaia had looked like undressed. It was pale next to the reality of it. Everything was hard, yet soft at the same time, as their skin touched and pressed. He couldn't stop shaking in Ihaia's arms, clinging to him like he might suddenly disappear. Tyson didn't know that sex could feel this good. Nothing he had imagined by himself alone in bed matched this.

Ihaia was all slow strokes and firm touches, drawing his world into an existence of kisses that rained down over his body. Tyson lay back as Ihaia moved him and shifted against him, staring up at the ceiling. The kisses and touches made him realize it came from him. It was him that Ihaia wanted, everything so physical. Ihaia's touch made him realize that easier than any words could. He was sinking in a passion that came from someone lost in love for what he was.

Tyson sank deeper, moaning out hotly as Ihaia went further. His hands clung to Ihaia's moist muscles as the pleasure blinded him, reaching new heights. Tyson saw a whole new dream.

❖

When Tyson woke up, he noticed how much time had passed. Ihaia was still lying next to him, something that was as real as the sensation of lying naked between the sheets. Now that he had finally got it, he wondered how he had managed to get someone so beautiful.

Was this love?

Tyson didn't know how long he had been staring, until he noticed Ihaia staring back, bleary eyed. A smile spread on Ihaia's lips as he reached out. Tyson warmed to the slow, easy stroke along his shoulder. All too quickly, Ihaia was pulling him back into his muscular embrace as they shared the bed under the blankets.

"Hey, uso."

Tyson smiled back, feeling the already familiar sensations of Ihaia's body against his. It was like somehow he had started working out the intimacies of his form, like he knew of his own body. He kissed again with Ihaia before settling his head down against his chest.

"When you were asking me about my dreams, I guess there was one that I wanted to say…but I didn't know how to say it."

"What was it?"

"I always dreamed that I'd find someone cool, like you," Tyson said quietly. "And that things would turn out okay in the end. That's one of my dreams, bro. I don't know if it counts."

"Sure it does. Nothing wrong with that dream. I think we sort of found each other."

Tyson felt the urge to kiss and touch Ihaia again and more, already starting to feel embarrassed at his morning desires. He let his hand play slowly across the smooth skin of Ihaia's chest. He tried to think of what to say next, knowing what to say but not how to say it. He felt Ihaia's voice against his cheek, as he breathed slow and deep. His arm was draped along the length of his back.

"Mates first, uso. Even if things hadn't turned out like this"—Tyson got the implication, lying there with him—"I still would have wanted to help you. No matter how messed up things are, there's always a way to fix things."

"I was serious when I said things were pretty messed up." Tyson wasn't even sure where to begin.

"We'll work it out together."

"I don't know why I'm so lucky…"

"Just let it happen. No pressure."

Tyson had to think about that for a moment. He was finding it difficult to believe that there might be another way of dealing with life's problems. Not that Ihaia was ignoring them, just that they seemed to run off him like water off a duck's back. Tyson caught himself staring, thinking about Ihaia's body again. Damn.

"It's not like I didn't drop you enough hints, uso." Tyson could hear the lightness in Ihaia's tone. He moved so that he could look him in the eye.

"You said you had a girl. How's that a hint?"

"I said I *came* from my girl's. She's my ex."

"You're bi?"

Tyson felt the muscles move under him as Ihaia managed a little of a shrug. "Never really been much into labels like that." Tyson wondered how that was possible, when he had struggled so much. "We known each other since forever, grew up together. Same church. I slept with her a few times and then found out she was pregnant. But I guess us being together wasn't what she wanted long term. Either way, I going to be there for my baby boy. He's three next month."

Tyson looked up at Ihaia's face as he spoke. The pride that he could see and hear made him look in awe. Tyson wondered if it was possible for Ihaia to make a mistake. He seemed so confident and laid back. The feeling of Ihaia's touch broke him from his thoughts, and then the quiet tone of Ihaia's voice.

"You said your mum was in hospital, uso…Why aren't you there now?"

Tyson felt a chill run over him, and he pulled himself closer to Ihaia. He started to explain things as best he could, wishing that somehow he could hide from it all. Everything seemed to come stilted and slow. Ihaia kissed his forehead softly, lending him strength. His voice was still quiet when he spoke.

"You should go to your mum. I can go down to the station and see what happened with Rawiri. And I can grab a paper on the way back."

Tyson tried to work out why it sounded so simple coming from Ihaia. "I guess."

"Nah, uso. You should be there. She's your mother. I'll meet you over there."

"I don't want to leave you, bro." Tyson felt so quiet and small.

"Hey, it's only going to be for a bit. Oh yeah, by the way. Marc was looking for you a few days back, when I was still hanging with Dodgee."

"What did he want?" Tyson asked, suspicious.

"Something about wondering where you went. He wondered if you had left town or something. What's up with that?"

Tyson muttered, "I sort of told him I had a thing for him."

"But he's not like that?"

"No. I didn't think he wanted to see me again."

"Seems like he's putting in a lot of work for someone who doesn't. I got his number."

Tyson remembered Marc's business card that he still had tucked away in his satchel. "Yeah, I think I do too."

"First things first, uso. Get in the shower and get over to the hospital."

Tyson managed a smile, even though it felt so foreign on his lips. "No, first thing is I want to kiss you again, bro."

Ihaia smiled as Tyson pushed himself up and looked down on him. Tyson liked the way that Ihaia was looking at him, that smile so easy on his lips, and his eyes so strangely intoxicating. There was so much he wanted to say to Ihaia, and to ask him. So many things that he wanted to do with him, and do again. He dipped down and kissed Ihaia with a depth that was returned with passion.

"You better shower, uso," Ihaia said after they finally parted. "Or I'll never let you out of this bed."

CHAPTER THIRTY

Tyson felt more focused than he had in a long time, but there was still an uncomfortable fear eating at him inside. The afternoon air was crisp and cool, still compared to the storm that had hit last night and left as quickly. Tyson tried to think that Ihaia would be true to his word, that he wouldn't suddenly vanish now they had finally parted. It still seemed surreal, what had happened. It felt weird that someone he had seen for so long had been staring at him, dreaming and wishing from afar, like he had been doing with Marc.

Tyson tried to keep his pace steady as he headed back to the hospital. He kept on the path that Ihaia had started him on. He tried to think of what to say if his mother was awake, like why he hadn't been there all along. How much did he have to say? Maybe he didn't need to mention everything that had gone down last night anyway. No one knew, other than him and Ihaia.

The hospital seemed eerily familiar as he went inside. The same clean corridors that he had bolted through came back to him. The hospital was more heavily occupied now. Tyson went back through the wards to where he had first seen his mother.

Tyson felt the nerves biting at him again the more he walked. As he counted off the rooms, each step was more difficult. The familiarity of seeing his mother sitting up in a strange place jarred him back into reality. She didn't see him at first, and then a weak smile spread over her features when he entered the room. Tyson faltered, feeling tears coming again. Seeing her reminded him of the fear and horror of the previous night, but the tears came from relief as well.

"Hey, you."

"Hey, Mum…"

"What rotten luck that I end up in here."

Tyson rounded, about to the side of the bed, feeling her hand come up and touch at his face. He tried to fight the tears, but the all-too-familiar burn lent him no strength to do so. Her touch seemed to only coax them out. Tyson was trapped between looking and not, fighting the fact that his mother was still lying in a hospital.

"Hey, hey, I'm going to be okay. I feel a bit rotten, but that will come right…"

Tyson lingered at the side of her bed, as even the quiet, unsteady tone of her voice made him cry. He didn't want to, but couldn't stop the tears. Being there made him realize how he had managed to tell her nothing of what had been happening with him. He had always expected that she would be a solid constant.

"How are your brothers doing?" she asked, wiping at the tears. Tyson tried not to let his voice sound so weak when he spoke.

"I haven't seen them yet." Tyson wasn't too sure how much he should admit, still fighting with telling her everything, wondering if that was even a good idea.

"The doctor said that you came in the other night. It must have been a big shock for you. I'm sorry, Tyson."

"Mum, don't be sorry…if anyone should be sorry—" Tyson stopped himself, leaving the statement wide open. He saw his mother's searching gaze. He broke it as he forced himself to move and get a chair. "I was so scared when I heard you were here."

"I don't think how rough things must be for you sometimes." Tyson sat at her side as she spoke, her hand seeking his out. "You're always so busy looking after things."

"I don't know if I'm that good at it."

"I know you are. You've always made things easy for me and your brothers."

Tyson took a deep breath, finding it hard not to say something about it, "I lost my job. But I'll get another one. I can cover the rent, even if I have to work more shifts. I mean, just while you are in here. I can still take care of things."

"I was going to say, you don't always have to be like that, Tyson. I've always appreciated the help, but you have to remember to be there for yourself as well. The rent will be okay for a little while yet. We have savings."

Tyson wondered why it had never occurred to him that his mother might be as onto it as that. She continued in that small voice, "The money you kept giving me, I put away. So we have a little while yet. And I can get support while I'm in here."

"I'm just happy you're okay," Tyson murmured. "I didn't want to stay that night…I mean, I was scared seeing you in here. It didn't seem like it was you. Sorry I freaked out."

"It's okay."

Tyson nodded, sitting in silence for a moment. He stared out the window of the small ward room, finally able to take stock of his surroundings. It was the same uniform cleanliness as the rest of the hospital, stark white. The windows let in a light that Tyson found strange, as the sunlight shined through haze and clouds. He hadn't seen much sun in a long time.

"You lost your job?"

"Yeah," Tyson replied, frankly. He wrote off any chance of a reference.

"I'm sorry. I hope the next one you find is a day job, and closer. It's funny how life sorts things out sometimes. Maybe you can work on being a chef now?"

Tyson frowned as he shook his head. "I don't even remember when I said that."

"Do you still want to do it?"

"I don't know." Tyson wanted to say something about Ihaia,

about himself and everything that had happened. He wasn't sure how to say that he had almost robbed a petrol station. Or that he had slept with a guy in her bed. Tyson knew that she could see the conflict.

"What's wrong, Tyson?"

Everything was too much, too quick. Tyson could barely make sense of it himself. He looked back at her, trying to find the words, trying to sort it out in his brain. He didn't want to keep it secret, not how Ihaia made him feel. That sort of secret was the worst to keep. But he was scared in a place deep within, feeling her gaze, scared of it.

When he looked her in the eyes, the words sidestepped inside him. His answer came unsteady.

"Rawiri's in trouble too…"

"What happened?"

"I don't know. Ihaia…I mean…a friend of mine. He's going to the police station to find out what happened." Trying to step around the issue of who Ihaia was was even harder than saying it. "I think Rawiri beat up his dad. It looked pretty bad."

"You care a lot about him."

"I just hope he's okay."

"You're always there to help him out. I'm sure he'll be okay."

Tyson frowned, idly studying the way the threads in the blankets ran. It was easier than looking elsewhere. All he could think about was the fact that he wasn't there. Probably when Rawiri needed him the most.

"I was going to find somewhere. I mean, we were. Rawiri and me. Like maybe find our own place."

"You still might be able to."

Tyson glanced up at his mother, confused at the light smile that he saw on her lips. He studied her for a time before she remarked quietly, "I know things look dark sometimes, Tyson. You're like your father in too many ways."

"I wish my father was still here."

"I do too, Tyson. But we're getting by okay by ourselves."

Tyson wasn't too sure of that, but he kept his mouth shut. He felt his mother's hand rubbing slowly at his, hearing the quiet sound of her voice. "It's pretty sad that I had to end up in hospital before we get a chance to have a really good talk. I haven't caught up on how things are with you in a long time. I promise that will change."

Tyson felt guilty. Everything pointed to telling her, all the paths led in the same direction. The hospital seemed still. Outside the sun was dipping behind and emerging from thick clouds. He stayed quiet, feeling the way his gut had gone tight. Why was it harder this time when he had said it enough times already?

"If you want to get your own place, there's nothing stopping you, Tyson. I can help you get set up."

"I don't know if I can now, if Rawiri is in trouble—"

"If it's not him, I'm sure you can find someone. Just let things happen as they will."

Tyson nodded, rubbing at his mother's hand in reply. He silently tried to psych himself up and find the momentum to move his lips and make those words. The effort felt titanic. If there was anyone he should be telling about things, it should be her, he thought. He prepared himself, glancing up at her. In the end, after all the struggling, he just grimaced and stayed quiet.

"Smile, Tyson. Thing's will be okay."

Tyson did his best, but he wondered how it could be true when he couldn't find the strength to say those few words to the one person he should.

❖

In some ways, going into the police cells was like going into the hospital to see his mother. Being there felt wrong enough, but seeing Rawiri there made it worse. Tyson kept himself as focused as he could, seeing those dark eyes staring back at him. Rawiri's hair was out, shaggy around his blocky shoulders. Tyson felt the emotions stirring inside him when he saw those eyes. He noticed fresh bruises on Rawiri's face.

Rawiri was standing up inside the small cell as the officer unlocked it. Tyson was scared enough being here, but it paled next to what he was feeling otherwise. Maybe if he hadn't bugged out, he might have been there to stop Rawiri. Tyson's head was filled with questions. What had he done wrong, or what hadn't he seen? When the officer motioned Tyson in, the questions fell aside, and he pulled Rawiri in for a tight hug. Something about it felt strange and stiff.

"Fifteen minutes," said the stout officer. Tyson glanced back, nodding. The cell around him was a stark copy of the other five in the snubbed end of the station. Nothing about them was meant to be comforting.

"'Sup, cuz?"

"What's up with you, bro?" Tyson looked Rawiri over, like he might work out somehow if he was okay. Physically, other than a few bruises in the face, he looked okay. "What happened?"

Rawiri shrugged. He sat back down on the bare bed. Tyson opted to take the floor opposite. He briefly thought how he hadn't ever expected to see the inside of a cell.

"Went over to get the last of my shit from my place. Ran into my father."

"Why didn't you wait for me?" Tyson searched his friend's face. The hardness he saw there shook him somewhat.

"It's done, Ty. Forget it. Wasn't anythin' you could have done."

"I could have been there for you. We mates. Mates don't keep anything from each other."

Rawiri shot him a stare, sitting stiffly on the edge of the bed. "It's not 'bout keepin' anything from you, cuz. I just went over there. He came out. I wasn't goin' to fuckin' take any of his shit any more. I'm so sick of him fuckin' me over like I was some bitch."

Tyson melted inside, getting up and sitting next to Rawiri on the bed. He put a hand on Rawiri's back, but his friend didn't much respond. Tyson could hear the emotion, but it was locked deep inside. He showed nothing in his stony features.

"Bro, why do you have to keep thinking like that? Things were going to be okay, bro. I was going to get us a flat and everything…"

"Too late now, cuz," Rawiri replied. There was a harshness in the blunt, uncaring way he spoke. "Hit him straight in the face. Didn't even see it comin'. Just kept at him over, again and again. Don't think he's ever goin' to touch me now, cuz."

Tyson saw something in those eyes when Rawiri looked at him. It was like what he had seen when Rawiri had pushed him over. A kind of pent, stormy violence. He tried to see something else in that dark gaze. He tried to see past the pain that he could see Rawiri was holding back.

"Felt good, cuz. Maybe a bit too good…Figure it's better I'm in here anyway. Was probably goin' to end up in here one way or another."

"Shit, Rawiri, don't say that," Tyson said.

"Ty, we grew up together, but you and me are different. I don't know, cuz, you got somethin' I ain't ever gonna to have. You can see all this shit for what it is, and you can still think you can get somethin' better. And all your shit about dreams. I'm just one of those feral horis that always gonna end up in the same place."

Tyson shook his head, shifting about on the bed to try and face Rawiri better. He tried to reason with him, even though he could see the peace Rawiri was making with things. "Bro, you and me can get out of here. We were going to get out of here. I had it all planned out."

"Cuz, if I hadn't fucked up my father I would have fuckin' shot someone, or hit up some place. You ain't like that, Ty. I deserve to be here."

Tyson fell silent, feeling the words hit him hard. He stared at Rawiri, as if his gaze could somehow cut through all the shit he was putting up, past that wall. Tyson wanted to hit him, try and break him out of it.

"You fuckin' kick a dog long enough, Ty, it's gonna bite you."

Tyson sat there beside Rawiri a moment, before putting his arms around him, trying to hold him like he had held him the night Rawiri had been beaten up. Tyson held on to Rawiri, trying to let him know somehow that it was going to be okay, where the words didn't seem to get through to him. He wanted to feel Rawiri hold him back and let go of everything inside like he had that night. Rawiri just sat there, barely moving. Tyson eventually let go of him.

"That your mate who came around before?"

Tyson didn't want to admit defeat. He didn't want to give up or let Rawiri just change the subject like that, but he resigned himself to it, murmuring quietly, "Yes. Ihaia."

"Sweet."

"A lot of things went down last night, Rawiri," Tyson said, still somewhat stunned that Rawiri hadn't even responded to his hug in the least.

"Damn fuckin' right about that."

"No, I mean…I lost my job."

"Your mother okay?"

Tyson nodded, resting his forearms down on his thighs, staring at his well-worn shoes. "Yes, she's going to be okay."

"Sweet."

"My mate Ihaia…well, he's like me."

"You mean gay?"

Tyson nodded vacantly, hearing the steady and rather emotionless tone of Rawiri's voice. "Yeah."

"Sweet."

Tyson wondered whether he should connect the dots and spell it out to Rawiri what he had meant by that. He felt the frustration and the way that it made him stumble around the point. Tyson thought that he had worked out how to talk to Rawiri better than this. His friend sat next to him, not giving anything more than what he was taking. Tyson looked at his face again, somewhat resigned. He locked himself up inside, not wanting to show the sadness he felt. He could see something of the same in Rawiri, silent and unspoken.

"Fuck, I would have gone all the way, cuz. I mean my dad. Either way, though, he's not touchin' me any more. Either he's dead or I'm locked up," Rawiri said. His voice was dangerously steady and dead. "I took care of shit, Ty."

"Yeah," said Tyson, resigned. "You did, Rawiri."

"That's what a man would do, cuz. Fuckin' stand up for himself and take care of his shit."

"Yeah."

"If you don't take care of things, then life ends up makin' you take care of it."

Tyson stared at the bare concrete of the floor, scuffed and aged, looking as if it had been there forever. He listened, hearing the words and making sense of them. In a sick sort of way Rawiri was making sense, but it was a sense that he didn't want to hear. Not in the way that Rawiri was saying it, like he had finally worked out the truth, beyond a doubt.

"I love you, Rawiri," Tyson murmured. "You'll always be my best mate. Whatever happens, bro, I'm going to be there for you."

Tyson felt the cool air of the cell, carried by a scant breeze from the high window, barred and slatted and all but rusted shut. The pause was long, Tyson still staring at his shoes. He noticed that one of his laces was undone.

"I love you too, Tyson. I know you my mate."

Tyson breathed deep, letting the silence fall over them again. He didn't want to look at Rawiri again, not now. Part of him was scared that he wouldn't see anything but that same staunch mask. The rest of him was scared that he would, and that it would make him want to cry again. Rawiri seemed as still as the cell. Tyson hoped like hell the officer didn't wander back as he tried to hold everything back.

"Get that flat, cuz."

"Huh?"

"Get that flat, just don't get it in our hood. Find somewhere else. Do it with your mate. Get your ass out of there, like you said we were going to."

Tyson finally looked up, searching Rawiri's expression again. He didn't see anything there, nothing beyond the flat, quiet sound of his voice. Tyson nodded a bit, pushing his hand through his dreads and breathing deep again. His throat felt too uncomfortable to talk.

"I'm going to find out from the officer what happens from here, bro."

"Cool."

"I'm going to be here for you."

"Sweet. I know, cuz."

Tyson felt their gaze touch, and finally saw what he had hoped for. For just the briefest moments, as he heard the sound of footsteps, he saw the pain in Rawiri's eyes. Anything that made him seem anything other than just some brutal criminal. Tyson could see how deep the pain ran in those dark eyes, and saw some of that staunch front drop. He wanted to hold Rawiri again, in the hope that he would feel something different from before.

"Time's up."

Tyson stood up, watching Rawiri stare back at him. He didn't move as Tyson headed to the cell door. Tyson didn't want to say anything, not trusting his voice. He couldn't get past the way Rawiri was looking at him, speaking more volumes than any of his brief words. When he finally looked where he was going, Tyson stepped out of the cell and heard the door bang heavily behind him.

CHAPTER THIRTY-ONE

Tyson smiled warmly, feeling Ihaia's presence beside him down in the grass. The sun cast dappled shadows down through the trees as they lay in the embrace of the long, uncut grass. It was indulgent lying there, doing nothing else but existing. Lying in grass that he should have cut weeks or even months ago.

It was good to be back with Ihaia, and with him there Tyson felt like there was nothing else worth thinking about. Overhead, through leaves, clouds raced, giving way to sun more often than not. There was a cool dampness to the air, but Tyson could sense it just like Rawiri had said.

Things were going to be different from now on.

Tyson was just happy lying with Ihaia, but it was something else to be able to lean over and give him a soft, slow kiss. Ihaia looked back at him, surprised and questioning. His hands were behind his head as he lay there, obscured partly by the length of the grass. Tyson matted it underneath himself as he moved and lay against Ihaia's body.

"What was that for, uso?"

"I don't know," Tyson replied. The sound of cicadas touched the air, but there was caution about them. Tyson felt the same thing within himself, although it was starting to slowly peel back. "It's just cool knowing you're here."

"You know I'm not going anywhere."

"I know."

"I told you things would be okay," Ihaia said. He moved to put an arm around Tyson, and Tyson snuggled into it. "You just got to try and not worry too much."

"That'll be easy with you around, bro."

Ihaia chuckled and let his hand wander. Tyson squirmed a bit under the touch. Despite the layers he was wearing against the still-cool temperatures, it was easy to feel the effects. He could feel the way it was making him feel frisky again.

"I don't know," Ihaia said, putting a hand up under Tyson's T-shirt. Tyson felt his stomach tighten with the touch. "Be hard to get anything done with you around, uso…"

Tyson lost himself in the dreaming look in Ihaia's eyes, only to be pulled back to reality by the sound of a car door slamming. He glanced back towards the house, managing to see a little way down the path down the side of it. A few moments later and he heard the regular sound of heavy footsteps, and he pulled himself up. Tyson tried to make it look like he wasn't making out with Ihaia in the grass, tugging at his sagging jeans. He wasn't surprised to see who was walking up the path, smiling and nodding staunchly in greeting.

"My man," Marc remarked, walking slow and steady at his usual swaggered pace. "Long time no see. Crunch."

Ihaia smiled and pulled himself up to his feet. Marc didn't look like he suspected anything, what with them both sitting in the grass. Either that or he didn't care. Tyson was about to greet him when he noticed who was following a little way behind him. He had expected to see Marc, sooner or later, but he hadn't expected who had come with him.

"Zadie?"

"Who you think drove him out here?" Zadie asked, smiling a tight smile. She was already taking out a cigarette, getting it lit up. Tyson looked back at Marc, confused, trying to make the connections. He caught quickly as Marc tossed something at him.

"You left that at my place," remarked Marc.

"What is it?"

"It's your basketball singlet."

Tyson checked it out, frowning. He felt guilty when he saw the unspoken words between him and Marc, the way that Marc was looking at him. He felt bad having walked out, remembering the night too sharply.

"I figured after...you know," Tyson said. "That you wouldn't want to hang any more."

"I was checking out your work the last month wondering where your ass was every Friday," Marc commented. He swaggered over, giving him a staunch, bearlike hug, before leaning in and muttering, "It's all good, my man. What goes between boys, stays between boys."

Tyson tried not to feel like he was under the spotlight, looking at Zadie and Ihaia. Ihaia was introducing himself, Tyson feeling a pang of protectiveness that surprised him. Marc clapped him heavily on the shoulder.

"I missed smoking up with you. I heard from Zadie that you lost your job. Raw deal."

"Yeah. I'm looking for a new one."

"Well, I tried to tell you about that," Zadie said, tossing a bit of her cigarette ash. "Before you stormed out of there. Thought Faye was going to piss himself with the looks you were giving him. There's a few places I can check, if you're still interested in trying to get into being a chef."

"I'm not sure," Tyson replied, wandering back onto the concrete and out of the grass. "I know I don't want night work any more."

"Might not have a lot of choice to start off with. But I can still look into it if you're interested." Zadie gave Tyson a questioning look, one that didn't give up. One that he knew she only wanted one answer to.

"Sure," he said, managing a bit of a smile. "Check it out."

"Yeah, and if you decide to go wander off again, my man,"

Marc said, putting a heavy arm about his shoulders and leaning on him a little too hard, "I know where you live. I'll track your skinny ass down."

Tyson tried to give him a look, as if trying to get him to realize things without him saying them. He wondered briefly if Zadie knew, or if Marc had told her. Given what Marc had muttered to him, he figured not. Tyson couldn't help but think how much easier it would be if everyone just knew and it wasn't an issue.

"You have problems again," said Marc, "you make sure you come to your people, my man. I'm not going to feel like a chump again, okay?"

"Nah, bro. I won't. I've figured out a whole heap of things recently."

"Sweet." Marc gave him a tight jostle that almost hurt before letting him go.

"You got anything to drink?"

Tyson glanced over at Zadie, nodding and wandering past her towards the house. "Yeah, probably got some drinks in the fridge."

"I'll get them, uso," Ihaia offered.

Tyson stalled and turned about, wandering over to where Marc had taken up a place on the ground. Marc pulled off his cap a moment, squinting up at him, before Tyson sat down next to him.

"Hear Dodgee is a bit off-limits to you now," Marc said, slapping his cap back on his head. "Siege been saying some shit about you."

"You seen him recently?" Tyson risked asking. "I mean, like in the last day?"

"Nah, saw him few days back. He was on a bit of a mish there. Why?"

"I'm sort of staying away from them all," replied Tyson. He wondered what Siege would do now he had pulled a gun on him. By how his hand had felt, he was sure Siege had felt that punch too. He didn't mention it to Marc. "Crunch is too."

"Yeah, I heard," replied Marc. He gave Tyson a look that he

understood instantly, and he just nodded a bit in reply. "Pity. Dodgee is some of the best. But what the fuck. Figure it's their loss if neither of you are hanging with them. Might make it a bit hard given this is your hood."

"I'm thinking of moving," Tyson said. He noticed Ihaia coming back out of the house, passing a bottle of Coke off to Zadie, who smiled in return. "I don't know where yet. Just somewhere else… make a fresh start somewhere."

"Fresh start with someone else?"

Tyson shot Zadie a look, hoping that she hadn't heard that, and then wondered why he cared if she worked it out. Somehow that would be easier than telling her. Marc was fixing him with a steady stare, waiting for an answer, before glancing off at Ihaia. The breaker was busy talking to Zadie, who seemed quick with smiles. Tyson tried not to feel jealous again.

"Yeah. Fresh start like that too."

"Happy for you, my man. I was serious about you not running off on me again, though. I figured we were friends."

Tyson frowned, shooting a glance back at Marc. Marc seemed nonplussed. "We are. I just figured…you know…after…that, that you didn't really want me around."

"How does that shit change things, my man? Friends are friends. That shit doesn't bother me." Marc nodded over towards Zadie, looking over that way himself. "Actually…your friend's pretty hot."

"Man…" Tyson replied, pulling a face.

"Serious. You sure you don't swing that way, right?"

"What are you trying to say?"

"I'm not asking permission, if that's what you mean, my man." Marc grinned. "Figured might be polite saying something, though."

"Bro, I'm not even listening to that."

"I won't ask again, then."

Tyson raised an eyebrow, taking in the brief look he saw on

Marc's face. He had seen that look in guys plenty before. It was a look that had made him feel lonely, the way they had stared at girls. He always wished that they had stared at him with that same sort of look. Tyson wasn't sure how he felt about Marc going out with Zadie. Not that he could do anything to stop it, really, but it felt strange given how he had felt about Marc.

It was easier sitting next to him right now. There was a time when Tyson figured that he would always have those feelings. He still did, but they seemed easier to bear.

Things were starting to feel different now.

"Just throwing out an idea here," Marc said, in a voice loud enough that Ihaia and Zadie could hear. Tyson was scared of what he was going to say, but his fears were quickly allayed. "I ran into this guy downtown who sings pretty good. Maybe when Dred here gets good with graff, and with Crunch being as good a breaker as he is, maybe you could all be a crew."

Tyson considered that a moment. There was something pretty sweet about being part of his own crew, forming something like that with Ihaia rather than joining up with Dodgee. He looked over at Ihaia, watching the way that he was thinking about it. There was an easy smile on his face.

"Sounds like a plan to me," Ihaia said, taking a sip of his bottle of Coke.

"Fucking give Dodgee a run for their money, maybe," said Marc.

Tyson caught himself trying to make excuses in his mind. All that usual self-doubt that always came to the top. Instead he just shoved his hands into the pockets of his oversized hoodie and nodded staunchly, smiling.

"Sounds good to me."

About the Author

Tama Wise is a Māori author of Ngāpuhi descent. He was influenced by growing up with hip-hop culture, as one of a generation of urban Polynesians searching for identity. Coming to writing in his teens, he was quickly drawn to what little fiction he could find that addressed race, sexuality, and poverty in an urban setting. Since then he has told stories of this world and others, weaving love, life, and a Māori view of things.

Tama has been published both locally in New Zealand and abroad, with short stories published in the anthology *Huia Short Stories 7: Contemporary Māori Fiction*, and more recently the *Yellow Medicine Review*. He lives in Auckland with his partner and two budgies.

Soliloquy Titles From Bold Strokes Books

Street Dreams by Tama Wise. Tyson Rua has more than his fair share of problems growing up in New Zealand—he's gay, he's falling in love, and he's run afoul of the local hip-hop crew leader just as he's trying to make it as a graffiti artist. (978-1-60282-650-2)

me@you.com by KE Payne. Is it possible to fall in love with someone you've never met? Imogen Summers thinks so because it's happened to her. (978-1-60282-592-5)

Swimming to Chicago by David-Matthew Barnes. As the lives of the adults around them unravel, high school students Alex and Robby form an unbreakable bond, vowing to do anything to stay together—even if it means leaving everything behind. (978-1-60282-572-7)

Speaking Out edited by Steve Berman. Inspiring stories written for and about LGBT and Q teens of overcoming adversity (against intolerance and homophobia) and experiencing life after "coming out." (978-1-60282-566-6)

365 Days by K.E. Payne. Life sucks when you're seventeen years old and confused about your sexuality, and the girl of your dreams doesn't even know you exist. Then in walks sexy new emo girl, Hannah Harrison. Clemmie Atkins has exactly 365 days to discover herself, and she's going to have a blast doing it! (978-1-60282-540-6)

Cursebusters! by Julie Smith. Budding psychic Reeno is the most accomplished teenage burglar in California, but one tiny screw-up and poof!—she's sentenced to Bad Girl School. And that isn't even her worst problem. Her sister Haley's dying of an illness no one can diagnose, and now she can't even help. (978-1-60282-559-8)

Who I Am by M.L. Rice. Devin Kelly's senior year is a disaster. She's in a new school in a new town, and the school bully is making her life miserable—but then she meets his sister Melanie and realizes her feelings for her are more than platonic. (978-1-60282-231-3)

Sleeping Angel by Greg Herren. Eric Matthews survives a terrible car accident only to find out everyone in town thinks he's a murderer—and he has to clear his name even though he has no memories of what happened. (978-1-60282-214-6)

Mesmerized by David-Matthew Barnes. Through her close friendship with Brodie and Lance, Serena Albright learns about the many forms of love and finds comfort for the grief and guilt she feels over the brutal death of her older brother, the victim of a hate crime. (978-1-60282-191-0)

The Perfect Family by Kathryn Shay. A mother and her gay son stand hand in hand as the storms of change engulf their perfect family and the life they knew. (978-1-60282-181-1)

Father Knows Best by Lynda Sandoval. High school juniors and best friends Lila Moreno, Meryl Morganstern, and Caressa Thibodoux plan to make the most of the summer before senior year. What they discover that amazing summer about girl power, growing up, and trusting friends and family more than prepares them to tackle that all-important senior year! (978-1-60282-147-7)